CARNAL NATION

carnal nation

BRAVE NEW
SEX FICTIONS

editors
Carellin Brooks + Brett Josef Grubisic

Arsenal Pulp Press
Vancouver

CARNAL NATION

ARSENAL PULP PRESS
103-1014 Homer Street
Vancouver, B.C.
Canada V6B 2W9
www.arsenalpulp.com

The publisher gratefully acknowledges the support of the Canada Council for the Arts and the B.C. Arts Council for its publishing program, and the support of the Government of Canada through the Book Publishing Industry Development Program for its publishing activities.

This is a work of fiction. Any resemblance of characters to persons, living or dead, is purely coincidental.

Design by Solo
Printed and bound in Canada

CANADIAN CATALOGUING IN PUBLICATION DATA:
Main entry under title:
Carnal nation
  ISBN 1-55152-083-4

1. Erotic stories, Canadian (English)* 2. Short stories, Canadian (English)-20th century.* I. Brooks, Carellin. II. Grubisic, Brett Josef.

PS8323.E75C37 2000   C813'.01083538   C00-910924-2

I shall at this point introduce two technical terms. Let us call the person from whom sexual attraction proceeds the *sexual object* and the act towards which the instinct tends the *sexual aim*. Scientifically sifted observation, then, shows that numerous deviations occur in respect to both of these — the sexual object and the sexual aim. The relationship between these deviations and what is assumed to be normal requires thorough investigation.

— Sigmund Freud, *Three Essays on the Theory of Sexuality*

The question we must ask is why no Canadian writer has seen fit — or found it imaginable — to produce a Venus in Canada.

— Margaret Atwood, *Survival*

brett josef grubisic

L.A. STORY: AN INTRODUCTION

LOS ANGELES — THE ZONE OF NOTORIOUS METROPOLITAN sprawl Bertold Brecht thought close to Hell and Bruce LaBruce calls an aging go-go girl — served as the accidental muse of *Carnal Nation*. Instead of overflowing with conventional sources of inspiration like legendary beauty or sophisticated culture, though, L.A. just happened to be the terminus for an odd commingling of people and events.

As far as we remember, the story actually begins in Canada with a letter of acceptance from the Canadian Studies in America Society: Congratulations, CSAS is holding its annual conference in Los Angeles, and can you present your proposed paper on the *CanLit: Conversion, Inversion, Subversion* panel? Why, yes, Carellin and I agreed, our schedules were free. On a Friday afternoon we departed from soaked-in-gray YVR and arrived at sun-toasted LAX. For the duration of the flight we stayed strapped into our narrow seats and talked incessantly; if Carellin's fear-of-flying anxiety kept her animated, I was nervous about the theatrics of delivering our paper, "Rapacity and Remorse: In/de-ferring Heteroglossic Homoeroticism in Susanna Moodie's *Roughing it in the Bush*." I wanted every pause to be perfectly pregnant, each raised eyebrow dramatically apt. This was our first presentation at a CSAS convention and we were thrilled: not only had we written something guaranteed to upset oldster orthodoxy, but with funding from the university and the Society, the entire weekend wouldn't cost us a cent.

In a city renowned for its teeming automobile popula-
tion, we waited an eternity to attract the cab that ultimately took us to our luxe weekend residence. And finding
accommodation had been problem enough until a few
weeks earlier. Though Professor K____, author of a career-
making Carter-era light-imagery-in-Emily-Dickinson
study, had generously offered to billet us, the idea of
spending even one minute discussing literature and/or
budget cuts in subdued tones while sipping from a single
glass of . . . whatever . . . was too much. No, no, we ex-
pressly outlawed that kind of socializing. We sought a different experience: innovative architecture, food, and drink
— not to mention garish nightlife, active street culture,
plastic surgery recipients, obscene extremes of income, re-
tail pornography strips, pollution-fogged vistas, monster
freeways, semi-automatic weapon fire, improbably thriv-
ing palm trees and sightings of obsolete stars. Truly, the
last thing on our minds was earnest, measured scholarly
chit-chat. So each of us had schemed for an escape route,
and M____, a former Canadianist, eventually showed us
the way out.

Carellin had met M____ at an English Department
book sale just before the eureka that led to his dropping
out and moving south. She'd introduced him to me, and
we'd all kept in touch (I suppose to remind ourselves about
the lives we weren't leading). The story Carellin and I
pieced together was that while making rounds at the stu-
dios in Culver City, M____ had played up a fake Oxbridge
accent as well as his pop culture savvy. He'd made con-
tacts (somehow: details are missing here) and immersed
himself in script doctoring. His store of arcane terms was
telegraphed widely (somehow) and had led (ditto) to a
writing credit in a Farrah Fawcett comeback vehicle,
Golden Girls 1849!, a dark horse, quasi-feminist historical
mini-series about a gaggle of enterprising and fun-loving
prostitutes working the California gold rush. It turned out
to be a remarkable — some said unfathomable — ratings

sweep, and was later sucked into a prime-time series de-velopment black hole when Fawcett (i.e., Lady Fidget, the madam) reportedly claimed that she couldn't relate to "any kitschy shit script." Anyway, from that point on, offers were M____'s for the taking. Carellin had told him about the conference and he'd responded by insisting we "make some noise" at his new home. He was lonely for dour Canadians, he said. We discovered too late that he wasn't speaking the strict truth.

In the short time M____ had lived in the palatial ex-panse of what he called with ironic and grotesque im-modesty "my little bungalow," he'd adopted startling new attitudes. At a table laden with bits of artfully-posed food we sat politely silent while he tossed around various pro-American pitches (or contra-Canadian ones, it was difficult to tell) about health care, currency design, unemployment rates, national character, and even guns and the military. It was as though he'd draped himself in ludicrous American jingoism in order to avoid standing out. (Later, we speculated that while his ersatz Britishness may have been his express ticket to Burbank, it soon became a lia-bility and so, pod-like, he'd come to embody what he imag-ined — in retrograde homage to Frank Sinatra? Charlton Heston? — as *Hollywood attitude*.)

Caught by house-guest *oblige* we stayed attentive for a while. Yet listening to most anyone for too long gets te-dious. Bored eyes wandering the room, I switched topics. I mentioned our conference, and was prepared to talk about it and related matters all night. Then M____ launched a full frontal assault.

"CanLit, huh?" he spat. "Canadian lit-er-at-ure, eh? It's got to be the most safe and polite and complacent writing on the planet: by the book anguish and paint-by-numbers resolution."

We sat silent, tense with anticipation. An academic through and through, once M____ had begun he always went on until he'd exhausted every possibility.

"Just think of its record on your essay's theme, sex," he continued. His shabby reduction of our deeply politicized activism hurt. Carellin — resplendent in black polyvinyl chloride despite the weather — recoiled visibly at the insult.

"Look at that bloody Victorian iceberg, Mrs Moodie in the wild," he exclaimed, one pale piece of endive speared on a fork of Scandinavian design.

"And," he exclaimed, freezing all artists together into one glacial chunk, "what about Emily Carr? More repression. Closed legs. Denial everywhere. Even the Group of Seven were a bunch of asexual landscape painters who canoed. So much for ancestry."

Several glasses into the Cabernet ("No one's really drinking Merlot anymore, but thanks anyway," he'd said after we presented him with our gift of British Columbian wine), M____ juggernauted through twentieth-century luminaries.

"It's still the same thing. Sinclair Ross, Hugh MacLennan, Margaret Laurence, Timothy Findley, Mavis Gallant. . . ." he paused to recall other CanLit deities. "If they step outside their decorous selves just an instance and mention sex for once, they're on about the destructive consequences of sexual expression. Same with Alice Munro. There's never any celebration, just naysaying and dire oracular predictions: *Enjoy yourself for a second and you'll pay the price.* God forbid anyone has a decent orgasm without losing an eye."

And, pursed lips presaging a *coup de grâce*, he turned to that most sacred of sacred animals. "And sex in Margaret Atwood is always dreary. Just dreadful," he asserted, the very voice of authoritative finality. After all, it was in the midst of his dissertation on homosocial femininity and counter-conventional heterosexual formations in Atwood's first volume of poetry that M____ had reached melting point. Evidently, extensive counseling hadn't resolved one significant issue.

In oracle mode himself M____ announced, "Atwood's never rhapsodic. For every one of her protagonists sex is either something to tolerate — think of that 'liberated chick'" (and here two sets of quoting fingers scored the air) "in *The Edible Woman* whose experience of bathtub sex consists of thinking how much it hurt her coccyx — or, big surprise, it's something that has terrible repercussions: look what happens in *Alias Grace* or *Life Before Man* or. . . . Beware! Beware! You just can't win. It's no wonder she became Canada's biggest literary celeb. She's the national temperament raised a few notches."

We begged off answerless, knowing that M____ didn't crave debate so much as an audience, and explained that the conference would demand our full, well-slept attention.

The following morning we presented our paper to a dun-coloured room and were greeted with silence — a pall of pin-drop, hear-your-own breathing quiet. Not a single question approached us, nor even one of those coughs that insinuates, *That was embarrassing, now let's all forget it ever occurred.* We felt as though we'd laughed at a state funeral. With M____'s pronouncements still ringing in our ears, we became more attentive to the other speakers than usual. It was only slightly surprising then that sex was nowhere to be found. To increase our reach we separated, Carellin taking the dreaded *CanLit: Before 1945?* session. (We flipped for it.) Two complete sessions and we heard nothing about sexuality in any form, excepting what we'd written. Landscape, weather, and nature, sure. Somewhat fewer words about colonial politics and the nation's absent modernism. We listened as speakers talked poetic imagery, one about fire, the other mapping the vicissitude of snow. Taking into account the wine, the city and M____'s undeniable penchant for overstatement, we wondered nonetheless about the sexual temperance of our apparently prim literature.

And then we left the conference, debating if we should drive to Silverlake for organic Portobello burgers or return to our host's for another verbose dinner.

> > >

Postmodern L.A. was as we'd hoped, exhilarating and de-
pressing — in short, a sweetly addictive narcotic. Our high-
light was drinking a toxic-and-not-to-be-repeated cocktail
while a woman sitting adjacent to us literally traced the
history of her Tijuana plastic surgeon's work. If we didn't
return feeling shaken or vaguely chastised regarding our
stillborn conference experience, we were at least curious.
We imagined another conference, *Representing Sex in
Canadian Fiction*, especially designed to solve our
quandary. Alternately, we rationalized that blanket state-
ments about national literary tendencies were pointless,
and decided that it's silly to discuss how sex-positive a national literature may be. I hypothesized, thoughts running
to *au courant* if partially retained theories of Michel
Foucault, that the very absence of explicit sexuality in the
nation's literature might signify Canadian writers' actual
preoccupation with it. And we happily formed an anti-
canon to M____'s pantheon of prudery, reciting sexually
ribald, celebratory, and explicit bits in novels by Susan
Swan, Heather Robertson, Barbara Gowdy, Mordecai
Richler, Scott Symons, Robertson Davies, and Leonard
Cohen. . . .

At some point during our conversations Carellin and I
began to consider the latest generation (more or less) of
Canadian writers, those born like us during and after the
1960s. Surely sexuality couldn't be a big taboo for these
wizened souls, a blush-inducing or vexing vice that's
hinted at but never brought into direct light. Since — as the
truism runs — this generation was born as the Sexual
Revolution and its aftermath raged, and grew into turbu-
lent adulthood inside what practically everyone agrees is
a far more permissive and less discreet culture (in which,
thanks to radio, TV, advertising, book stores, and the nearest cineplex, sexual images and discourses are ever-appar-
ent, available, and even a chore to avoid), does it not make
sense that such a demographic pie-slice would have
markedly different and maybe far more relaxed views

about sex than that which preceded it? Then again, we asked, since it's so often fused to love and always experienced in the body, might there perhaps be a surprising degree of intergenerational continuity regarding sex acts despite the innovations wrought by history?

In any case, we wondered how writerly types of the famed X generation would represent that provocative and infinitely broad topic, sex. To a group for whom sexual activity is no longer the Great Private Topic, and rather just the opposite, what could it come to mean? And if sex had become just another commodity, would it be given a remarkably different value? To get outside our own heads we asked around; and then after hearing others express interest we began to seek fiction submissions. *Carnal Nation*, the concrete result of our cross-border experiences and post-mortem talks, features a wide sampling of writers born between the early 1960s and 1970s who've spent some time thinking about the meaning of sex. Having a wealth of perspectives, the anthology can offer scintillating and disquieting glimpses; it reflects an impressive variety of approaches to thematizing and understanding sexuality — and showcases the literary manoeuvres of young writers who exhibit no reticence about addressing the often visceral facts of sex. Giving M____ something to respond to (while answering Carellin's and my questions, too), the stories exhibit breaks with the discreet sentiments of past literary endeavour as well as some continuity. Apparently, the urge toward sex is, like love or anger, one of the brute facts of human existence; it's our historically-shifting ways of mapping and understanding it that are intriguing.

While the stories in *Carnal Nation* cannot be said to represent the perspective of an entire generation (as if anything could), they do provide insight into the multiplicity of roles sexuality plays, as well as the shapes it can take. These roles are always polymorphous, and so give that ever-popular social category "normal" a mythic and faintly

nonsensical status. Sexual experience remains good or
bad, and, no big surprise, a complex, volatile mixture of
the two, but it never holds to a single position long enough
to calcify into any cultural creed; carnality *is* incontinent,
to paraphrase and redirect William F. Buckley's damning
diagnosis of President Clinton. Longed for or feared, sex
has intimate connections to pain and solace; to self-defi-
nition, self-deception, and self-revelation; and to tear-worthy
tragedy as well as laugh-worthy comedy. Passed through
the mysterious filters of femininity and masculinity, pro-
tean sex absorbs prefixes, becoming asexual, heterosexual,
homosexual, or bisexual. In the stories compiled here, sex
assumes a central place, and emerges as an essential fac-
tor in race relations, career decisions, conjugal bliss, employment status, marital strife, family genealogy, and even
vacation plans.

Finally, any wisdom to be gleaned from these fictions
is linked to the indisputably mercurial contours of sex:
"Don't you rely on me," it whispers like a puckish and enig-
matic fairy-tale spirit throughout *Carnal Nation*, "I'm always around and you always need me, but I cannot be
trusted for long." Now there's a case of *caveat emptor* if
there ever was one.

I

derek mccormack

THE ACCESSORY

"I'VE BEEN WATCHING YOU," THE MAN SAID. "YOU DO BEAU-
tiful work."

"It's nothing," I said, boxing his buys.

"That's not true. What you do is beyond wrapping, it's
like, what's that Japanese thing?"

"Origami? I can't believe you know about that. Nobody
knows about that." I cut reindeer paper.

"Not everyone in this burg appreciates art." He leaned
across the counter. He was blue shaven. Blue eyes. "So how
do you do it?"

I drew the paper skin tight. "You really want to know?"

"Of course I do," he said, holding my gaze.

I creased ends into envelopes. I folded the scissor cut
under. "It's sort of like sewing. No rough edges should
show."

"Interesting," he said.

I measured out ribbon, looped it under and around. "I
always leave an extra inch. And I always cut the ends at
angles."

I held ribbon between thumb and index finger. Made a
loop, then another, then another. "I can do bow ties. Or
plain ties. Depends on which loop you use."

On another box I ran the ribbon in parallel rows, tied
the ends and ran them across the scissor blades. They
curled. "I like Texray or Excello," I said.

I made rosettes. Glued one to each gift. Beauty set,
fountain pen, clock. I swallowed. "These for your girlfriend?"

"Nah," he said.

"Wife?"

He laughed. "Nah."

I was red as wrapping. I could smell my deodorant. "Well," I said. "Thank you for shopping at Turnbull's."

"Listen, I gotta run," he said. He slipped a fiver in my hand. "We'll talk more later."

I leaned into the aisle. Watched him disappear into Radios.

"Where are his receipts?" Behind me. My manager.

"Receipts?"

"You didn't ask for them?" he said. "How do you know he paid?" He got on the horn. "Tall guy. Duster coat. He's coming through Brown Goods. If he tries to leave, pinch him."

I sank down, folded the fiver into a swan.

"He give that to you?" the manager said. "That your kickback?"

"Kickback for what?" I said.

> > >

I took off my shirt.

"Keep going."

My pants.

"Keep going."

I shivered. "I told you I don't have anything."

The security guys laughed. One guy snapped on a glove.

"What's that for?" I said.

"Brown goods," he said.

annabel lyon

STARS

"IS THIS LOOKING LIKE A PANTHER TO YOU?"

Elijah, Meredith's husband, was painting the archway over the new *Adults Only* section of his video store. Lily, Meredith's sister, looked on.

"It's a little humpy," Lily said. "More like a buffalo."

Past the archway, in the old storage room, stood empty video shelves. Stacked against one wall were a dozen cardboard boxes, waiting to be unpacked. Lily had volunteered for this, since the boxes made Meredith furious.

Elijah stood on a three-step ladder. He had a gauze pad taped over one eye. He held a pot of silky pink paint. Pink like dawn over elephants, Lily thought. She liked Elijah very much.

"Meredith is so angry with me," he said, studying the animal-shaped space he had left on the wet pink wall. Later he would fill in, black.

"May I browse?" asked a man in a shirt and pants, peering past Elijah on the ladder, into the little room.

"This is my point," Elijah said. "This money, we need. Will we get types? I'm not saying we won't get types. Take this person here, for instance."

"Excuse me," the man said, affronted, walking off.

Elijah sighed and lifted the paintbrush up and down like a soup ladle, trailing pink threads. "Please picture us as children," he said. "Your sister and I, just graduated from university, freshly wed, going into business. Beautiful movies, Fellini, Kieslowski, Kurosawa. This was two years ago. Do you know, for breakfast this morning, she called me a pimp?"

"She has a point," Lily said.

The browsing man came back. "Okay," he said, holding his hands up like they were threatening him with a gun. "Just, when does it open?"

Lily ate a wide, pale tortilla chip. Paper bags of these chips stood on shelves by the till, along with big jars of almond caraway biscotti and little jars of angry hot salsa, all home-made by Meredith. They had been her idea for stimulating business.

"Faith, hope, love. Never," Elijah said. "Tomorrow."

Later, they unplugged the neon, turned off the overhead set, and locked the till in the safe. They had to check the titles against the packing slip, make sure the movies were in the correct cases, and arrange the cases alphabetically on the shelves. They worked fast, smiling crookedly, like union elves.

"It's a whole culture," Elijah said. "Stars, suicides. I've been reading the literature."

"Goodness," Lily said, thinking of Meredith. "What literature is that?"

He pressed three fingers against the bandage over his eye, as though to sop loose blood. "Breasts can be arty," he said.

She showed him one of the cases. "Is that even legal?"

He blinked, inky-eyed, and took it from her. "I told them not to send me this shit. I'm phoning Ray." He held it up to the light.

"Ray'll take care of it," Lily said, nodding. Elijah jumped up and bounded into the main room. She watched him lean over the cash desk and root for the speaker phone. Dialling out. "Who is he, exactly?" Lily called.

"Ray!" Elijah shouted at the phone. Lily heard him laugh. "No, I promise!" he said. "She went home." He returned to the little room, smiling. "Well, Ray," he said. "You know."

>   >   >

Ray was a tired man with a dirty look around his eyes. He had a leather jacket and the ghost of a handsome smile. He shook hands with Elijah but stood off from Lily, warily. "How many of these you got?" he asked.

"I'm her sister," Lily said, and then he shook hands with her, too.

"Sweetheart," he said, picking up a case and stowing it in a nylon sports bag, "these slip in."

Elijah went back to the cash desk. This time he closed his eyes and dialled by feel. He squeezed his eyes harder closed and mumbled. Lily couldn't hear. She turned back and saw Ray had been watching her watch Elijah. "How'd you get into your line of work, exactly?" she asked.

He went on popping videos into his bag, nodding. "Your sister asked the same thing, more or less. How did I end up as me? Women always ask, men never do. What do you make of that?"

"Men can imagine it?" Lily said.

"I used to deal, at university," Ray said. "I hate movies. I like cars. It's a cartoon life, what can I say?"

Lily waited. He had a tan, she noticed. Not so frail.

"You seem like a nice girl yourself," he said.

> > >

Out of the store, into the dust and dead grass and yellow jello sunlight of late afternoon, Lily walked where bees bigger than thumbs purred by her ankles, along the long highway, between the ditch grasses and the shoulder, until she got to Meredith's house.

"Have a good time?" Meredith asked, looking past her for Elijah's car.

Lily closed the door.

"I see," Meredith said. "He stayed behind to watch a few."

"Oh, Merry. He did not."

"He is most certainly watching some movies."

Meredith had a floor-length robe and delicate hair. She

collected books of photographs. They littered the coffee table like big silver pizza boxes.

"You're all dusty," Meredith said.

Lily followed Meredith into the kitchen and watched her spoon sugar into a glass. She added a teabag and a slop of milk while she waited for the kettle to boil.

"No more teapot?" Lily asked.

"You saw the bandage."

"Can I have a bath?"

"You can have a bath."

"Can I have an egg?"

Meredith eyed her reproachfully.

Lily got an egg from the fridge and separated it neatly into two wineglasses from the drying rack. "You want the white?"

"Stop bothering me," Meredith said, settling on the sofa with a vase of gin and a *Cinemonde*.

In the bathroom, Lily smeared the yolk onto her face with two fingers, glossing her eyebrows and the fine hair at her temples, avoiding her lips. She ran a bath.

"The boundaries of art are not at issue here!" Meredith called from the living room. "Did he give you that line?"

Lily shifted in the tub.

"Alternative erotica my ass!"

"He didn't give me a line," Lily called.

"I don't want to know!"

Lily got out, rinsed the egg smear from her face, and danced with a towel.

"On the counter, in the blue jar?" Meredith called. "I have some nice talc. Please don't use it."

Lily went into the living room.

"Your face is all pink," Meredith said. "You smell like me."

"Gimme clothes."

In the bedroom, Meredith went into the closet and stayed there for a while. Lily tried on a pair of big silver mules. They stuck out from her heels like planks. "Nice,"

she said, clogging a little on the hardwood. She snapped
her fingers, wound her wrists over her head, nose to bicep,
eyes closed, and shuffled a spin. The dress hit her in the
face — a sleeveless, backless bind of pale green silk with
the finest zipper she had ever seen. It was cold to touch.
She put it on.

"Don't sweat," Meredith said.

Back in the kitchen, Lily tried to sit down in the dress
while Meredith unplugged the frantic kettle and shoved
her tea gear behind the toaster. She opened a tin, inverted
a hockey puck of cat food onto a saucer, and collapsed it
with a fork. "You always liked Ely."

"Yup," Lily said.

"Dissuade him from those movies."

Lily said nothing. She shimmered, just breathing.

"Lucas!" Meredith hollered. Lucas was the cat, a patchy
tabby with ripped ears and a pretty smile. He drifted in,
star of his own silent film, and nuzzled the saucer. He took
some meat into his cheeks and chewed. Lily wished she
had a tail so she too could turn her bum to Meredith and
trace such indolent arabesques of contempt.

In the living room, Lily and Lucas shared a chair. She
wound a piece of her long hair around his paw. He kicked,
yanking. He tried to jump to the floor and tripped, jerking
Lily's head down. Her dress went crazy with lights.

Meredith shook her head as they untangled themselves. "Only you could sprawl a cat," she said.

They heard Elijah's Bug come chewing up the gravel
driveway. A door slammed. "You don't say," Meredith said.
They arranged themselves. "Do you wax?" Lily asked.

Elijah stood radiant in the doorway, scratching his eyebrow with one finger. "Women are bread and coriander,"
he said.

"He watched the movies," Meredith said.

He frowned accusingly at Lily, then brightened. "Hey,
you like my shoes?" She was still wearing the enormous
mules.

"Ritzy," Lily said, swinging her legs so they flapped and flashed against her heels. "They're you."

"Judas," Meredith said to Lily. "You just encourage him." And to Elijah: "Did we get any good ones?"

He went and knelt before her. He lifted her feet in his cupped palms, one at a time, and kissed them. He rubbed her arches with his thumbs.

"If I did one of those, would you take me out? Me and some popcorn?"

He decked her a look.

"Isn't he full of shit?" Meredith said.

"I like him," Lily said.

"Oh, you," Meredith said, vicious. "I know all about you. When are you going to get a job?"

"Here we go," Lily said.

Lucas spilled to the floor and ran. "That's a smart cat there," Elijah said.

The doorbell rang. "There's Ray," Lily said quickly.

"Oh, Lily," Elijah said, and Meredith said, "Oh, Lily, no."

It was Ray. He had changed into chinos and a heathery grey polo shirt under his leather jacket. "I found you," he said.

Meredith put her fingertips to her hair, then let her arms drop to her sides. "You've never even had a boyfriend," she said, frowning.

Lily smiled at Elijah.

"She's trying to hurt me," Meredith said.

"You're killing me," Elijah said. His hand drifted up to his eye.

Ray leaned on the doorjamb, smiling at his feet. He seemed to be trembling slightly. "Am I going?" he asked, looking at Lily.

"Lillian Gish, don't you dare," Elijah said. He was pale around the mouth. "Do you know what he is, really?"

>   >   >

Ray was a good dancer. He could anticipate. Lily danced like someone tossing hair from her eyes. Close up, she could smell the leather of his jacket. Later they walked down Main Street, into a crowd of movie-goers leaving a cinema. Lily still wore her sister's pale cool dress. People watched her pass.

"I'm going to call you Slim," Ray said. He took off his jacket and gave it to her. "For me, okay?"

She had been thinking of the time she kicked in the face of Meredith's TV, when she was first dating Elijah and bringing home all those foreign films. And now, as if an hourglass had been turned — the first swirl of interest, whisper of grit — a new suggestion of collapse, and the inevitable sly mounding beneath.

They walked for a while amongst the moviegoers, paired quiet as animals in the bright night.

michael holmes

LAST CALL

FRIDAY, OCTOBER 3rd
11:59 PM

PUSSYSWOGGLED.

The guy she's led over the hard, beaten, red and black carpet, through the amazing dark — weaving him, deep into the club, past small tables where other girls hang on the every word of whomever, past security, a dogleg right, up a step and through a narrow entrance way, stepping high and delicate and side-stepping around the high heels and calves and swinging hair of women contorted every-whichway — pivots and eases back, nonchalant, cool as anything, never breaking eye contact.

He sees himself this way: irresistible, formidable, quick-silver, his face hard and cold and perfect. His smile is coy and his jaw is strong; his eyes burn, transfix, draw her down into his lap. He could make her laugh or break her heart; she'd confess any wicked secret, say anything to win a moment more of his attention, admit weaknesses only he can kiss and make better — he fulfills her darkest, dampest fantasy.

This is all her doing, of course. And she's good, very good, at what she does.

He's feeling fantastic and when he feels fantastic he always wants to take out the new ones for a test drive: shower his magnanimous attentions, share all of his bad self. There's plenty to go around, baby.

And so he lowers his powerful, beautiful self, easy into the tight alcove.

Actually, no. He flops, this guy. Tries to plunk his drunk butt down.

She watches him — eyes spinning, red and white and blue, flying saucers — misjudge the edge of the black vinyl and red velvet-backed booth's worn, plush, built-in chair. And she doesn't laugh when his elbows keep his ass from plopping on the sticky black vinyl tile below and his face contorts into a surprised puppy's disbelief. And she doesn't even flinch or sneer or break eye contact — she's seen and felt it all before — when an arcing fountain of lager burps up and ejaculates out and over her right ankle. Squishing a bit, Molson Golden seeping under her heel, soaking into her black stiletto, dripping another five-and-a-half inches to the floor, she shifts her weight and spears a million foamy bubbles: all the tiny, dishevelled men in red neon and blacklight reflected and refracted there, this guy and the one in the next alcove and the one directly across and the one next to that, pop.

Perfectly strip-pokerfaced, she just thinks: Smooth move, Ex-Lax.

Scrabbling back like a baby turtle, he becomes a jellyfish on the imitation red velvet, flicks his ash to his left and takes a swig of his green-bottled beer. Goofy now, he wipes the excess with the back of his smoking hand.

"It's twenty, okay?"

His tongue draws left to right over the edge of his teeth and just under his rubbery lip.

"Okay?"

He blinks the only choice he has left, pulls at his casual collar, loosens the knot of his pale tie.

Jesus, he's so old.

She smiles and growls and tilts his head back by chucking his stubbled chin. He thinks of a million brilliant things to say, trolls his love-lines — they're all good. But he can't pull his eyes away from how pneumatic she is, can't stop thinking: Monsterbagos, huge fucking melons. So he says:

"You're so fucking beautiful. . . ." And then he adds: "I like this song."

It's Prince. She crinkles her freckled twenty-year-old nose and shrugs. Whatever.

She produces a small beige towel from out of nowhere, drapes it over his lap.

Suave, he knows he has her now: "Don't know about the little freak's new stuff, though. Where you from? How you doin'?"

Not about to answer, she rolls her eyes and bends her knees, looks into his okay face and smiles vacantly, taps his hand. He butts out his smoke and she lifts his arm and lets it fall into his lap. She eases her ass onto the armrest. Puts her arms around his neck.

"You've been through the drill, right? You can't touch me. I touch you."

He blinks, stutters his soundless mouth around something pat to say next.

She helps him out: "What do you do?"

His head's swimming in the smell of her, baby powder and lilies and sweat and smoke. It's divine, his favourite smell in the world.

"What? Oh, I. . . . Um, contracts mostly, I make deals. . . ."

He nods and swigs more beer. The wheels turning, his nostrils flare.

It's the shrimpy Artist's last verse now. "Darling Nikki" almost done — onstage, Nikki Sin's bunching up the ratty duvet between her thighs.

She thinks: Just like she does every time. Every guy in the place trying not to look like he wishes he was that filthy piece of cloth.

Her new guy laughs, narrows his eyes. "You know, if you touch me, then I am touching you."

She shrugs again.

"So what do we do about that?" He thinks he sounds like the smoothest motherfucker, like butter, like silk. He's sweating beads of beer and Sex-On-The-Beach and Orgasms.

My new guy's a talker and he's smashed. Bad combination, good combination — depending on how you want
to look at it. Okay. Fine. She plays the card he's thrown,
uses a finger as a pointer and touches her wrist and shoulder, her knee, her elbow. Using her deep throat and the kit-
tenish squeak she learned from Marilyn Monroe movies,
she says: "Okay, you get to touch me here and here and
here. And here."

Nikki's gone to light applause, drunken slurs and hoots
— all the impossible noises guys learn from teen sex
farces, even a couple Blur woo hoos. The DJ's doing his
game show announcer voice now, his tenor rising in fake
excitement to get a response from the crowd. The Steve
Miller Band plods into its groove: fuck, fucking Krystal's
first of three, overindulgent '70s shit, the stuck-up cow.

She runs her hand over the guy's short spiky hair and
sighs — she hates long, moody dances, hates this fucking
interminable song. Reaching over his lap to grab the other
armrest, she swings her cleavage around his cheeks as she
vaults her left leg over his right knee. He sinks deeper into
red when she's standing straight up in front of him, her
long-nailed, French-manicured fingers tapping at the
snaps on her hips, her heavy tits braced in their pink-lace
underwire bra.

His eyes race from the slope her left toe begins, up,
and then down the other side of the perfect V and then
back up again.

She unsnaps her magic thong and with a flourish pulls
the cloth out from under the table she's set for guys like
him. He follows the sleight of hand like he's supposed to,
up across her taut tummy until he sees the pink cotton kiss
the tattooed Balinese weaving that frames the body art of
her belly-button ring. Ta-da!

Jesus.

When his eyes finally drift down, a soft honey brown
heart has replaced the thin V of pink. The illusion's so perfect he doesn't notice the faint blue shadow of stubble, angry

pricks of red. In fact, he's so entranced by the perfect sym-
metry of her, the miraculous fold and tuck of her genital
disappearing act, that he doesn't notice her cracking gum
as she defies gravity by unveiling her huge new breasts.

And then he does and he's very, very pleased.

Like, Christ. Pam Anderson and David Copperfield,
rolled into one. So many illusions: like, in this light you
can't even see the scars.

She's listing with the music and readjusting the hand-
towel, taut, over his uncomfortable lap; he's squirming and
blinking rapidly, taking off from the launching pad of her
magnificent nipples, over her belly and between her legs
again. Completely taken, he's thinking: Where does it go?

I mean, it's like she really is a living, breathing Barbie
doll.

His jaw drops and he sucks in enough breath for an ex-
tra-point team's worth of drunk, horny guys. For a moment
it feels like it's not enough, that he's suffocating, even his
pants constrict him and he spreads his legs wider, looking
for relief. His cheeks balloon as she shoots her index finger straight into her pubic heart. When he pops and hisses
out the air, his eyes follow. The kick's up, and it's good! She
smiles and shakes her long blonde hair.

Christ, I'm good.

This is the part she likes best, the stunned, stupid look
of amazement a guy gets when he first falls for the miracle of her snatch. The pale look of disbelief that quickly
becomes pure, blind desire; his new obsession, the beginning of a game of peek-a-boo that will end only when he's
broke.

I don't care if his girlfriend or his wife swallows, I'd bet
a thousand she won't, can't do this. And that means he'll
keep coming back, to me, for more. The old guy's gotta
have it.

She pivots 180 degrees and bends and touches her toes,
grinds, slowly, down. He slides his hips even lower,
charmed, to follow her lead. The bulge under the hand-

towel grows; it's tenting now, slightly peaked, aching
closer. His tongue wants to snake across the salty small of
her back, across the electric, thick black lines that fan out
there in another tattooed V. She shimmies back up. Inch
by inch, closer and closer, she comes. Soft, tiny white fuzz
dances on the first hint of cold, sweet gooseflesh. She's
moving closer to the immobilized man's laboured breathing, the fat roll of his hot wealth. His back bows and his
neck strains forward: he's ready, this is it. She sinks the
trick — still doubled over, the blood rushing to a head happily occupied with thoughts of the new stereo she's going
to buy tomorrow — by running both hands up the insides
of her spread thighs. His gaze skirts, from the pink rose-
bud in his face, up onto the track, the valley between her
tanning-booth bronze hillocks, then sleds forward, fast
along the Vaselined slick. His eyes crash to a halt against
the padded tips of her two fuck you-fuck me fingers. The
perfect nail on the right one wags: drum roll, please. She
winks and she winks: Janus-like, one for an invisible audience and the guy working security, and one the other
way, just for him.

The finger on the right does the honours, reaches all
the way back to tickle her asshole, then dives into the track
he will remember and long for, for the rest of his life, but
never touch.

She draws the greased digit forward slowly and her lips
part. A garden of delights springs out, and then, there it is,
the rabbit out of the hat, the warren, the flower released
from its sleeve, breaking ground.

The tiny, wet, perfect hood of her clit.

Jesus. Jesus, he thinks, I gotta see that again.

One hundred dollars later and she's hovered over
every inch of him. This fallen angel's hands have spread
out and pushed off his shoulders, the back of her wrist has
caressed his cheeks, all of her lips have spilled intoxicat-
ing perfumes into his mouth, always stopping just before
they kiss. Her naughty finger has grazed his lips before dis-

appearing, deep, to the quick, between hers. Both of her thumbnails have raked up from his knees, up high on his inseam. They never got past the crease in his pants that folds over the place where his balls are cupped. Her head has dipped into his lap a half dozen times, long bleached locks have brushed the length of his cock.

He wants to explode.

He thinks he needs another drink.

He might explode.

He definitely needs another drink.

"Another?" she says, tired, bored, hoping for a clip of three-minute pop numbers.

"Uh, yeah. . . . Maybe." His cock's only half-hard now; he's lost some fuel, some lubrication, can't quite maintain. "But how 'bout I buy you a drink first? Gotta check on my buddy, too. You could come sit. Take a break. Talk."

She's relieved. She'll take his money and the drink, then move on to someone else, make him wait for her, for later, another time.

He'll be back alright. And you don't want to overload him, you know? Spoil the surprise?

Doing up the right snap of her thong, the lethal weapons she knows her breasts have become already holstered, she says: "So, um, that's one-twenty."

"Oh, yeah." He's lit another smoke and balled up the hand-towel. Doesn't know what to do with either. She relieves him of both and takes a crimson-lipsticked drag while he flops around, struggling for his wallet.

"Oops, not enough cash. Card, though. Right, put it on my card."

"There's a twenty percent service charge, you know."

"Whatever. And bring me an extra $200 and another Molson's, okay?"

"Yeah, but I'm not allowed to buy you a drink. Ya gotta go through the waitress, okay?"

"Okie-dokie."

Jesus, did he really just say that?

"Okay, sure, I'll bring your card and cash to you and you can buy me that drink. Where you sitting?"

"Watermelon row," he says, rolling a tiny foil ball between his free thumb and forefinger while he grins.

"Pardon?"

"Um, you know, watermelon row. Right up front. By the stage." His perfectly capped teeth flash from within an overplayed wink and nod.

"Never heard it called that before."

"Sure you have, it's an old nudie bar, burlesque kinda thing."

She lifts her razor thin eyebrows

"You know, like the Tom Waits song."

She cocks her head, sniffs, "Well. . . ."

"Jesus, ya gotta hear the guy, he's brilliant." He sings, froggy, bourbon voiced: "Chesty Morgan and a Watermelon Row, raise my rent and take off yer clothes. . . ." Coughing then, sputtering, he nods. "Watermelon row, you know, it's like the first row."

She purses her lips, almost amused: "Whatever. I know the song. But, like, I think you've got it wrong."

"Nah, I've listened to that album a million times."

"Well, it's Rose. Rose, not row."

"Say again?"

"Rose! Watermelon Rose. It's a chick's name. It's about a girl. Some old stripper."

"Nah, no way."

"Uh huh."

"You're shitting me."

"Nope."

"Naw, you don't know what the fuck. . . ."

The conversation's over because she's stopped listening. You couldn't pay me enough, shitfuck.

She's just noticed the white stain that runs down the guy's leg. She must have missed it in all the goddamned black light and neon. Shuddering with disgust, desperately wanting to bathe, she turns and walks to the bar holding the guy's credit card far away from her body, as delicately as possible, between her right thumb and her magic finger.

Who knows what the old fucker's got all over it.

Scott Venn tries to stand, to follow the night's newest fine lady. The scold in his unevenly drunk head pushes him back down into his seat. He blushes, hoping none of the other peelers writhing on the laps in the adjoining booths saw that.

Many of them did.

Few care.

Scott burps, opens his mouth wide, and stretches it around the beer gas to make an envelope. Bitch, he thinks. I hate Tom fucking Waits.

michael v. smith

GUCCI

I'M NOT SAYING IT BOTHERS ME, IT'S NOT TERRIBLE, AND IT'S not the end of the world, but why women? Yes, I was bored with the usual line-up of jeans and fat cocks parading through the park, the back room, the dungeon party, the police station, or wherever, and I was bored with my movies, bored with my books, bored with the pictures I either conjure or buy. Bored. I bore myself in bed. Except lately. There are women there, in my mind, undressed, or with their skirts raised, knees wide apart, and my mouth doing things it's never done before. Women are suddenly getting me off. Is it purely the novelty? When I'm tired of pussy will I start fucking dogs?

Tonight, Brady and I are at the bar, in the basement, watching the stripper. We like this new guy; he's got tricks we haven't seen before. After that kid with the ornamental gourd some months ago, everyone's been putting a grocery list of products up their butts, from vegetables to canned goods to frozen fish. And lately it's tubes with lube (our favourite being the neon orange pylon two weeks back), but how interesting can that be after the first time? Okay, the second or third. Once is a freak show, twice is an experiment. Three times, I say, is pure indulgence. The best you can get out of a crowd on the third strike is a weary ho-hum.

But this guy, dimples in his face as big as those denting his ass, this guy's got a real talent. He's a showman. For one thing, he can dance; he has moves I can't stop watching. The slick hair is in and out of his eyes, half-closed in a delirium I prefer to think is more erotic than narcotic. And his thighs, his naked thighs bump the wall behind him as if he was hip-checking the bar. The song is "Upside Down," which I have to admit is campy but not that hot, only I don't care, he's tasty. He's dangerously sweet.

"Who gets the front?" Brady whispers in my ear. He's grinning at me through his freckles. Manly freckles. Brady's got a thick neck which makes him look more masculine than he is.

"You do," I say.

He chuckles. "I don't know. I'm not sure if he can handle me." He's leaning against my arm. I think I smell the joint in the front pocket of his jacket. "But you're right. We wouldn't want him to see your luggage. . . ." Meaning my foreskin. Brady likes to say I got enough skin to make a set of Gucci luggage. "He might think you're moving in."

"Oh, fuck off," I say and push him away. "You've got no idea what I look like."

He crosses himself. "Thank God."

I don't know where he found it, but the stripper has one of those old bottles of Coke. Glass bottle with the cap still on. Full of pop. He stuffs it inside him, bottom first.

"You're just jealous that I, who is — am . . . are — ten years your junior, am also unmutilated," I blather.

Brady's laughing at me. "Got a little bit flustered there, did we?"

I can only point. The boy on stage has successfully buried the Coke bottle completely up his ass, so only the small round bottle cap is exposed, looking like a tin asshole. I think, Industrial Chastity Belt. No rear entry. Unless you have an opener, which, casually, the stripper materializes from his mouth. Wish granted. I'm telling you, the honey's got a flair for fantasy. He's got magic.

I look around the crowd to see if others are getting him too, if they're noticing what he can do. Brady sees it, he's interested again. The guy to my left, with a belly the exact diameter of the cocktail table in front of him, has a hand in his pocket. He's focused, big time. It's the guessing game of what will happen next. That's what keeps us hungry for them, when they've got mystery happening.

Diana sings her second chorus and the stripper feigns boredom with the music. He shrugs and jumps off the stage. The Coke bottle doesn't budge. Naked, with a weak spotlight following him, he twirls his way to the emergency exit, light flaring off the bottle cap as he spins. He walks out into the street. He's naked, on a downtown sidewalk, with a bottle up his ass, as the bar door closes behind him. We're left alone with the music and the spotlight trained on a red Do Not Exit sign.

I smile at Brady and he returns the grin, which, I'm sure, means he too is wondering if the guy's coming back. And in how many pieces. His attention turns again to the door.

"You know," I say, taking advantage of the surprise element of this moment, "I'm gonna have sex with women."

Still watching the exit, Brady cocks his head. He might not have heard me. He could still be puzzling the fate of the stripper, but something in his demeanor says not. Then the door opens and our five-minutes-of-famer saunters back in with a cigarette, lit, hanging low off his bottom lip. A few men clap. The stripper shakes his magic ass, which has, yes, still got its pop.

"You're just perverted," Brady hisses. When I notice his cheeks are red, burying some of the colour from his freckles, I wonder if he's kidding and flushed from the alcohol, or genuinely pissed off.

"There are lots of bisexual people in the world, Brady."

"But are you bisexual? No, Mick. If you fuck women, it's just perverted." He does sound angry. Then, as a guy in overalls approaches the stage and hands our stripper a five dollar bill, Brady, thankfully, elbows me and laughs. "Kidding," he says.

Before I can respond, the dancer, on a beat, flips — boom — onto his hands. Now the music makes sense.

Upside down — flip — you're turning me, you're giving love. The boy is doing a hand stand, triceps straining, ass clenched, and the neck of the bottle perfectly upright. He's holding the opener between his teeth, poised in such a way that it's clear to all of us he's waiting for someone to step out of the crowd and pop his cap.

Collectively, we pause. In shock and excited at the prospect before me, I clutch at Brady's arm as he, the bastard, rises from his chair. He's beating me to it. Whether deliberately or not, Brady stands beside the boy so the audience can still watch as he slips the bottle opener from his teeth. The dancer's face is growing ruby with the effort, but somehow, he's still wiggling in time with the music. His hips sway, the contents of the Coke jiggling at the neck. As Brady lifts his arm to clutch the glass neck, the bottle rises four inches out of the dancer's ass, then, like a near miracle of anatomy, it shrinks again, disappearing to the cap. He's swallowed the thing. By sheer will, sucked it up again. My jaw drops. Brady's hand remains where it was, hovering above the boy's split legs. The man across the way has stopped tugging inside his pants. We're stunned.

When Brady covers his mouth with his free hand, I know he's got the giggles, which could be disastrous. *Don't ruin the show*, I pray. I'm furious with jealousy, but he can't stop now and ruin the momentum. The bottle slides back up, mechanically, right out of a pornographic James Bond flick, and Brady pulls himself together. He's risen to the occasion. As he sets the bottle opener to the cap, I'm wet in my pants. I think I hear metal touching metal. And then there's a slow wet fizz hissing out as the cap drops to the ground and Coke sprays over Brady's face, down the boy's legs and across the wall. A Coca-Cola ejaculation.

Brady dashes out of the way, lifting his shirt to wipe the spray from his face as he returns to our table. Coke still dapples his ear. "Clean yourself up, will you," I snap.

"What's that, Mick?" He's all nonchalant.

"I hate you."

"Now don't be mean." He nearly sounds hurt, except he's turned back to the stage. He's a glutton. Being part of the show isn't enough.

The boy has removed the bottle and righted himself. He's splay-legged on the edge of the stage, holding his drink up to the spotlight like a frisky child in a commercial. I'm sure he's a hustler, though he's got this not-quite-corrupt look, as though he's taken the money, but hasn't yet done anything to merit it. I love him. I want to have a body that can do those sorts of dirty tricks. Not that I would. Only — think of the confidence I'd have, knowing I could draw anything in and out of my ass without hands.

Snapping his neck back, he tips the bottle over his head and pours. Straight down his throat. We see the Adam's apple bob. He swallows. As he he drinks the remains of the bottle someone in the back shouts, "I coulda had a V8," but we aren't listening. We love this. This is real, the kind of real that takes you out of yourself for a while, that makes you special for having witnessed something others won't ever get to see. That's why you can't repeat a show successfully. They're only special once. If the audience knows what's coming next, the moment's killed.

When he drains the bottle, he tosses it to the big guy with the hand trapped in his pocket, and, surprisingly, the bugger catches it. Everyone's a showman tonight. I wonder if the glass feels greasy in his palm. I wonder if it smells.

Diana Ross's voice fades into the distance. Show's over. The stripper picks up his clothes as the bartender's voice comes over the crackling speakers. "Give a big hand for the original Coca-Cola kid, Mart-y."

There's a weak smattering of applause. We know the show was awesome, though nobody claps all that hard. They never do. I, for one, don't want to seem over-enthusiastic. The private moment happening in your head between you and the stripper is sacred. A public display of what it meant to you is not cool. Only drunks show pleasure.

I look over to Brady, who's throwing me his best shit-eating grin. "I did good, didn't I?" he asks, waggling his eyebrows.

"You have no idea what that was, do you? You have just participated in the ultimate consumer experience," I say.

"It looked like a sex show to me."

I say the words slowly. "Low-brow. Transgressive. Product. Placement."

He blinks at me like he has no idea what I'm talking about, then snaps himself lively, saying, "Hey, I got an idea. Can I buy you a Coke? Suddenly, I'm thirsty." He stands.

"You're not really getting a Coke? You've got a full beer."

"I can't stand it any longer, I've got to ask him." Brady's looking round the room.

"Who? What?"

"Where'd he get that cigarette?" And with a quick pat on my back, he's gone.

Now Brady loves to say he doesn't pay for sex, he's too good at it to need to, but still, I'm a wee bit jealous. What if he did go home with the stripper? It's not unheard of. Strippers have feelings, too.

I'm not saying I'm in love with Brady, I'm not. Let me make it clear, I am not in love with Brady. Hell, I dated Tori for years and still can't say what love is, exactly. I've been a mite bit clueless. Two years of living together, I didn't even know Tori was a woman. Finding out after the fact that your ex-boyfriend is transgendered, your boyfriend was a girlfriend in his own mind, well, it puts a strain on an individual. It's like finding out your husband was a Nazi, or a serial killer, without the bodies. What I'm saying is, it's a shock to the system. Suffice it to say I have yet to absorb the full impact. So, love Brady, no. But there's a possibility, I'll admit, that something more is going on. With me. It's some kind of puzzling on my part, which isn't new. I've got a tired habit of getting curious about friends who are better left as friends.

It's the same for all of us. We get to wondering what he looks like naked, then boom, next time you're both watered to the gills, you're grabbing his dink at the urinal. He usually likes it, or let's say, shows appreciation, until the next morning when he's sobered up and either you have a big ugly talk about boundaries where he says he needs his space or he cooks you an amazing breakfast and doesn't return your calls. Which is fine, because you've followed the pattern so often it's what you expect and, by now, it can't hurt you.

Thankfully, that hasn't happened to Brady and I due to a new approach I've taken regarding friends and relationships: Don't get your hopes up and you won't get involved. So I'm cautiously not in love with Brady, and I'm not curious about him either.

He returns to the table, grinning. "You'll never guess what I just saw."

"His dink."

He turns his chair towards me and leans forward for a complete confession. "More than that," he says excitedly.

"What did you do?"

"*Nothing*," he says, sounding offended. "I couldn't find him, that's all, so I went to the can to relieve my dingle and there were these two guys talking. I don't recognize him because he's got his clothes on now."

"You are so shallow."

"No, he's got his back to me, so, you know, there's nothing to recognize. Anyway," he flaps his hands in front of him, giggling and scrunching up his face, "you *won't* believe this," he says, his voice sounding both excited and horrified. "I thought he was just standing there talking, he's with that guy who caught the bottle, they're standing real close at the urinal. Well, when I got closer, I peeked. He was pissing into the Coke bottle. The big guy had the bottle in one hand and a twenty in the other. No big deal, right? Who knows what he wants it for, but I'm a nurse, I see piss in cups all the time. Well, before I can finish up — okay, I haven't even been able to start, I'm too distracted — the big guy hands the twenty to the kid and *takes a sip*."

"Brady!"

"I'm telling you it was gorgeous. I'd have pissed my pants if I hadn't had my dick out already."

"So did they leave together?"

"No. The big guy left but the kid had filled the bottle and had to stop, right, so he's *still* got more to pee. I guess that Coke goes right through you. He turns to the trough and I'm telling you, I couldn't resist, I had to ask." He pauses for dramatic effect.

"What?"

"Where he got the cigarette."

"Oh. And?"

"He says to me, a cop, and grins."

"*No* way."

"Well it's a joke, of course, so I laugh. And then I got one. A line. I look at him and ask, 'Do you want to tell me the truth now, or are you gonna keep it all bottled up inside you?'"

I gasp, "You didn't."

He only laughs, squeaking, as he holds his chest from the effort.

"I can't believe you. You're shameless."

"Oh, you'd do the same thing."

"I wouldn't dare."

"Well, that's why I'm a lot of fun," he says patronizingly, "and you're the ugly-can't-get-a-date stepsister." I sneer. He continues, "Now listen, I got a real close look at our friend Marty, and I've figured out what makes him look more virginal than he is."

"What's that?"

"Make-up. Maybe you could try some to help you with your little problem."

"Very funny."

Brady gets all serious again and says, "I should get his phone number."

"Why?"

"So you can call him and get some Mary Kay tips, dearie." Times like this, I have to remind myself that Brady really cares or he wouldn't say such nasty things. Cruelty is a skill you acquire to protect a soft heart, and when shared with friends, being bitchy is no more than a skin-thickener. We're dogs, play-fighting.

When the stage lights come on again, I'm glad for the distraction. Brady slaps his hands together and rubs them. "Here we go."

"I don't know if I've got it in me for another one," I say. "Not to sound boring."

"But you are, Blanche, you are," he says, quoting from *Baby Jane*, which I've never seen. That sort of camp shows your age. I'm about to tell Brady as much when the speakers crackle to life and "I Just Called to Say I Love You" fills the room. The next guy is a blond, which I like. He has a phone, with a receiver in his hand. You don't need to draw a diagram to know what's coming. "Oh, no," I say, not hiding my fear.

Brady's got a similar pained expression. "Doesn't look good. There's only one thing to do." He taps the corner of his mouth with his pinkie, a gesture which has somehow come to mean that he's hungry for sex.

"You want to go to the park."

"Well, now that you mention it, I *could* get some fresh air."

"Oh, Brady," I say. I'm not interested in following him there. I like it fast and dirty, just not tonight.

"Now, Mick, I'm not going alone."

I point to my chest. "Tired."

"I've got a doobie," he whispers, leaning over the table, which only draws attention from the weirdos beside us, "and I only smoke half a doobie and that means I need someone to help make sure I don't smoke the whole doo-bie and you're my friend so you're going to smoke the other half."

"No."

He leans back, as if shocked. "Don't make me slap you in front of all these nice people," he says, maternally.

That's enough to convince me. "Okay, but I'm not stay-ing late." I say this every week, though my intentions are good.

He's already standing, slipping his arms into his jean jacket. He gulps back a couple more swigs and leaves some behind.

On stage, the blond has his balls twisted in the white spiraling phone cord. I sigh inside, dying a little with each tired act. I'm afraid the Coca-Cola kid isn't even enough to save me from a night of unsuccessful masturbating. I'll be re-creating my women-driven fantasies. I can't help but suffer a twinge of guilt, knowing I don't do girls in real life. Maybe I could beat off thinking of Tori. Middle ground, though we haven't had sex since she's come out as trans. Although her body might not be any different, her tech-nique may have changed. Can I picture that? Does a fan-tasy life answer to morals or is my guilt fucked up? I'm telling you, sex isn't easy, even in my head.

"Are you with me here?" Brady asks.

We're on the street, moving at a good clip towards the park. There are two bright stars to my right and the rest of the sky is cloud. I sniff. "Yeah, yeah, I'm thinking."

"Don't strain yourself."

"I'm thinking about my marriage."

"Why, honey, I didn't know you cared," he gushes, wrapping an arm around my shoulder.

That's not funny, and I realize, as fast as Brady popped the cap off that bottle, he's hurt me. I cover up by saying, "I mean my ex," and slap him on the arm to behave.

"But you know," he says, "I don't want to be married. I did that." He's more serious now, I can tell, because he has a hand in his pocket digging for matches. Brady's most down-to-earth moments happen while he's smoking a joint. The edge comes back as soon as he splits the last stub of the roach between his fingers and offers you half to eat.

"Not to sound shallow," he says, "but after my ex, Ronnie, died, I started having sex again and I'll tell ya," he chuckles, making his voice rise and pitch, "it feels mighty good." He flicks open the lid on his lighter. The butane tickles the hairs in my nose.

"Did you and Ronnie break up before he died?"

"Yeah, the day before," he says dryly.

"No, really, Brady, were you not together when it happened?"

"I was in the can taking a dump," he says. He's so damn hard to pin down, sometimes I could choke him.

His voice gets an apologetic softness to it. "No, we were still living together and everything, though he was bedridden a long time. I just call him my ex 'cause it's easier than explaining every time what happened. Nobody wants to hear your husband died of AIDS. It puts a real damper on the date."

He passes the joint. "I don't want to do that again. Ronnie was great, mind you, but you can't trust fags. They're always running around and lying, telling you they love you when they don't, and telling you they hate you when they do. There's no figuring them out. I've given up. That's why I have family. Right, my ugly-can't-get-a-date stepsister?"

"Honestly," I say before I can catch myself, "is that how you feel?"

"Honestly?" He makes his head wobble like he were spinning from the neck up.

"Come on."

"Sure. Sure, that's how I honestly feel."

Strolling into the cruisy part of the park, he offers me a stub of the joint. "Give you a bit of a body high later." This is the part of our routine where we chew the last bit of paper and pot and make plans for morning brunch. Tonight, everything's dark from the cloud cover. The trees are solid black, like paper cut-outs. And the men moving ahead of us, strolling the lane, are solid masses. There won't be much scrutinizing going on. Brady calls this a Veronica Dumont night, meaning VD. You can't see what you're getting.

"Well," he says, "time for the meet 'n greet. It was nice knowing ya." He extends a hand like he wants to shake. Not our usual thing.

I clutch my heart. "Are you leaving me for good?" I say, all melodrama.

"You couldn't get so lucky." He squeezes my shoulder, since I haven't taken his hand, and then he's off, into the bushes, leaving me to wander alone. I'm no more in the mood now, even with a buzz coming on, than I was when I started out tonight, but for argument's sake, I head for my usual spot, behind the big tree trunk that encroaches on the walkway. There's a narrow path into a clearing where it's very dark. The less I can see, the easier it is to fantasize, the quicker I get off. Job done, buddy can you drive me home?

I'm there only ten minutes, getting colder, when I decide to warm my hands up by masturbating. I hate the way men jump like they've been cattle-prodded if you touch them with frozen fingers. My cock, your cock, it's all the same temperature, so I think, what better way to keep them toasty? Unfortunately, I have more hands than dick, so while my pecker grows cold, my hands don't warm up. I'm ready to go home, be miserable and fall asleep when a dark outline pushes through the pine branches. Three feet away from me, I see who it is and whisper, "Gucci," to warn him it's me. I'm shy here, I don't talk loud enough. He's unbuttoning the fly to his jeans. "Gucci," I say a little louder, but whether he hears me or not, he opens his palm towards me. I step forward knowing that tomorrow morning will surely hurt, hoping, this time, tonight will be enough.

truman lee rich

MASS
PRODUCTION

for Dodie Bellamy & Kevin Killian

READER COMES TO THE PAGE WITH OR WITHOUT THE KNOWLEDGE that the Author is also Michael Turner. Reader decides to read on.

Character picks up the remote, turns on the TV.

KXXXXXXXXXXXXXXXXXXXXXXXXXXXXXXXXXXXXXXXXXXXXX

Reader assumes it's late, that the station's signed off. Character lowers volume . . .

kxxxxxxxxxxxxxxxxxxxxxxxxxxxxxxxxxxxxxxxxxxxxxxxxxxxx

. . . taking note of the channel, which happens to be Showcase.

Character wonders what the owners were watching before they left town. Remembers their taxi pulling up at 6:30 AM. Remembers driving past the night before, a blue light pulsing in the window. Assumes the owners aren't morning viewers. Character reaches for the *TV Guide*, scans Friday night. Decides the owners were watching Radley Metzger's *Camille 2000*. Character thinks: Pretty soft stuff. Character presses 03.

The face of Macaulay Culkin.

Character exchanges remotes, presses VCR, then PLAY.

A door bursts open. An untucked couple — a man and a woman — fall to the floor.

Character raises the volume, goes to the TV, kneels before it. Character is giddy, reminded of the girl in *Poltergeist*. A tiny voice, somewhere deep inside, squeals: They're heeeere.

The woman is struggling to undo his belt, the man is working on the buttons of her blouse. Or: the *woman is working* blah, blah, blah, the *man is struggling* blah, blah, blah. Author leaves it to the Reader to decide.

A car pulls up. Character goes to the window, sees it's the Chungs from across the street, then returns to the TV. The man is sucking on the woman's breast. Character is curious about the preceding scene, what the owners last watched before switching to television. Character presses REW.

The man sucks saliva off the woman's breast, while struggling to do up her blouse. The woman shoves the man's erection back in his pants. Together they leap from the floor, take three steps backwards, where the man opens the door with the suction of his foot. They back out so fast they take the door with them. Semen flies off the face of an Asian man into a new penis, a pink one. . . .

Character presses STOP before the Reader is reminded of *Time's Arrow*. Author wonders whether the Reader will have read Martin Amis; at the same time, recalls the old gag: Don't think of a purple pony. Author debates whether this paragraph should be parenthesized, rewritten, or chucked altogether. Something for the Editor.

Reader breaks down into splinter groups. Some are bored and don't care where this is headed; some are excited by it and don't care what happens. A dozen bored Readers return the book to the shelf, though many continue flipping. Janice Levitt, of Newmarket, Ontario, has decided to purchase the book on the basis of this story and the one by Nathalie Stephens. But McGill University's Robert Lecker, who has taught the work of Michael Turner and seems to like the idea of Truman Lee Rich very much, has come to the conclusion that he won't be assigning *Carnal Nation* as a course text, no matter how much he likes the work of Steven Heighton.

Character stares patiently at the CBC test-pattern while all this is happening.

A knock at the door.

Character goes downstairs. It's Mr Chung from across the street.

—Yes, Mr Chung.

—I have complaint.

—What's the problem?

—You don't live here.

—I'm looking after the house while the owners are away.

—My wife upset.

—Oh?

—She can see out her window.

—I don't understand.

—Through your window!

—Oh. Then I have a problem. She shouldn't be snooping.

Character goes upstairs, makes for the blinds. Just before shutting them, Character spots Mrs Chung. She drops her binoculars, jumps back, lowers her Levelors.

Character is annoyed by the high frequency tone that accompanies the CBC's test-pattern. Readers with perfect pitch will recognize it as a high-F. Character pushes MUTE, then presses REW. Character is curious why the owners have heterosexual and homosexual porn on the same tape. Reckons owners made their own mixed tape (or had it made for them). Character is glad to see the owners have such broad taste and thinks they're better for it. Character wonders what else might be on the tape. Recalls one of the owners bragging about the infamous pony loop. After ten seconds at REW (approximately twelve real-time minutes at SP) Character hits STOP, then PLAY.

The pink penis is being jerked up and down by a small hand. That, or the penis is very large. Character assumes that because the pink penis is the same one that came on a man's face earlier, and because that man happened to be Asian, and that Asian men generally have smaller hands than Caucasian men, then it is more likely that the penis is large but not immediately as large as it might have seemed had it been a pink hand jerking up and down and not the one on tape.

The camera zooms out to reveal a man on his back, his legs open to the camera. The Asian man is kneeling at the prone man's hip, his left hand jerking. The man on his back lifts his head, stares into the camera. Amateur stuff, the Character thinks. You can see right up his nose.

Character has been around long enough to know what's going on. The prone man is no amateur. His name is Casey Donovan, and the section of beach he's lying on comprises the first-storey view from Chris Eamon's Fire Island time-share. The Asian man is Terence Chan, a handsome young actor who came and went very quickly during the late 1960s. Nobody knows what became of Chan, although Bruce LaBruce claims to have met him in Hong Kong while touring *Hustler White*. Character assumes the loop is probably an out-take from Wakefield Poole's classic *Boys In The Sand*, which was filmed on Fire Island many years ago. Character continues to watch Chan's hand. Character feels nothing for the scene and presses FFWD.

The pace, of course, is frenetic. The hand — a total blur. For fun, Character presses PAUSE, just to see if the hand stops on something that resembles a hand. It doesn't. But a beautiful abstraction nonetheless. Character goes downstairs, gets the Polaroid from the dining room, then runs back up, two steps at a time. Character removes the flash setting, turns off the light, and focusses the view-finder inside the TV frame. Character presses the red button. The exposure is a long one. The image spits out.

Character gets a felt pen from the owners' study. On the bottom of the photo, Character writes: MOM, THIS IS ME JUMPING UP AND DOWN AT EXERCISE CLASS. Character places the Polaroid and photo on top of the TV, makes a mental note: Pick up some stamps. Character switches on the light, presses PLAY.

The hand continues at its frenzied pace, though nowhere near its FFWD speed. Donovan sits up; Chan swings around and assumes the reverse-cowboy position. Despite his small hands, Chan has a rather large penis. It hangs there semi-flaccid as Donovan attempts to work himself inside Chan's ass. But Donovan's having problems. His penis keeps slipping, getting softer and softer each time. Character knows this isn't Chan's fault, because he's seen Chan take bigger cocks before. Chan's such a pro. He looks straight into the camera and laughs. The scene cuts away to the jerk-off finale. Character guesses that's why it's an out-take. Presses STOP, then REW.

Convinced the pony loop must be somewhere on the tape, Character decides it's time to go hunting. Clothes form a small pile. Character is now naked. What to do while the VCR rewinds? Character goes downstairs to get some dope from the fridge, sees Mrs Chung in the window, waving frantically. Character thinks: This is fucked. Considers going back upstairs, but Mrs Chung looks distressed, in need of immediate attention. Character opens the door a crack.

—Everything okay, Mrs Chung?
—Yes, my husband very upset.
—I closed the blinds.
—Yes, yes. I saw you. Can I come in?
—I'm a little busy right now.
—I have my own drugs. My husband very upset.
—Do you want me to call the police?
—Yes.

Mrs Chung enters the house and goes straight to the kitchen. She pours herself a small glass of water and places it on the stove. She opens a few drawers before she finds the cutlery. She takes out a spoon, then goes over to the stove, turning on the gas. From her coat pocket she takes out a small plastic box, the kind you keep fish hooks in. From her other pocket she takes out some surgical hose and lays it next to the box. She wiggles out of her coat, letting it fall to the floor.

Character doesn't know whether to keep on watching or go upstairs and get dressed. Character's forgotten about the phone call. Mrs Chung waves Character over.

—This is A-one shit. Real highliner stuff. You must try.

—I don't know, Mrs Chung. I think—

—You wanna smoke instead? You will smoke some, yes?

Mrs Chung turns back to her rig. She removes from her box a small square of tinfoil and a syringe. Carefully, she opens the tinfoil and dips her spoon into its contents. She places the spoon over the flame. Character and Reader both get the picture. Character opens the fridge door, gets the dope from the freezer, and goes upstairs.

The VCR has rewound. Character presses PLAY, then begins to roll a joint.

A meadow, some pine trees, a broken cattle fence. Not a cloud in the sky. The image is many generations removed from its original print. From the tones, Character reckons it's early seventies Kodak stock. 16 MM as opposed to 8.

Character lights the joint, takes a series of short tokes. Downstairs: a running tap, some humming. Character places the joint in the ashtray.

A young woman in jeans and a gingham top. She reads hippie. She steps out from under a tree, shading her face with her hand. There's a groove to her walk that suggests she's out of it, a hype.

The hiss of slippers, the creak of stairs. More humming.

—Hello! Hell-*ohhhhh-oh*!

A pony is being led towards the camera. An older man in a cowboy hat is holding the reins. When the pony gets to within ten feet of the camera, it is turned lengthwise. The pony has a very substantial penis, even by pony standards.

—I'm in here, Mrs Chung!

The young hippie approaches the pony, kneels down. She's totally fucked up. The man continues his grip on the reins, as if the hippie can't be relied upon to control the beast herself.

—Can I lay down beside you?

—Of course.

Mrs Chung lies down beside Character, her eyes glazed. She looks right through the TV. Meanwhile, the camera closes in on the action: the young hippie takes the pony's penis and brushes it free of straw and woodchips. Once clean, she gives it a few strokes, then puts it to her mouth. Mrs Chung looks at Character.

—You like horses?

—Sometimes.

Author wonders if this is relevant to the Reader, to that particular Reader whom the Author finds so difficult to write for.

—You like to ride?

—Oh yes, very much.

Author wonders if this story would benefit from a particular setting, a town or a country, fall or spring . . .

—When was the last time you rode?

. . . whether ages should be given, if it should be generational, class-driven . . .

—When I was little.

. . . whether ethnicities should be reconfigured or completely neutralized?

—Mrs Chung!

Not nice to leave things so messy.

kxxxxxxxxxxxxxxxxxxxxxxxxxxxxxxxxxxxxxxxxxxxxxxxxxxx

Author likes things the way they are . . .

—*Hey!*

. . . its Character . . .

XXXXXXXXXXXXXXXXXXXXXXXXXXXXXXXXXXXXXXXXXXX

. . . so sexless.

tess fragoulis

SEX ON
THE ROCKS

"THERE'S A PORN FILM BEING SHOT DOWN AT THE BEACH," announces Karina, who hasn't been seen since last night, as she bursts into the cheese room. She flops herself onto her bed and rests her hands behind her head. "Right by the rocks where the old men fish every morning. You should have seen the looks on their faces."

"*Kapetan* Manolis told me there was something weird going on down there, but I didn't believe him," says Petros, who is learning how to hunt squid from the old fisherman whose hands are permanently dyed purple. "Said the lights scared off his lunch."

"Who's making it, Greeks or foreigners?" asks Ariadne, who by this point believes everything and nothing she hears on Nysas. She has become acclimatized. Or more precisely, she has become indifferent to those fine lines that separate the real from the imagined. She sits at the edge of Karina's bed and smoothes down her friend's mussed hair. When Karina lifts her head to tell the story, a fine layer of sand dusts the pillowcase.

"The really tall, bald French guy. You've seen him. He wears those little round sunglasses with the red lenses all day and night and goes up to women he fancies, asks if they want to be stars."

> > >

Ariadne has heard so many pathetic come-on lines since she came to work on the island that they have ceased to make an impression on her. But she does remember the bald Frenchman and his red-lensed squint, sizing her up from a distance on the beach. He walked up to her as she was about to enter the water and looked over her body as if it were a lace tablecloth hanging outside a shop window. He reached out to feel the texture of the needlework, running his forefinger along her arm to get her attention.

"Are you an actress, *mademoiselle*," he asked unctuously, "or just a natural?"

Ariadne stared at him, one eyebrow raised, letting him know without a word that she'd heard it all before. She turned her back to the Frenchman (and what a back — *magnifique* — tanned and straight, sloping down into a perfect ass, the pornographer noted), then dove into a wave and swam until she could no longer hold her breath. She cracked the surface of the water and arched backwards, dunking her head to smooth her tangled, snaky locks, and then rubbed the salt out of her eyes. When she looked towards the shore, the Frenchman was still standing there, staring at her through a camera with a very long lens.

For the first time in all her months on Nysas, Ariadne felt exposed. This was far worse than being spied on by her landlord, *Kyr* Georgis, who the villagers said did it with his goats at night. At least *Kyr* Georgis had the excuse of ignorance coupled with an underdeveloped brain, which left him at the mercy of his basest instincts. The bald Frenchman with the long lens knew very well that he was invading, stealing, and did it anyway, in the full light of day, with a dirty smile on his face.

Ariadne rose out of the water to her waist as if a retinue of nymphs was holding her up by her feet. The Frenchman, still peering through his camera, waved at her, then raised a thumb to indicate his pleasure with her pose. Ariadne raised her middle finger in front of her face in reply, jabbed it towards the sky. She then disappeared underwater, swimming among the sea's children, letting them guide her. She emerged refreshed at the far end of the beach where the waters were mottled with squid ink, though her skin remained clean. She didn't see the director applauding, didn't hear him yelling, *"Bravo, ma petite,"* or ordering his hunch-backed, horny toady to go into the water and bring her back, grab her by the hair like a caveman if she refused to cooperate. The toady stripped down to a pair of white, stained underwear and walked into the water warily. He had barely submerged himself up to his waist when a *medusa*, a jellyfish, stung his balls. He ran towards the shore screaming. The nymphs were on Ariadne's side.

> > >

"What were you doing at the beach this morning, anyway?" Ariadne asks nonchalantly, deciding not to share her encounter with the bald pornographer with Karina and Petros because she is in no mood for stupid jokes.

"I met a Yugoslavian guy at the Tartarus last night," Karina begins. "He was badly dressed, like all his clothes belonged to someone else, and he wore a pair of those horrible Speedo beach slippers. He was so proud of them because they were new that I didn't even have the heart to make fun of them."

Within the oligarchy of the cheese room, the blue and white plastic flip-flops merited as much disdain as Petros' tattered bikini briefs with the corny and vulgar decals stretched over the crotch announcing, "Rugby Players Have Leather Balls," or even more offensively, "Rub here and your wish will come true."

"Really? You fucked someone in Speedo beach slippers? Ugh." Ariadne grimaces, slides her index finger across her throat, while Petros gives the thumbs-down signal. Under the laws of the cheese room, Karina has committed a grievous crime and will have to die.

"Shut up, *malaka*. He took them off before he got into bed. His name was Miro and he waited for me outside the restaurant until closing, then walked me back to the village. We sat down on the church steps and he pulled out a bottle of retsina. . . ."

"And told her she was the most beautiful girl on Nysas. . . ."

"I wish you'd just get laid, Petros." That shut him up good and tight. Petros' luck with women was worsening as the season wore on. It was either the fault of the underwear itself or the rumour that there was nothing in it.

"Go on, go on."

"Well, I hate retsina, it gives me a headache, but I'd had a bad night at work and I guess I wanted to forget. So I took a few swigs and when he asked me to go home with him, I just followed."

Home for Miro was a small army tent at the campsite on the beach, the least favoured of all places for Nysas' seasonal grunts. No fuck was worth the mosquitoes or the sand in the crack of your ass. Only the most inexperienced tourists — those who lived in large cities — still laboured under the illusion that a sandpaper fuck was romantic. Karina was halfway down the road to the beach when she realized Miro wasn't taking her to a *pension*. She turned around, looked at the lights of the village and decided she was too tired to walk back up the hill. And Miro held her hand so firmly and tenderly that she didn't want to disappoint him — or herself for that matter. "That Yugoslav was damn cute," she tells her friends.

"You should have known that commies never have money for rooms," Petros taunts, challenging Karina's naïve surprise when Prince Miro held the flap of his one-man tent open for her to crawl into like a kennel.

"Well, I didn't stay long," Karina continues. "As soon as it was over, I crawled back out of the tent to take a swim, to wash off his sweat and the sand that clung to it. He was snoring like a mule by that point, and you can imagine what that's like inside a tent. I thought my head would explode."

"It was probably the retsina," Ariadne offers.

"That, too."

> > >

As Willendorf Karina emerged naked from the tent, she was blinded by lights set up on the beach. When her eyes adjusted to the glare she saw the tall, bald Frenchman. He was barking orders through a megaphone to a couple rutting on the sand under lights hot as the mid-day sun. "*Plus vite, plus vite,*" he commanded, and the cou-ple complied. It was not often that Karina got the chance to watch two people fucking without a sense of guilt. Not at all like the few occasions earlier in the season when she'd spied on Petros through half-opened eyes while she pretended to be sleeping. She recognized the couple from the Tartarus, where she'd served them and the Frenchman the night before. They were not a particularly attractive pair, but were obviously confident enough to share their most intimate moment with the world. That, Karina thought wistfully, must be true love.

As she stood there watching, feeling a little aroused de-spite the objectivity she was trying to feign as a not en-tirely innocent bystander, she considered crawling back into the hot, cramped tent with the snoring Miro. But be-fore she could decide, she was approached by the horny toady, whose jellyfish encounter was already old news thanks to the endless appetite on Nysas for such personal injuries. In his best Maurice Chevalier, he asked Karina if she wanted to be an extra.

"You must stand in *le cercle* and shout for *le* couple *qui baise* when I say. *Très simple.* You want?" Without waiting for her response, he took her by the hand and led her to-wards a circle of naked people. The toady then demon-strated the cue for her and the other extras. Karina smiled nervously at the man standing next to her, a burly brute whose body was covered in a coat of black kinky hair and whose engorged penis made him look like the painted satyrs who danced around ancient amphoras. She looked at the other people surrounding the couple — who had momentarily stopped rutting and were now chatting ca-sually — and realized that they were all chosen for their mythological attributes. Across from her stood fleet-footed Hermes, blond, curly-haired, with a tattoo of a wing on his ankle. Next to him was Poseidon, his beard dripping seaweed. By him stood Artemis, small-breasted and muscular, her eyes darting back and forth in search of prey.

When the toady gave the signal — two hands raised in the air like a conductor sustaining a high note — the gods, some drunk, some sleepy, collected around the couple and let out a triumphant cheer that echoed through the valley, up into the village. Karina's cry rose above the rest.

> > >

"You mean you were actually in it? You? Naked?" Ariadne guffaws and shakes her head in disbelief.

"You have a problem with that, Ariadne, my girl?"

"She's just jealous," Petros answers for her. "All that excitement and she missed out."

"You know, they asked me, too. Yesterday afternoon, at the beach."

"Oh sure, Ariadne," Karina drawls sarcastically. "It's always you they ask."

"Well, they did," Ariadne begins, then backs off. Though she did not appreciate the bald Frenchman's attentions, and would have never consented, she feels slightly annoyed at having been replaced. "When do we get to see it?" she asks over-enthusiastically, trying to rise above her sulkiness.

"I don't know, but I gave Jellyfish Boy my address. 'Send it to my mother's house,' I told him, 'or she won't believe that I was actually here.'"

Everyone laughs along with Karina, then Ariadne asks, "What about the Yugoslav?"

"Who cares about the Yugoslav," Karina replies airily, "now that I'm a porn star I can have anyone I want."

"So can we tell people?"

"Can I have your autograph?" Petros unzips his fly, and

the sparkly purple lips of his "Linda Lovelace Eats Here" briefs pucker at her.

"Fuck off, Petros. I wouldn't touch your wee-wee with a ten-foot pole. And you know how it is. Everyone already knows," Karina gloats. "As I walked back up to the village, Father Theodoros was in front of me, running up the hill, tripping over his robes, crossing himself and panting. He'll tell the old ladies, they'll tell everyone else and *Kyr* Georgis will bring me flowers."

"What the hell was the priest doing down there? That's disgusting."

"What do you think, Ariadne?" Karina rolls her eyes.

"I'll bet he was wanking off under there." Petros smirks.

Karina nods. "Praying for our sins, while committing his own."

"Poor bastard."

>   >   >

Miro the Yugoslav wakes up from his deep and drunken sleep, after the pornographers have packed up and left, after Karina has disappeared, and wonders whether he brought anyone back to his tent last night at all or whether he just dreamt it. He puts on his brand new Speedo beach slippers, lights an American cigarette and walks towards the shoreline. He splashes his face with the warm salt water to clear his head. There are already hundreds of naked bodies baking in the sun, stretched out on their straw beach mats and colourful towels like corpses laid out in a field after an attack. Miro goes back to the campsite, strikes his tent and decides it is time to go home. Something about all those motionless bodies has given him an uneasy feeling that he can't explain. He boards the ferry later that afternoon without looking back and completely forgets that anything happened the night before. Just like Karina.

r.m. vaughan

MANNA

THERE IS A SHORTAGE OF WATER, AHMED IS TOLD BY THE policeman, and you must go home and wait for the sirens to call you. And you must bring a proper jug or bottle, no buckets will do, and what a stupid boy you are, standing here with your shredded plastic bag, wasting everyone's time.

That bag will not hold a drop, the policeman sneers, and then you will be back at my door in less than a minute, with more water on your face from crying just like a foolish girl than that bag will ever hold.

Whose child are you, to be raised so stupidly? Go away now, before I find my stick.

But Ahmed lingers, tracing the shape of the watching eye, the holy signal, in the dust with his toes. The sun is the perfect flame at the centre of the holy eye, and it watches him, and the moon is its brother. Ahmed makes a circle inside an X inside a circle. His toe finds a stone.

Stand there then, you born fool, stand there and maybe the precious rains will come, the policeman laughs. Wait for your rains, idiot boy.

The policeman's laughter is clean and willowy, so unlike his curses. It is almost a kind sound, Ahmed thinks, like music. And will there be rains? Above his head, only gulls gather to circle and scream, no clouds.

The policeman goes inside and sits at his desk. Ahmed hears the policeman talking on his telephone. The policeman's bright voice curls and rolls with patience. Perhaps he is reciting a poem, like teacher in school? Or flattering a woman, a lady.

The policeman rises from his chair. The chair lets out a fat squeak. Ahmed can see the top of the policeman's cap bobbing behind the windowsill. He listens while the policeman fills a kettle from the tap, strikes a match, and lights a gas jet. The flame makes a tiny pop.

Here, Ahmed whispers, here there is water for tea.

On the street, a noisy pack of older boys form a line. Some carry stones, the taller ones hold boards and shovels over their heads. Ahmed watches, uncertain if the boys are angry or playful. Will they begin a game of war?

The street quickly fills with shouts. Grandmothers bring empty bottles, old men wave handkerchiefs. Water, they shout, water today! There are no young men, no girls on the street. Only boys, only the old ones. Water today!

The boys with boards and shovels crowd the policeman's door. Who will make the first step inside? Ahmed hides under the policeman's window box, picking dead flowers off long, dry stems.

These people are bad, Ahmed tells himself, but I am a good boy. The policeman will beat them, maybe he will shoot one or two, but the policeman will not beat me. The policeman will praise me for being patient, he will bring me inside and give me tea, and these boys will be sorry after they are beaten that they did not wait for the water siren. I will sit on the policeman's guest chair and have apples and tea. I will tell him a joke.

The policeman's door opens slowly. The boys tense, raising their boards and shovels a few inches higher over their heads. The old men nod at the grandmothers, who only grin. Now, someone shouts from a window, Now!

The policeman steps outside. His pants are loosely fastened, the two ends of his wide belt dangle off his hips. His bare chest is damp and his wet, dark hair stands up straight. Water runs down his neck, and soap clots behind his ears. Bath salts sparkle on the policeman's long arms. All around him, the smell of lavender and pine cools the air. But where is his leather stick?

The grandmothers look away, and the boys cover their mouths and giggle. The old men shake their handkerchiefs at the boys and walk back into the shade.

Ahmed looks at the policeman's bare feet. The bottoms are pink and smooth, clear water runs between his thin toes.

Ahmed is ashamed of the policeman's weakness, ashamed that he wanted to be the policeman's favourite.

The boys fall back and onto each other. They stumble down the street, laughing louder and louder with each step. The policeman clumsily fixes his belt, his eyes refusing to look down. He does not see Ahmed under his window box until the street is empty.

Still waiting, he asks Ahmed.

Ahmed makes a pit with his toe and buries the brown flower petals in the dust.

The policeman bends down to smile at Ahmed. He jostles Ahmed's pointy shoulder with his wide forearm. Ahmed shoves back. The policeman laughs quietly.

Soon, boy, soon, the policeman sighs, standing up. Soon enough.

The policeman goes back inside, shaking water out of his ears.

On the front step a puddle of grey water, a blot the size of two feet, lightens as it sinks into the wooden planks.

Without thinking, without shame, Ahmed squats and makes a circle with his lips. The water tastes of mud, shoes, and, curiously, apples.

sonja ahlers

LET'S ERASE THE HUMAN RACE (& START ALL OVER AGAIN)

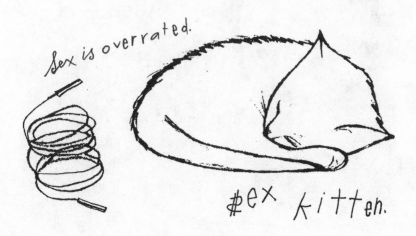

sex is overrated.

#ex kitten.

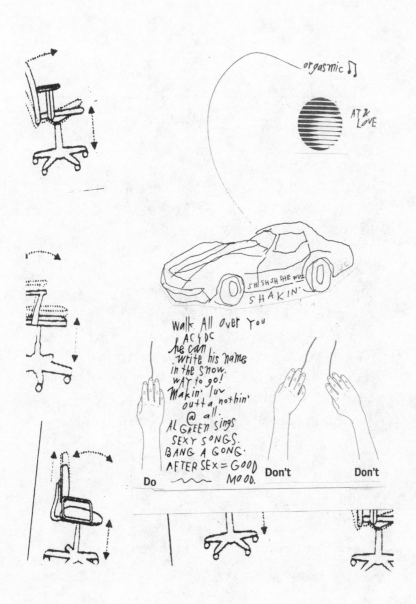

Hey Mother Fucker! Get Laid! Get Fucked!

We were at the high school dance and "Mony Mony" came on (not Billy Idol's version) We all start screaming the usual: "Hey mother! get laid! get fucked!" during the chorus. One genius inserts our principals name so now it's "Hey Mr. Allen! Get laid! Get fucked!"
After one whole round of that, the gymnasium lights FLICK ON totally assaulting our GOOD TIMES. "This dance is OVER!!" shouts the vice-principal. oh-vah

The End

THINGS TO DO

1. have sex
2.
3.
4.
5.
6.
7.
8.
9.
10.

Group Sex →

It never
works out →

I'm driving out of
my element

Bad Scene ←
no thank you. ←

Group Hug ☑

ALL DAY
YOU DREAM ABOUT IT →
May all your → dreams come true.

adidc

Se

Lamb of God, take away the sins of the world.

you are doing my head in

you are doing
my head in
& sick nurse—
now
you have a side
    kick
she is all boring
toplessness
she is sick
in the head
& we are shaking
on it

black & **Lavender**
tiles like in a
bordello

That's your job
as you become
unbecoming
trickier   slier
unfeeling & unfeeling
You forget
it's done
You forgot.

WE FUCK
& FORGET

Cosmic cash
machines & psychic

I fell in love with her on knowing her.
The nonchallant sense is excellent.
I like very much you who are very bright.

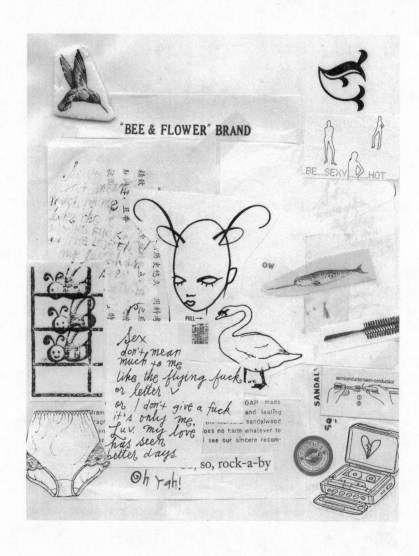

Wifebeater Part I

He was a wifebeater don't
you know ? You can see for
yourself - it's in her nose.
Aquiline with a prominent
hump - that's what. A bulb.
The reason why is 'cause she
would not have sex with him
one night. He was drunk &
she awoke to a punch in the
face.
Maybe maybe & just maybe
that's how I came to be.
No, impossible - I was
asleep in the other room.

all

Jewel sucks.

it

phylo
i wonder
if popping a zit

on his back means that you
love him. I know that my mum
used to pop zits off of my dad's back
they are divorced now & she hates his
guts.

okay that crap aside. wanting to be his siamese
twin wanting to crawl inside his skin wanting to
be together non-stop always always close-
r. & the drinking & the drugs are so safe with
him i don't feel afraid anymore
like i would pull open my ribcage to let him
inside.
& when we are apart i think about him nonstop
& close my eyes & breathe & feel myself
falling behind closed eyes tightly shut.

I don't want to keep you @ arm's length but
I've been in the past. A Vietnam in
heart. A raging like
consumption. I've been taken over before.
I don't know if I can allow that to happen
again.
But wouldn't that make me dead ?
it is better to have loved & lost
than to never have loved @ all

Well, I never said that
some other fuckhead did.

the warmth of a
human's touch.

people that
seem really
SEXY like like
on the outside
are inept in
le sack.
E.g. Marilyn
Monroe kissed
like adolf Hitler
according to one of mine

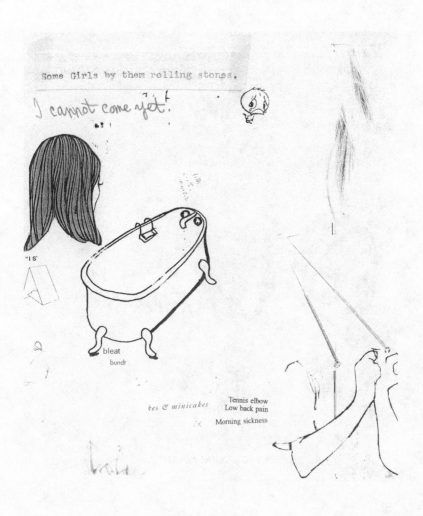

Some Girls by them rolling stones.

I cannot come yet.

"IS"

bleat
bundt

kes & minicakes

Tennis elbow
Low back pain
Morning sickness

1980

I love you

Sometimes I Worry about You

over the phone. I took a picture. I think it was the first time I ever
tried to photograph a telephone conversation.

True Story

Once
the boy
of my supposéd
dreams...
well - he said
to me

I love you.

I didn't believe him
@ the time.
No - I didn't believe
him @ all

I thought he was lying
or saying it so that I
would fuck him (or let
 him fuck me).
Or b/c he knew I wanted
to hear it.
Truth is - I was right.
On all counts.

Madonna
+
Spicoli

II

clint burnham

FREE COUNTRY

SIMON PASSED THE JOINT OVER TO MARIA. MMM, NO THANKS. That's enough for me. I hate it when the filter, when the cardboard gets all. . . .

What do you mean you don't like the grey rotting soggy cardboard? How could you?

Yeah, well, anyway. Indian music played.

There was this guy, Simon goes, god, you know there was this guy at work today, name of Hal, and he goes, we were talking about free trade or whatever and he goes. He's a real asshole, he was going on and on about something and I just felt like saying fuck you, you know what I mean?

Hmm. You wanna go into the bedroom? She rubbed her fingers on the palm of his hand.

Uh, yeah, unh-hunh.

She pushed up her top and reached a hand inside.

Whatcha doing? Showing off your belly-button.

No, just — and she pulled a bra-strap over one arm, then the other. She moved over quickly and sat on his lap. Mmm, this is nice. They necked for a couple of minutes, then he stood up. She squealed delightfully as he twirled her around. He had a bit of a head-rush from standing up quickly and from the dope and from the Indian music. He squinted a couple of times, wetting the rims of his eyes, and let her down. She bent over the table and blew out the candles.

He stretched out between her legs and pulled down her jeans. She still had her tank top on and she leaned back on her elbows, watching him. He drooled onto her lips and began licking them slowly. His mouth was very wet and soon so was she. He kept licking her, trying different tongue and teeth techniques, biting, penetrating, stopping something when she flinched and pushing his face hard into her cunt when she moaned. He rubbed his face from her asshole to her clit, licking everywhere. She pushed his head away and he moved up next to her, kissing her with his face still wet. She wrapped her legs around him and pulled his body against hers. He put two fingers into his mouth and put them between her legs, sliding them down her clit and lips and into her. He moved back down to bite her hair, and slid two more fingers into her. He curled them inside her.

He rolled over and she sat on him, grinding her hips against him. She bent her head over his cock, drooling onto it and then moving her hand up and down it. She took some lubrication and wiped it on his ass, sliding two fingers into him. She then flipped him over and sat on his ass, rubbing herself against him. She picked up the whip and flicked it gently on his back, then harder, raising red welts and he bucked under her.

Then she turned him over and grabbed his cock, sliding it into her cunt. He kept still, his hands folded behind his head, as she fucked him until she came. Then he pushed up into her, and she kept coming. She lay on him, shivering in small spasms. He rolled out from under her and lay on her ass, penetrating her and fucking. He panted after as he lay on her, their sweat cooled from the breeze. He rolled off her.

Pass me some Kleenex? They lay together for a while, then she stood up and moved to the window, looking at the traffic. A tall guy across the street approached the corner. He wore an orange safety vest and a turban, his grey moustache flat against his cheeks from a strap.

She turned around and looked at the empty bed. She bent over and grabbed a sheet and tossed it onto the bed. He walked in, and stopped to pull on his shorts. Well, if that was breakfast, that's it.

Hey, did you want something to eat?

Yeah, that'd be great.

Okay, great. He turned around and walked to the kitchen.

So you wanna get some tunes going here?

Yeah. She pulled a blue plastic milk cart out from under the table, and looked at the cassettes. She took one out and got it into the ghetto blaster. Aretha Franklin filled the small kitchen, and the phone rang. Up, oh, I'll get it.

He put two slices of bread into the toaster oven and sliced some cheese.

She picked up the phone in the hallway. Yeah, Candace? . . . Oh, not bad. So what are you up to? . . . Yeah, sure. Okay, yeah, sure, come on over. . . . Yeah, okay, see ya. She hung up the phone.

So's she coming over?

Yeah, you want some juice? Yeah, she thought she had to work today, but it turns out she didn't.

Oh, yeah, so what's she up to?

Well anyway, yeah, she wants to come over. We were thinking of going out, look at some fabric stores. Or she wants to, anyway.

Fifteen minutes later when they heard the knock she said, Coming. She hurried down the hall and opened the door. The hall was narrow and she knocked a Kewpie doll off a nail on the wall. Oh, just a sec. She picked up the doll and put it on the bookcase.

Candace came in and they hugged. So how's you guys doing?

Oh pretty good, we were just having some lunch. You want something?

Yeah, you want a beer or something?

Oh, yeah, I guess so.

He opened the fridge and pulled three beers out. He twisted the tops off and passed two to the women.

Oh, so's you don't got any cinq-oh, eh? Candace laughed.

They walked into the front room. No, what is that, oh, you mean 50? He wondered if his face still smelled like pussy juice.

Yeah, that's what we used to call it, cinq-oh. Or cinq-oh cinq-oh, you know. Yeah, so what you guys been up to?

Oh you know, the usual. Maria walked over to the stereo and turned the radio on. A hip-hop show was on, some bootleg 2Pac, and she turned it down a bit and sat back down. Just you know, doing stuff. I finished — she turned toward the window and stuck her head out. Hey you watch what you're doing there, buddy!

They all looked out the window. A neighbourhood drunk, a blond guy with a moustache, was on the ground. A guy in sunglasses and a black bomber jacket looked up at their window.

He's a racist. Are you a racist, too?

Maria hesitated. No, but he's no threat to you. He doesn't know what he's saying. He's just out of it.

Simon started to roll a joint. Jesus, you know, that guy's always shooting his mouth off and saying stuff.

Yeah, but usually the people around here don't take him seriously.

He's going to get into trouble, well, he probably already has.

Yeah, but did you see that time last Saturday? There was this big scene, and someone was yelling at him from their car, and this woman she like, was saying, what do you need, you know, doing the social-worker thing or the bible thing or something. And so she gives him a mirror, just pulls this mirror out of her bag and goes and gives it to him right there.

Oh, yeah? No kidding.

Oh, yeah, a real commotion. And I don't know, what's he going to do with a mirror?

Simon licked the joint to finish it and flicked a match. He took a couple of puffs and passed it to Candace.

Oh, jeez, I don't know. Three on a match, eh?

Oh, no, that only counts if you light three smokes with one match, like three separate cigarettes, eh?

Oh, yeah, oh okay. Ha ha, oh, I don't know. Oh what the hay, eh?

May as well party.

Yeah, really. You know, Candace, I was telling Maria about there was this guy at work, and he's like this total asshole, and he's going on about stuff and just a real jerk.

Oh, jeez, you know there's always these guys like that, you know they're like, let's get a beer after work. And you know, I've like known them for two days, and they're already just in your face, going on about how let's get together. Course usually they just take a couple wigs and that's it.

Maria took a drag. That's enough for me. Oh jeez Candace, we've just been smoking too much lately.

Oh, yeah, it's getting tragic.

Assuming tragic proportions. Gonna have to stop.

We're going to go dry for a while. Simon opened the hotel and dropped the roach in it. A week anyway.

Yeah, real heroes.

So, but what were you saying about that guy, Candace?

Hunh, what, the guy?

Yeah, the guy who just wanted forty winks?

Hunh, oh, no, I said a couple of wigs. Don't you say that? Yeah we used to say that all the time, in the bar, you know, in the valley, they'd go have a couple wigs, eh? Yeah, c'mon, they'd go, have a couple wigs, you know, like swigs.

Oh, yeah, that's hilarious. Maria took a sip of beer.

Hunh, pretty interesting. It's like when these people have their favourite sayings, and they're always going, whatever. Like there was this salesman I saw last week, and he's always going, bottom line. Or, Let me be honest with you. Everyone's living these clichés.

Yeah, well, you know like it's a free country, eh?

Oh, yeah, I know, I'm just, I dunno.

Candace picked up the comics on the table. Hey,

Snoopy, jesus, I haven't seen him in a long time.

Oh, yeah, it's hilarious. D'you ever notice everything they say is with exclamation marks?

I think they get paid for that. They get paid more for anything that's not a period.

They do not. Who told you that?

I dunno. I just heard it somewhere, I read it somewhere.

No. It isn't true. Maria leaned back in her chair, laughing.

He drained his beer. Okay, well then remember, well this is probably before your time, but in the early '70s there was the *Donny and Marie Show* and *Sonny and Cher*.

Yeah, but later it was just *Cher*. Remember that? I remember Cher's show. She always had those great Bob Mackie dresses.

Oh, yeah, weren't they great?

Yeah, but remember the big backdrop she had, too? Her name this big C? Yeah, those were the days for variety shows, that's for sure. Bobby Vinton, you know, he had that song that goes "Moya really Krakatoa, means that I love you so," in Polish? I don't know, it goes something like that.

Yeah, right. What's your point.

Okay, well, so like I was saying, there were these two shows. One of them *Donny and Marie*—

The other one *Sonny and Cher*. Oh wow, Simon, I don't know. That's pretty good. So this is all about some consipiracy or something?

No, it's just like I remember my sister saying to me, that she liked —

— wait, don't tell me, she liked *Sonny and Cher*?

No, she liked *Donny and Marie*.

Yeah, well, it figures. Didn't they do that song, "I'm Not Lisa, My Name is Julie"?

No, I think that, oh, maybe. I don't know.

But they did have that good song, "And They Called It Puppy Love."

Yeah, I think that was a Donny Osmond solo effort. I

remember it in the fall, when I was going to Grade Five. 1972 I think. Our school didn't have a gym, so in the winter every Wednesday afternoon we went skating at the rink. It was really cold there, too. I remember when I'd go to hockey practice Saturday mornings, if the janitor hadn't got there, and some kids put their skates on at home, so they didn't have to lace them up there. You know, the whole getting your skates tight enough thing. And these kids would be crying, it was colder inside than outside.

Oh, you're crazy. Don't pay any attention to him, Candace. He's out of control. Enough, grandpa.

In my day, he squawked.

Maria stood up. You guys want some coffee? Candace, you want some coffee? I was going to make some. I'm bagged, I don't want to spend the whole weekend tired.

Oh, sure, if you guys are having some. So hey, Simon, did you guys go dancing in your snowmobile suits?

No, we had sock hops, I remember those, and rubbing my hand against some girl's velvet ass, I mean she was wearing velvet pants or something. That was my first sexual experience. About a year later I was laying on a toboggan and I felt something, too. I had to beat this kid up, 'cause he was there with me.

Maria called out from the kitchen, wow, you've progressed so far. At least we don't need a sled, no.

Hey, watch it! Yeah, so Candace, what, d'you mean people used to wear their skidoo suits at dances?

Oh, yeah, they still do, if someone has a wedding or whatever in the winter and they're going to some tavern. They just unzip their suits half way down, and they'll dance all night.

Crazy. Maria came back out from the kitchen. Well, I know that when my parents used to curl, I can remember sitting up in the caf, and the old guys'd be there, they didn't have a licence so they'd just have a mickey of rye and pour it into their coffee.

Yeah?

Yeah, I guess they were still playing, or waiting for a
rink, you know. Or it'd be a bonspiel, and they'd go down,
and they'd be fucked up.

Hilarious.

Yeah, well, I think once one guy cracked his knee. Or
maybe that was the time my dad broke his leg. Or he had
bursitis or something.

So you want to get going, Maria? Oh, you're making
coffee.

Oh, no, let's forget that. I've just got some water boiling. Let's go out. It's so beautiful out, I just want to go and
sit in the park.

Hey, yeah, you want to go on the swings?

Hunh, are you serious?

Oh, yeah, he's serious. We'll see Simon. He's never going to get a job anyway, so he figured he may as well not
grow up.

hal niedzviecki

THE DAY WILL COME

FOR A WEEK, THEY PRETENDED HE WAS MORTALLY ILL.

Don't leave me.

I couldn't, love.

You won't leave me?

I won't leave you.

Hold me.

I'm holding you.

Ahhh. . . .

Does it hurt?

Stay with me.

I'm right here, love.

One day she said she didn't want to do it anymore.

It's a stupid game, she said. Enough is enough already, she said.

It isn't a game, he said.

> > >

You want to know what people look like. You want to know what people who could say such things and act such ways could look like. You do want to know, don't you?

> > >

He was fifteen. His brother was seventeen. He called his brother zitus. His brother called him fattie or pig boy or piggo or fat boy.

They were playing ping-pong. They were playing ping-pong in the basement.

It's not that big a deal, playing ping-pong.

They were playing intensely, hardly speaking, grunting as they lashed at the ball.

Take — that — pig boy.

Shit! Ah — ha — huh — at least — I'm — not — a — zitty! . . . ha!

He was up a few points but he knew he would lose. He always lost to his older brother. The games went to twenty-two, twenty-three, twenty-four points — but his brother always won.

And that's the way he wanted it to be. Eternity. Forever. An inevitability you could count on your whole life. The kind of solace in assurance you don't find again — that perfect moment, that teetering instant before you fall. It wasn't about ping pong. It wasn't about winning or losing the game. Patterns of circumstance. The snow swirling, TV warming up, disconnected image slowly forming into the anticipated, fluctuating picture. Play it safe. Take it easy. You're perched on the edge, unwilling to take that step, chasm echoing through the unknown, what you imagined, the way it might have been, the solitude of victory.

He was fifteen years old. This was as good as it was going to get.

I'm — on a — comeback — fatso!

No — fucking — way — zitus.

But something strange happened, didn't it?

Your brother flubbed an easy one.

And the score was nineteen to twenty, you. So the ball went to him for game point. And you could hear him clear his throat — he was a phlegmy teen, allergic to dust — and he bounced the ball once and nobody spoke and he served a fast slider almost off the side of the table but you were there — incredible — and it nicked the net as it stumbled back to his side and fell dead like a shot partridge; the perfect return, you won, silence.

Then the scream, your mother, upstairs.

>   >   >

Some people say death is the great equalizer. Some money. Others TV.

They watch a show where each team has a captain and the captain answers the question and then you have to agree or disagree with your captain's answer. If you're right you win the money for the team and then the captain decides if the team should risk it all on the next question. Whatever the captain decides, you have to go along. The captain is the captain because the captain was the contestant closest to getting the skill-testing question right at the beginning of the show. The skill-testing question was: how many spaces are there on a Scrabble board?

That guy looks familiar, you say. Doesn't the host guy look familiar?

Turn it off, she says. Jesus Christ.

>   >   >

It's raining outside.

He checks his watch. He checks the time displayed in the right lower corner of his computer screen. He moves from his watch to the on-screen time until he gets dizzy. Forty-eight seconds pass. He closes his eyes, thinks about meeting someone new, someone he will never see again. Meeting and fucking her.

He goes into Betsy's cubicle.

What time you got?

Betsy stops typing, squints at the screen.

I got 4:39.

He always asks her the time. It doesn't occur to her that he has the same computer, the same relentless display, the same view of the passing minutes.

Or it does.

She looks up at him, smiles.

Bored?

Uh me, he mumbles, nah, just, you know — he holds up his wrist. Taps the glass. My watch, he says.

Betsy nods.

Neither of them has windows. They don't know how dark it is. They don't know how the rain whips down, how the men and women scurry past each other.

> > >

They drive to the next city to visit his brother. On the way, he tells her the end of the story:

My brother's just standing there. And Mom's hysterical. I punch my brother in the shoulder, but he doesn't move. So I push him out of the way and I walk into the bathroom and there's Dad half on and half off the toilet, eyes rolled up into the back of his head. And Mom is trying to — I don't really know what Mom is trying to do — get him back up on the toilet maybe — I'm like just standing there, and my brother — he doesn't do anything — and then Dad all of a sudden spasms his arms around and snaps out of it. I don't know what happened then. I guess he pulled up his pants. He said he was fine, you know. He said, get the hell out of here.

> > >

You take the call. It's a mistake. Your door ajar. Post-coital intrigues, multinational mergers, the frenetic buzz of cubicle murmurs, suspicions swirling into flickering cyberspace messages orbiting an ever more temporary permanence. Betsy across the hall, ears pricked.

A sharp pain? you say. No, no, you say, it's all right, I'm — not busy. Don't worry about —

You look down and see that your fingers are reflexively tapping two letters, "A" and "S," over and over again. The screen is slowly filling, variations on a pattern, a prolonged sentence featuring recurrent usage of the word ass.

Your father died of a heart attack. What could you do? What could anyone do? A certain blockage. A repression not unlike love.

Comes and goes? you say.

She takes a tiny white pill every night before bed.

When you were first married, you used to place it gently on the tip of her extended tongue. It excited you, sexually.

She explains about a pain that has no central locus, no defining principle.

You're on page two. Your document autosaves. You type: AAAAASSSASAASASASASSSASAASAASASSAS. You're favouring "A," you notice, an imbalance in your finger strength, you wonder if it will get worse as you age; increased inaccuracies leading to indecipherable emails; a kind of muteness; a precondition to retirement.

Uh-huh, you say.

Starts and stops? you say.

You don't like what you hear in your voice. A certain plaintive type of whisper likely to be noticed, ears pressed to thin, hard, grey-carpeted walls.

A week? you ask. Just a few days?

The lines on the screen blink up, one by one, and then disappear.

I see, you say.

An open door. A call, potentially monitored. Pain flaring in the flexing joints of your fingers. Eight hours a day in a room made of portable walls. You don't mind the work. It passes the time.

I see, you say again.

She doesn't say anything.

She says: Are you typing something?

I'm keeping a record, you say. Transcribing the call.

—

Kidding, you say.

It's like a burning, she says.

You stare at your fingers, in motion. It's not a question of love. It's not a matter of insincerity. It's a place you want to go, it's a place you don't know how to get to.

You want to be the patient.

You hang up. Your fingers slump over the keyboard, just barely twitching.

Betsy looms in the doorway.

Getting a cup, coffee, she says. Her face is just right: concern, understanding, warning.

You pick up a random stack of papers from your in box, make a face.

No thanks, you say.

When she's gone, you head to the bathroom, lock yourself in a stall, masturbate.

You get up off the seat and drop a wad of clotted paper in the bowl.

Flush, wait, look in just to make sure.

> > >

She rubs her hands all over, combs his hairy chest with her fingernails.

C'mon, big boy, she says. C'mon, my big furry big boy.

He puts it in her.

That reminds me, he says. I was watching this show. . . .

Uh-uh, she murmurs.

He does it slowly, his fingers on her thighs.

This thing about this sub-culture, this, like, underground community called the Furries. They call each other, uh, Furries.

Furries, she kind of sighs.

He picks up the pace.

Yeah, he says, and they're like, obsessed with, uh, whaddya call it? — it's like when animals act like people, you know, whaddya call that?

Anthr — oh — po — uh — morph — ah — ism.

Yeah, that's it. He's really thrusting, talking between grunts.

And when they get together, he pants, they have these, like, meetings, conventions, you know, and everybody comes dressed up as a character, you know, like from Disney or whatever, and they have these panel discussions on rodents and marsupials and *The Lion King*. And there's — uh — but there's — uh — big — uh — split — uh — between the — uh — the ones who — uh — think — who

think it's like — uh — a sex thing — and the one's who —
uh — yeah — who just do it — cause they — uh, yeah —
cause they — ohh — love their — ah — characters.

Fuck me, she says.

> > >

Of course, we all know our parents are going to die.

Probably before we do.

Which is why we can't help hating them.

They think they've taught us love and devotion but
what they've really taught us is a devastating loneliness, a
perfect understanding of despair: I will die before you. I
will leave you to your irretrievable self.

He wishes he had a baby. He wishes he was a little boy.

On the outskirts of the city there's the giant fruit made
out of wood. On the second floor of the fruit there's the
restaurant where his family used to stop for pie.

He slinks out of the office, bumps into Betsy.

Leaving early?

Uh, he says, doctor's appointment.

Betsy shrugs, smiles unpleasantly.

> > >

She's waiting for him outside the apartment.

She's wearing those shorts he likes, her skinny legs
flowing out of her ass like forking rivers.

Where are we going? she says.

Get in, he says.

martine delvaux

TAXIDERMY

THE HEAD OF HIS PENIS RUBS AGAINST THE INSIDE OF HER mouth, brushes up against the entrance to her throat. Her cheeks tighten as she wraps herself around it like a glove, a prophylactic. She strokes the velvety softness of the flesh, the fleeting wings of a butterfly, the fur on a sleeping kitten's ears, kid gloves on the hands of an elegant woman. She circles it with the tip of her tongue, moving her lips as if sliding on a ring, a collar, a noose. Up and down. Up and down. And as she does this, as it slides between her lips, she flies, she escapes away from him, out of his reach, of his gaze. His injunctions against her dreams. Thoughts begin to travel, rescuing her from the scene. A spiral of memories trickles out of her like a slow stream of blood out of a hanging rabbit's eye, out of a girl's body.

They have known each other for years, and for years he has been driving her crazy. She is but the last in a string of women collected like so many insects, women found in the village where she grew up, little women chosen for their beautiful heads, girls whose bodies and minds he would be able to manoeuvre, entering them surreptitiously like a gust of wind or a fatal infection. Girls as farm animals, and he, the master holding onto the reins, yanking the bridle to pull the bit as far inside as possible. They would become older and wiser, or they would go mad, caught in a diabolical merry-go-round.

Her mouth moves up and down, up and down, *a Ferris wheel in a country fair, like the one that stood in the church yard of the village where I grew up, along the highway that stretches between Ottawa and Montréal. Where my mother and her husband had bought a yellow brick bungalow that sat in front of acres of grass and dirt tracks. Where my mother had a garden. Cabbage, squash, carrots, cucumbers, peppers, beans. Take the stems off, honey, take off those little tails so that we can have the beans for lunch. One head one tail, another head another tail, four thousand fucking heads and tails until I give up, until I throw them all in the garbage, until they find them and punish me, taking away the money that they had promised to give me later that day when we went to the fair. I apologize for my crime, show regret, paint strong disappointment on my face, until my stepfather, moved by my representation, hands me a dime, the only one that he is willing to grant me. One dime for having disposed of the beans. And then, when we arrive at the fair, I head for the gambling tables, the games where I can make my money grow, standing tall amongst the grown-up men who pat me on the head, running their stubby fingers through my hair, their dirty nails across my scalp. I proudly play at these tables until my dime turns into twenty under their burning eyes.*

Sometimes, he offers to pay her: twenty dollars a head. A whorish arrangement, a cold deal like the hire of a contract killer. When he does, she chuckles at his proposal and takes him up on it, takes him in and makes him pay for how he empties her. But this time, there was no discussion about money, just a nudge out of sleep and her drowsy compliance, her exhaustion as he moved her body into position, forcing adequate access. He pushed and pulled until she was under the covers, her head at his feet, until he thrust it in her face and, gasping for air, she took him in her mouth. A night deeper than before, her breathing stifled by his bodily heat, under feathers *heavy like the comforter that I used to hang across the tops of two chairs when I was a child, a tent where I would hide with a lamp to read the sex scenes of my favorite romance novels, trying to replace gardening chores with a forbidden education. A pleasure away from them.* Come closer. No, move this way. There, that's better. Yeah, that's good. . . . Oh, no, swirl your tongue. No, not so fast, yeah, there, that's better, now suck, suck, suck harder. Come, go, speed up, linger, she had to master the mechanics, she needed to concentrate, get it right, do it better, think, focus. See it in your mind, visualize it like an illness, like your own. Imagine a pleasure different from his. *Dick and Jane, as their glowing eyes meet in the darkness, as their hands inadvertently touch along the rail of the bar. An electric current runs through them as the feeling of love whisks them off their feet into the red Camaro that will take them to ever after happiness* while she mourns the loss of Cinderella stories, glass slippers, and white horses. For a shining fraction of a moment, he made her believe that he was Prince Charming. But now sitting beside him, uncomfortably crouched over, her body is folded into a cramp, hiding bedtime stories in the curve of her stomach.

My hands separate. The left one keeps holding the book as the right one opens up my pink cotton shorts, either from the top or from the opening inside the leg, along the thigh. His eyes are tightly shut, his arms spread out, away from his body, away from hers. Christ-like. Her hair hangs in her face, in her eyes. In his presence, she is alone. A lost child, a lonely orphan. *My fingers begin to move in awkward circles, surprising me. Sweat runs down my legs. My back and my hand become cramped with tension as Dick and Jane undress, as Dick pries open Jane's legs and crouches down between them, cocking his head so that his tongue can stretch out, as it starts moving in awkward circles, slow and then fast and then slow again. I make it last, I hold it back until it cannot be prevented any longer, until Christmas comes and fireworks explode like on Canada Day.* She feels a tingle in her left arm, a bruised elbow, a cramped leg. Her face is flushed, her upper lip covered with a string of sweat. He cannot tell, he cannot see how she becomes Tinkerbell, how she can fly over, away, escaping in the crisp winter night. In the pit of her stomach, a heavy stone that could drag her to the bottom of a river, where drowned kittens lie asleep after having caught their death of cold. *In the morning, I would find a bed of ice on the surface of the water that I left in their cage for my rabbits to drink. I had been given two young ones: a male, mostly black, and a female, mostly white, brother and sister, purchased from a farmer down the road. My pets. Adam and Eve. My stepfather had made an insulated shelter for them to survive the winter. When the spring came, their cages were placed in the backyard, right under my bedroom window. Soon, they were fully grown and I would be woken up at night by unfamiliar sounds. As the rabbits moved, the cage's metal frame would hit the side of the house, she fighting him off until there was nothing else to do but to give in, give up. Give it up. Empty battles, meaningless words, phantasmic resistances.*

For years now she has tried to evade him, pushing herself away when he pounces, disappearing in a corner, flattening herself against the wall of her cell. "No, I don't want to, not now, not today," she says to him. "Yes, now! You have to. You know you have to," he answers, his fingers tight around her neck. "You're mine now. My little kitten. My baby girl." His words drown her. She is not armed against him. She is without resources other than her own imagination and silent anger. His strength and persistence triumph over her endless struggle *and soon, a string of rabbits was born inside the row of cages, an ever-growing incestuous family. And then, one night, weeks later, new noises, male voices, heavy footsteps, a commotion different than usual. Almost as in a dream, until there was silence and I must have fallen asleep.* She is like a sleepwalker, both awake and withdrawn, present and absent, at once full and empty, inside and outside herself. *The next day, I walked to the back of the house in order to feed the rabbits before going to school. My morning chore. The cages were empty. Only the originary male and female remained, only them and a pile of red slimy flesh in a corner in one of the cages. Horror. A cold sweat covered my body. I shook in fear. "One of the females must have given birth when they were taken away," my mother explained when I called her at work, in a panic. I hung up in a stupor. Dead babies. My babies. The rabbits had been taken by a neighbour to be butchered and one of the females had given birth out of fear.* Muted, she circles over her own body like a hawk, until it is all over, until she can head down and touch her prey, take it into her mouth and incorporate it. Her tongue a knife. Her teeth pliers. She could scratch, bite, tear, cut, scream, cry, and spit out the piece of pink flesh. *The rabbits would soon be served to us for dinner, pale tender meat in a reddish sauce. "You'll see," my mother said as I fumbled around in my plate, "rabbit tastes like chicken. You should eat it." "My head hurts," I said. Aborted foetuses, menstruating children. Rabbits taste like slimy bloody babies, tight little bodies of blood-injected flesh covered in a transparent viscosity, an organic lens through which light is diffracted.*

She cannot see herself anymore, there is no-one there. No speculum could reveal her, inside or out. There is nothing here. She is nowhere. Only a shell, a robe of skin. *The man who butchered the rabbits was known as "the stuffer." He sometimes worked for the happy few who wished to proudly exhibit the prey that they had successfully caught during a weekend hunt, drunk men in plaid shirts who put up a picture of their wife between two dead birds. He had such talent that the dead animal's gaze seemed to stare at you, dark bullets straight into your eyes, from wherever you stood in the room. As if their bodies had been emptied out while they were still alive and something remained of their soul. In still motion. A collection of these mummified animals had been set on a sideboard in the bar of the village hotel, a hole where the men would meet and drink themselves silly. A raccoon, some wild rabbits, a squirrel, the head of a deer, ducks. . . . Even a white rat. The hotel was not far from home and sometimes, on my way back from school, I would sneak in and stand in the doorway, mesmerized by the smell of dust and beer, wishing that I could be inside the stuffed corpses, behind their eyes of glass.*

Sometimes, I would see him, the stuffer, I would catch his gaze through the crack of an open door, prying my body open. She looks, but there is nothing to see. His body beside hers, his cries, his moans. The numbness has spread throughout her jaw, pins and needles inside her gums, her cheeks. An eclipse: she is blinded by the absent reflection of his gaze. She keeps her eyes wide open in a blank stare, looking straight ahead, losing herself in a false horizon, as if there were no future, no hope, only the abyss of a live death. In and out, in and out, merry-go-round. He moans and moans like a bruised animal. And for a fleeting moment, the hunter becomes the hunted. She holds his life; in her mouth, the meaning of his existence. Only she knows the stuff that he is made of.

The day following the night of the rabbit killing, the night of the day when I found the dead babies, the stuffer dropped by our house in order to get paid. My parents did not particularly care for him, but they were cautious and nonetheless wanted to seem polite. "Do you want a beer?" He followed them into the living room. I could hear them from the kitchen, where I stood beside the bag that he had dropped on the floor as he walked in. It exuded the smell of dried blood. I carefully pried it open, all the while listening for voices in the next room. I slowly unzipped the canvas, enough to slide my hand inside. The teeth scratched my wrist as I blindly fumbled about in the bag, unable to make out what I was touching. I ran my fingers over pieces of cold metal, afraid of hurting myself, until I could not hold back any longer and pulled the panels apart, yanking on them as if my life depended on it. When the time comes, she recognizes the sounds and follows the rhythm, stages a ceremony rehearsed numerous times. She knows by heart the moves that he has taught her. Soon: his body tightens, his thighs flex, his neck folds back inside the pillow, his hands push on her head. Her mouth becomes a frozen scream.

Silently, I lifted various instruments from the pile of objects covered in dark red crusts, until I could distinguish their shape.

A saw, pliers, knives. A stapler and scissors. Packets of saw-dust and clay. Needles and thread. Styrofoam. Wire. Brushes, paint, varnish. Lost feathers and bits of fur. A pair of glass eyes. And then, this one object that I was unable to identify, a long metal rod whose ends were rounded in the shape of a baby spoon. I pulled it out of the bag to have a better look. The curved parts were filled with a thick transparent substance that had congealed and dried. Like egg white. She clenches her jaw and passes it through her teeth, thick saliva stick-ing to the edges of her lips. A violation. She slides it quickly in and out, in and out, while he spills over her face, across her cheeks, into her hair. Her mouth is full with the taste of salt, swells of sea water, raw oysters, running noses, and buckets of tears. He lies on the mattress, his arms spread out away from his body and from hers. Her eyes squeezed shut, she receives, spits and then swallows what is left in her mouth. She scrapes the inside of her cheeks with her tongue, dreaming of tearing it off with her teeth, of open-ing the skin, of emptying the shell, of amputating the in-side from the outside, of severing tail and head. *Mesmerized by what I had found, I didn't hear him enter the room. When I noticed his shadow hovering over me, I let out a scream. He took the spoon out of my hand. "It's a skull-emptier," he said. "Hard to find. I made it myself." I took a few steps back under his gaze. While keeping his eyes on me, he put the instrument away, zipped the bag shut, and walked back towards the liv-ing room. "Your daughter is very pretty," I heard him say be-fore I ran outside, "very pretty eyes. A lot of stuff must go on inside that head. You shouldn't let her out of your sight." He left that night, but he would endlessly return, looking for a new prey, the smell of blood on his merciless hands. Until he caught me, and skinned me.*

He sleeps, perchance he dreams of someone other than her. She wonders what thoughts travel inside his head when the lights are out, when pleasure has brought him rest. He sleeps and her eyes remain open. She stays awake under the feathers, in the cuckoo's nest, hanging off the edge. This is where she lies, years later, between his teeth, his claws. He thinks that he owns her now, grown up and beautifully accomplished, wearing a uniform of dead rabbit skin. She feels the aura of his heat, recognizes the faint smell of manure under a layer of cold sweat. She can hear the ice forming in the wind, the swaying of the tall trees. There is not a soul in sight. This house stands alone in an endless field like an open-air jail. He weighs on her, his body a millstone around her neck. She struggles to breathe until she gently extricates herself from his hold, pushing his limbs away from her, resisting the urge to hit, to scream, to pull the fur out of his forearms, his legs. She smoothes her hair, tears away the knots until her scalp begins to bleed. Deeper and deeper, from the surface to the inside, she digs her nails, ploughs her flesh. Tracks run on the surface of her skin, staging a strange network of communication. A ceremony. A preparation.

She runs her tongue on her lips, and breathes in an emanation of dried blood. A stabbing pain pounds inside her skull. She closes her eyes on dancing winter stars, fractals of pure white snow. She gets up from the bed and moves toward the closet, toward the canvas bag that lies on the floor. She slowly drags it inside the room, parting the stained flaps. Her hand deliciously slides between the teeth as she caresses the cold smooth metal, holds it between her fingers until she feels a new-found warmth. Then, she pulls the instrument out, holds it before her and sees her own reflection, her shining face in the moonlight. She can hear the ice forming in the wind as she leans over him, her knees on each side of his body, as if she were riding a horse. Up and down, up and down, merry-go-round. Her mind is clear, her hand is steady. A gesture a thousand times rehearsed. What she sees he will never see. What she is he will never be. *My head is full*. Her head is empty.

r.w. gray

BACK

I

WORDS TO REMEMBER LATER: RIPPLE, THIRST, ASKANCE, RICOCHET.

Sometimes I go too far just so I can see the way back.

In the bathhouse, stumbling into the dark room, the one with the holes in the doors. A little drunk and following a pretty boy. He's wearing a towel like everyone else, but also, for some reason, a long-sleeved shirt (remember a shirt worn by someone you loved once, maybe blue and a little frayed, the kind of shirt that makes you sad when it walks away).

Come back, but it comes out as a whisper.

Following the cute boy into the dark room and finding at first only a troll facing a corner. Looking around to the other side of the troll, find the cute boy on his knees. Watching from the side, watching as a line-up of plain men begins to form. Move from corner to corner, avoiding the hands that reach out to touch chest, ass, crotch.

Standing in the dark, seeing the troll. Seeing the cute boy's legs, his toes curling around the answer to a question not asked. Watching his calves flex, watching his legs spread a little and then pull back together. This boy with the lovable shirt.

Why is he willing to kneel there for just anyone?

Found walking towards that end of the dark room.

Found coming up behind the troll he's blowing, trying to get a better view of the other side.

Standing where not much can be seen, troll looking over his shoulder, then down the length. Thinking, shouldn't he be looking at the cute boy? But no, he's checking out the bulge under this towel, checking out these pecs, he's reaching back to grab this nipple like he barely cares that he has a cute boy down in front of him.

Troll turns a little too far to see, and cute boy stops going down on him to look up. String of saliva hanging from his lower lip, and he looked right in these eyes . . .

. . . and the   mirr   or   cut
both ways. I reach to my lower lip to wipe away saliva, and go down on the troll again. Waiting for the next plain guy and spitting the last into the corner.

2

Lost count. Stopped listening.

Yeah, you like that. Kiss those balls, yeah. Like that.

Half-listening to make sure the story doesn't go the wrong way and thinking about carpet beneath feet like a cat's tongue. Thinking about line-ups, the accumulation of people turning their backs to you.

Harder.

Working on the seventh or eighth ugly man. Cums in my mouth — *Fuck!* — and his legs are shaking, so it's looking like he might fall. Watching the falling man and sitting on my hands to keep from jumping after him.

Spit his semen in the corner with the others. Accumulation hides in the dark.

Looking for the next ugly man in this parade, but instead there's a woman, white towel wrapped around her waist, breasts naked in the dark. Two quiet suggestions at the wrong dinner party.

She doesn't say a word, just unwraps the towel, opens it like a coat to draw me in, like she's shy and doesn't want to expose her ass to the man behind her in line. I catch only a glimpse, this creature between her legs, and it mumbles something through thick lips, something that sounds like

Take a deep breath

so I say *excuse me* to interrupt and take over the conversation because you know how these things can talk when
you don't show them who's boss.

But she takes the upper hand, steps up to the bench I
am sitting on so I have to lean back. Facing heaven, she
moves her cunt over my lips to lips, grinds the last word
all pumice so my lips thin out and I just know it's harder
to smile through thin lips but I'll have to try. Nothing to do
but stick my tongue out.

You're welcome someone says but her thighs are slapping like wings against my ears and it might have been

Want some talcum or *My kingdom cum.*

She rubs hard hard against my face, uses my chin, my
nose to hit the right spots. Her thighs slap my cheeks, her
legs the wings of sarcophagus girls looking for ascension
— all punishment for not letting this tongue leave its
mouth for possibility. Someone's beating out a rhythm. No,
it's my head banging the wooden wall behind me, three
taps of the egg before she'd break it hard, my mother and
her ritual morning. *Eat them before they get cold.* Bumps
there now that won't go away, as if bone grew thicker to
protect in case of her return.

Her legs shake just like the troll's, but rapidly, and not
much to spit out but the taste, acquired they might say, but
wondering where she acquired it.

She steps down from her last word, stands in front of
me as she tucks the towel around her waist again. Her face
reads nothing about the story still ringing in my ears.
Raises her hand to wipe her juice from my face

Wipe that smile off your face mister
but in mid-gesture decides not to. She walks away.

3
Stunned by the shadow flung where the body just was, no
doubt. Looking to see next in line coming out of the darkness.

A little boy, couldn't be more than six.

Looking right through as he undoes his towel; undone stepping towards me. *Me, too, me, too.*

andy quan

INSTRUMENTAL

Flute

JONATHAN WAS A FLAUTIST. HE HYPNOTIZED ME. SOMEHOW, as the orchestra played, and the soft glint from the lights above reflected along the length of his polished silver flute, I was transfixed. Waited for him after the performance. Until he came out of the dressing room hall, still in formal tuxedo, and paused in front of me. I followed the colours from his chin to his shoulder: pink, white, black. Those stripes of formality have always made me weak.

I could see right away how strong his lips were, holding back a torrent of breath that, when released, became bright melody. In a soft light, I could see the shape of his lips pursing, the muscles around the mouth tensing and moving forward. Suddenly, I was caught in a gust of wind. I was floating in the air, notes and melodies vibrating out of my bones and skin. The air around me warm. Cool. Moist like the leaves of a fern after a sudden morning rain.

He played every part of me that night: arms and legs, the edge of my ear, each finger, my Adam's apple. The pressure of the air would pulse, strengthen, and ease. The stream of air would widen so I felt I could jump and bounce off it like a trampoline. Then narrow like a spotlight into a finger, a match, a needle. A thousand needles and me so perfectly balanced upon them that I remained unpierced. Whole.

Bass

You know the bass guitarist. Just out of the spotlight, hiding in the half-light at the back of the stage, a calm eddy in a rushing river, an indentation in a cliff face where the wind doesn't reach. The drummer on one side, arms multiplying like an Indian goddess; on the other, the octopus fingers of the pianist splaying through sea air; saxophonist centre stage right, a brass fury of horn and sweetness; centre stage vocalist playing huge sporting games with energy and sound, taking it in, giving it all away.

Amidst all that: him, feet less than shoulder width apart, a slight rock from time to time sliding into a sway. The legs and hips are toothpicks. The torso is a carriage. The shoulders lean forward to create a space below, then fall back to lift the infant into a cradle. Just awoken, his yowl turns into a hum. The arms are mismatched socks. The right arm tightly tucked against the body, a chicken foot, a claw. It reaches under the round thigh of the bass and grabs and plucks and strokes the dark centre. If it was pubic hair instead of electric cord, it would be braided by now, unbraided, curled, frizzed, straightened, gelled, spiked, waxed, bleached, and coloured. A body wave for good measure. The left arm falls down, crooks up into a V. The fingers are the long legs of a dancing spider or a cranefly skipping across a pond in the middle of a yellow-green glade, tall grasses, pollen in the air; you sneeze and the insect skitters. A saunter turns into a sprint.

Above this activity, the head is passive, a fixed globe, a longitudinal smile, a gentle curve that doesn't quite break into a grin. He's not showy; if he wanted the attention he'd have taken up a different instrument. But it's he who has the power, and no one knows it, not even the other musicians. They're carrying on; he's carrying it all. He's the railroad tracks under their train, the rope stretched tight beneath their strides and flips. Do all the acrobatics they want, humans still can't fly. He knows this.

The short scales, fourths and fifths, chromatic drops, back to the tonic. He's there, he's under them, he keeps it moving. If he stopped, the audience would know something was missing. They wouldn't know what it was.

> > >

He's like this in bed, too. He doesn't look like he's doing much. I mean, yeah, he seems to be enjoying himself, his foot tapping time, the upward turn of his mouth, but suddenly there's this vibration that has filled up your mind with runs and scales and intervals, and he's playing you like strings. Your body is taken over with pleasure and it's not your own.

Boom boom boom. This is dry sex; if it was wet, you might get electrocuted. As it is, there's a crackle in the air, feedback and circuit clicks, up and down the length of you.

He reaches over. He's getting into the groove. But first things first. Here he stops, he's tuning you up at the base of your torso, at the place where your legs meet, at your groin. You've got to twist and turn and loosen so that the pitch falls into place just so, so that all the strings are sounding off the same vibrations. That's what he's doing, bringing you further and further into pleasure, his ear on your stomach. *Ping!* Sharper, sharper, that's it. *Ping!* Now, that one's too sharp, bring it down, flatten it out. His breath warms your skin like a soft wind coming up on the outback. He's playing your nipples, the folds of skin near your armpit, the bounce in the muscles in your chest, the waves of your abdomen. He's bringing it all into tune.

Saxophone

I'd thought of a saxophone player as flexible, easy, groovy. Improvisational. But that wasn't the case at all. What he did, he did well, but he stayed stiffly to what he knew. He played sax; he wasn't a multi-instrumentalist.

So there we were. I tried to move his hands out of position; tried to coax his body out of its slightly hunched and twisted stance. No luck. I gave in. He started on the smaller parts and worked his way up. The tips of my index and middle finger in his mouth. The top of his teeth resting just over my fingernails, his bottom lip curled up over teeth pressing up into the first segments of my fingers. His right hand above the left, holding my forearm, his two thumbs balanced on one side, the fingers starting to rock and play on the other.

First one arm, then the other, both legs, his mouth on my toes, my feet, then the whole torso, finding reeds and mouthpieces at all extremities, keys to press with his fingers. My body makes soft clicks, cavities half-open and close at different pitches. His right hand always above left, thumbs trying to cradle behind, little fingers itching to press any key they can find.

I reach out to play with him as well, his long, lean torso slowly covered with perspiration, a slick golden glow; my hands polish the surface.

He plays the knobs on my spine, lowers me down to the ground, and positions his mouth over my groin. It is then that I realize that the fingers are less important than the mouth, that the music all comes from there. *Embouchure* is the word for it. The way that he presses his tongue and lips around the mouthpiece and reed, the exact configuration of the muscles in his cheeks and mouth, the way he blows, the way he brings the instrument to life, the way he makes love.

Blow. Blow. Blow me.

Sounds come out of my ears and nostrils. All the pores of my skin.

Piano

He was kicked out of the academy after Leonard, the harpsichordist (and part-time piano tuner), broke down in tears in the master's office. In front of the assembled authorities, he confessed that he'd been forced into it, that it was not his fault, and that, yes, he did it, but can't you see, Patrick was "too forceful, too persuasive, too threatening, too too too." His speech suddenly lost meaning and turned into musical sounds.

Faced with the blubbering mess in front of them, and unwilling to expel a student they knew would go on to great things (as he did), the headmasters instead (gleefully) took the opportunity to bid adieu (insincerely) to Patrick.

No matter. Patrick really had to admit that blackmailing Leonard into retuning the academy's priceless Bosendorfer to the seventeen tone scale of Kazakhstan throat-singers was worth the punishment, and besides he never could handle this classical shit. Years later, he'd grin cheekily at the memory, pleased at his skill, that he had found Leonard's weak spot. Though Leonard was afraid of his own body, and more so of his desires being discovered, Patrick had firstly seduced and secondly explored Leonard's young, nervous body until he found the hairless, soft, wrinkled folds of skin between Leonard's anus and scrotum. He experimented with gentle tonguing and hungry devouring till he found that the optimum technique was somewhere in between. Patrick thought of the action as the sharp vocal intake of breath you make when you see someone you really really want to fuck. Applied to Leonard, it would send him into a different world. Patrick wondered if Leonard had found people in later life who had sent him back there.

> > >

Patrick developed his classical repertoire regardless, could pick out pop and folk tunes easily, and was much amused by punk rock. Still, it was as a jazz player that Patrick was in demand. He would choose only the most glamourous, young, up-and-coming stars; and if chosen by him, they knew their careers were set into ascendancy. He would match his playing to their voices like a master choosing frames for a Renaissance painting.

During his piano solos, he would steal the attention. He would become the painting and they were simply the frames, as he exploded into colour and movement, as if painting music onto a canvas of air.

Effortlessly, he told stories of swelling emotion, lost loves, and broken dreams. Even though he had never lost a love, nor had a dream dashed to the ground. No matter. That's what a virtuoso is — a conduit for something, someone, somewhere much much bigger than the instrument itself, the player or the channel.

>   >   >

When we met, it was like the tiniest music, sparse notes from a music box, a child's melody with too much empty space in between. Later, he said he was getting to know me, and never let anyone in too quickly.

The next was scales. Arpeggios. Octaves. Hanon finger exercises. Who would have thought that a virtuoso needs to do the basics? Formula scales. First, both hands travel up two octaves together, then separate like wings until they are four octaves apart. They come together once more, climb two and descend two, part and rejoin, and fall back down to the beginning. Up and down. Up and down, that's what we did. Elevators. Escalators. Take-offs and landings.

He was testing me, he told me when it was clear I had passed. Like a doctor trying out each joint, a full physical examination. Here, he scrutinized tone and texture, age, sonority, action of the keys, and the type of wood I'd been made with. What kind of hall I was suited for; long and flat, or tall and round with a cupola in the ceiling.

He gave me lessons. I had stopped when I was a teenager, as an act of rebellion. I was slow at the beginning, but there was memory left in my fingers.

Not just the fingers, he scolded. It's so much more than that.

His aim was to play around, expand our repertoire, see if we could do a few duets, maybe some public performance, see what it would be like if he accompanied me, or if I accompanied him.

He explained that the art of playing is to share, that

music is not meant for one set of ears: a few is okay, but more is better. That means that each time music is more than practice, it is an event, an occasion, everything is to be remembered, every detail is to stand out. It is memory as well, he added. You play something like it's the first time you've heard it, the first time you've played it, like you are remembering the deepest emotions you've ever experienced, dark or light, and in doing so, you are making new ones.

> > >

The first time I undressed him: in a dressing room, with an unkind light glaring off a mirror in one corner. To start, I was content with his hands, long, muscular fingers. Soft palms with a touch of electricity about them. I placed his hand onto his long neck, the pronounced, sky-coloured veins from his wrists up the back of his hands reflected the sinews and veins in his neck.

I lost my patience. Undid buttons, belt, zip, shoelaces as quick as highway traffic, while he stood bemused. When I snapped down the elastic of his briefs, hands on each side pulled straight down to his ankles, his cock stood out, a perfect straight angle, like the torso of a concert grand piano, the lid down, one long, shining object with a gracious curve at the end.

I stood back and saw a person with so much energy that fat couldn't stick to him. Pleasing lines at all angles. A hairless torso, with shadings of hair down the legs, the forearms, a tidy arrangement at his groin. A scar, faded brown with a hint of white. Prominent nipples, dark aureoles low down on the chest. I fell close to him, a long, wet kiss, inside my head a jazz-inflected melody, a small French impressionist jewel from Satie or Debussy or someone whose works lay undiscovered.

> > >

The first time I fucked him: I had never stayed so long inside someone. Against the wall. On the bed. On a chair. Him on top, lowering himself onto me. Me on top, pushing his legs up to his head. On a diagonal, entering him sideways.

We paused for breath. "A music teacher at the academy called me an invert, said homosexuals bugger each other, and that is unnatural. I said, 'What is natural? Is music unnatural because it is created by men? What left in the world is still natural?' With him scowling and confused, I said, 'And your cheap polyester shirt is certainly not natural. You'll have to get rid of that.'"

I think he told me this because he sensed that fucking was new for me, even though he made me feel like a veteran. Could he have known that I had never felt so natural before, music of water and air, the tones of weather and bird-song, wind whistling through shapes of rock and wood?

He drew me out of my reverie, shifting his ass forward and back, clenching and releasing his buttocks, a coquettish swing side to side. Suddenly it was a bawdy Slavic dance, an off-kilter ragtime, a humming kazoo solo in the middle of a Teutonic aria.

Then it was rock music, '70s guitar, flesh slapping against flesh, heads thrown back and swaying. If we'd had long hair, it would have been flying every which way.

We came at exactly the same time, me inside of him, him shooting up, a perfect arc that touched my chest and fell down onto his.

>   >   >

The first public performance: it was at a popular gay resort with vistas of washed out yellows and greens, an ocean filled with small whitecaps that would burst into spray. Flecks of salt on all windows and woodwork.

The resort was fully occupied with gay travellers: couples, friends in pairs and threesomes, a handful of single men, all wealthy enough to escape to here and all hungry enough to want these surroundings of testosterone and chemical heat, constant cruising, tropical cocktail laughter.

Saturday evening was spent around the pool and spa. Clothing was optional and no one opted. Fluorescent glow-sticks lit buckets of condoms and lubricant. We staggered our entrances, wanting to warm up the audience, I strode by a row of three, my hand like a paintbrush on a fence, touching a different part of each: shoulder, chest, abdomen.

He zig-zagged through couplings and threesomes, not intruding and getting involved, a light stroke down the side of someone I knew particularly pleased him, hot breath on the small of the back of another.

I beamed with pride as I watched him weave through the gathering. He had an energy that I knew was recognised. Even without knowing why he was famous, they knew who he was.

By the time we met, all eyes were focused towards the centre, towards us.

We performed a full symphony in dramatic E flat minor, translated to four hands, arms, legs, two tongues, cocks, assholes. *Allegro con brio* to start, fast but not too fast, to set the pace for them to follow, some watching and masturbating, some attempting imitation. *Adagio assai*, we slowed down so that all around us were deep sighs and intakes of breath. *Scherzo*: we stepped up the pace when we felt their hearts and lungs were ready for it. Dancing, dancing, in, out, up, down, side to side, all directions to build up to the finale, *allegro molto*, fast fast fast, until you reach that plane where you don't think anymore, you only feel, and what you feel is pleasure. Then, a trick to confuse the audience if they didn't know their symphonies: *poco andante*, the most tender exchange of tongues. Then *presto,* this is the fastest it gets: sweat flying in every direction, mixing with ocean salt, the water from the whirlpool and swimming pool rising up, a mist turning into a hard, cooling rain of bodies, every man you've ever wanted, slick and shining. The wind sweeps up, the sounds of palm leaves rustle together in an imitation of a great crowd. Around us everywhere, applause.

nathalie stephens

AUTO-DA-FÉ

JEANNE D'ARC KEEPS CALLING. I WATCH HER WALK AWAY from flames. "This way," she says, keeps saying, over and over again. Her arms a windmill beckoning. She is wrenching sky from the clouds, blue on her fingertips.

I kneel with my face to the gravel on the road. Pebbles encrusted in my cheek and a boot on my neck. Laughter.

Press your fingers into me. "Loving you is hard," you say. "Harder," I say.

Isabelle blows Ferdinand. The taste of human flesh, burning. "Pig!" Someone shouting. (There are people watching.) Trails of smoke in Toledo. People crowding the plaza. Ferdinand fucking Isabelle between the pages of a book. Me reading the whole time, smelling olives.

I am drawing pictures on the wall, and you are watching from a distance. I lie down on top of you, pelvis to pelvis. Me on top of you, not breathing. The sun strikes the wall orange. "Fire!" Someone saw.

A tooth among the ashes, golden, catches the glint of a falling star. Sparks the Andalusian night sky. There is no one left to see. I tuck constellations into my mouth, bring them home to you. We slip underneath stars and sleep until people come to claim them.

I am swimming with my two hands inside of you. Tasting salt. There is blood on my face. You notice. Caked dry. Dirt mixed in. "What have you been reading?" Corpses ground to dust. A small dog barking. Everywhere, eyes seeing things and me not listening. "Nothing," I say. *Nada.*

A word wound up inside like a knot. Crease of skin. Crumpled earth. Made smooth by a voice in flames, reaching. *Soy yo. Soy yo.* A name branded into me and your face attached to it.

larissa lai

POMEGRANATE TREE

THE FIRST TIME I TOOK SOMETHING, I WASN'T CONSCIOUS OF reasoning, only the thrill of illicit behaviour for the pure joy of it. It was a wind-up toy I took, a duck on a tricycle with a whirlygig atop its foolish, flap-mouthed head, a nineteenth-century European fantasy of eccentricity and madness, made on the eastern rim of the Pacific Economic Union in what used to be China. It was an awkward shape and rattled loudly, but I had lots of space beneath my overcoat and a very steady, quiet foot.

In no time it became an afternoon diversion. I racked up a considerable collection of wind-up toys — a plastic goose that ducked its head as it moved and scooped its neck down, then up and forward as it came to a halt; a wind-up frog that jumped helter-skelter across the small desk beside my bed and tumbled gleefully to the floor; a small-scale replica of the Hindenburg; an elephant that twirled around and balanced a beach ball on its nose; an alligator that snapped its jaws as it scooted forward; a panda bear that marched and beat a drum to keep the time. At the beginning, I promised myself I would never visit the same toy store twice, but my passion for these quaint, odd toys got the better of me. And there was a shopkeeper who had better taste than anyone else, who brought in wind-up fish and butterflies, grasshoppers and spiders. The precision of their movement, their life-likeness, was more accurate than that of toys anywhere else and they delighted me. Later, when I looked at the price tags, I realized that I was costing him a pretty penny. At some level, I must have known he suspected me, but by then I couldn't help my-self. The adrenaline rush that accompanied the thrill of re-bellion had become an addiction I couldn't shake.

One particular Friday, he had a green wind-up snake that slithered across the floor on its belly with such real-ism I had a shudder of recognition. I loitered until he dis-appeared for a moment, I thought, into the storeroom, and then I snatched the thing up and dropped it into my over-coat pocket. He had me by the scruff of my collar before I knew what hit me. To this day I have no clue how he could have gotten there that fast.

"Get your greasy fingers off me, you ugly bugger!" I yelled. But I didn't have to say much more because sud-denly there was a small explosion like a pop can bursting right beside the cash register, and then flames spreading rapidly up the walls and over the counters. He dropped me and ran to save his cash box. And then Evie was there. She grabbed my hand and we ran out the door laughing like idiots. In the distance, I could already hear sirens wail-ing. Evie pulled me into a dark narrow alley. We ran and we kept turning corners until I completely lost my sense of direction. Having been raised to believe that it was far too dangerous to walk in the city, I had no idea about these alleyways, no idea that the city was connected by them, that it had this whole internal maze, an alternate organiz-ing principle beyond its bustling, commercially prosper-ous facade.

We tumbled out of the maze onto a dilapidated street on which many houses were abandoned. The walls of some had crumbled, leaving steel and concrete beams exposed and rusting. Others were hopelessly covered in a black fuzzy mildew that seemed to thrive on cheap aging stucco. A few were occupied. There was no electricity. Torches and candles burned in the windows. Evidently, there was no running water or functional sanitation system either. The street reeked of raw sewage. Numerous scrawny cats and the odd stray dog roamed the boulevard; in the gutters rats fat as small footballs scampered, sleek and foul, their yellow eyes gleaming.

"Better stay with me until the dust settles," Evie said.

"I can't. My brother and father —"

"Will have to do without you. Didn't you see the video camera in the corner of that store? If you're going to do that kind of stuff you have to be smarter."

I knew where we were going because of the tree. It wasn't tall — barely the height of the house. It sloped a little towards the porch, so that it protected and obscured the house at the same time. Its branches were knotted, growing away from the trunk in contortions that spoke of age and grace. Dark leaves fluttered a little in the evening breeze, revealing their slightly paler undersides and the faint red of their veins as though blood flowed from the trunk, down the gnarled branches and into their fine tips. The most striking feature of the tree, however, was the fruit, which glistened round and red against the foliage. I thought they were apples at first, a strangely round, squat variety, much smaller than those I was accustomed to, cultivated from Saturna's Bright Beauty seed. At certain angles they seemed to emit a dull glow, but perhaps this was a trick of the moon and the candles that burned in the window of the house behind the tree. Pomegranates, swollen with blood and seeds. Evie reached up absently, picked one, and dropped it into her pocket.

We passed beneath its branches, down a wood plank walkway that led to the back door of the house.

On the back porch sat an old woman in a rocking chair, smoking a pipe and reading by the light of a single candle. There was something oddly familiar about her face, although I was quite sure I had never met her before.

"My eldest sister, Sonia 14," said Evie.

"Nice to meet you," I said to the old woman. She lowered her pipe and nodded at me politely.

We stepped in through the screen door. The kitchen was lit by four torches, one on each wall. In the corner by the stove was a heap of cabbages and a small basket of pretty radishes, round and red. Before the kitchen table, on long wooden benches, sat six other women all in their late teens or early twenties. They were chatting rapidly in a language I could not quite get a hold on, though I thought I recognized a smattering of Chinese, a few words of Spanish, some French, some English. Four of them were busy wrapping a seasoned mixture of pork, bamboo shoots, and black fungus into wonton wrappers. Two held infants in their arms — girls, if their ragged baby dresses were any indication. At intermittent intervals along the benches were four makeshift cradles made from old fruit crates, in which four other children slept, quiet and peaceful in spite of the chatter and raucous laughter. But the uncanny thing was that, except for pimples, scars, and wrinkles, all six of the women's faces were identical to Evie's.

"Sonias 116, 121, 148, 161, 211, and 287."

"Your sisters."

"Yes."

I nodded hello, but my stomach churned. A gaunt cat rubbed up against my right leg. Another came up along my left.

"Just kick them away," said Evie. "The place is crawling with them."

"How come you're not also called Sonia?"

"I am. I'm Sonia 113. I changed my name when I escaped. It's weird though, never quite comfortable."

I didn't know how to respond so I said nothing.

"You hungry?"

"A little."

She moved towards a little stove that sat in the corner and lifted the lid of the pot that sat on top. Whatever was in there, there wasn't much left. She scraped some into a bowl. Sticky rice with *lap cheung, ha mai*, and *dong gwu*. It was still warm, though a bit dry. As an afterthought, she reached into her pocket and tossed me the pomegranate she had picked on our way in.

I sat down at the table and dug into the dry bowl of rice.

"You're lucky it's dark out," she said. "In the daytime we eat out of cans because we can't risk anyone seeing our smoke."

I wondered about the eight of them and their children, living in such secrecy so far from the inhabited parts of the unregulated zone. Were the Pallas Corporation's security people looking for them? Who were the fathers of these quiet children?

I finished my rice, and broke the pomegranate open. The dark seeds lay dormant and silent within their glistening red casings — rubies or blood pustules? I broke a few away from the tension that held them packed to the others and popped them into my mouth. Crushed the taut skins between my teeth and felt sweet juice gush into my mouth. Swallowed. I had no idea how a pomegranate tree had come to grow in this temperate climate. It was an unnatural transplant that made no sense in the cold rocky soil of this once upon a time country called Canada. But I was accustomed to eating strange fruits without questioning their origin, as my parents had been before me, and theirs before them. I put my questions aside and hungrily gobbled the sweet red seeds.

When I was finished, Evie picked up a half-burnt candle that sat in an old brass candle holder beside the defunct electric stove stacked with chipped bowls and plates. Put a match to it and headed down the hall towards the stairs. As she walked, the salt fish scent she left in her wake was subtle but unmistakable. No wonder cats followed her. I followed her, too.

My head brimmed with questions. How did all the Sonias escape from the facility? How many more were left inside? Where did all the infants come from? Why did the corporation use the same genetic material for so many workers? And why, of all of them, was Evie the only one that bore that distinctive smell?

There was a hallway at the top of the stairs, and at the

end of the hallway, another door, which opened into a narrow stairway to the attic. The steps creaked under our feet as we climbed.

"Who helps you?" I asked.

"There are these students. . . ." she began, but then she stopped. "I think you have enough information for now. How do I know I can trust you?"

The ceilings were low and slanted in the little attic room. The floor was strewn with books and papers. In the corner slumped a stained, beat-up futon, without sheets, and with the stuffing poking out of the holes. A ratty synthetic quilt and a couple of limp grey caseless pillows lay haphazardly tossed on top.

"You can trust me," I said. And then I paused because I knew it wasn't true.

She sensed my hesitation. "That so?"

"No," I said. "You're right. It isn't." Quietly I told her about my first international literary coup; the poem I sold to Pallas to use for advertising.

As I spoke, her eyes narrowed and darkened. I could see something bitter rise in her chest, see her choke it back as she waited for me to finish. And then it burst out of her. "How could you?" she sputtered.

"I don't know," I said defiantly. "It just happened."

Her fury frightened me. I thought of the ancient Sonia sitting outside in her rocking chair, the three younger ones downstairs making *sui gow*. How many were there working in the dark factories and what did they have in them that gave them the wherewithal to escape? I wondered if their backs were drawn with scars in the shape of wings, like Evie's.

Meanwhile, Evie ranted. The worst rhyme I have ever heard, and playing right into the hands of the enemy. Not to mention massacring your own talent. How could you? But her hand reached out and touched my face and her fingers burned against my cheek. She leaned forward, mouth full of fire, hot against mine, which was cool like sweet tofu, so cool, delicate, barely able to hold its shape; a collision of hot and cold, red fingers tugging at cool ivory buttons.

We rolled onto the tattered futon, coarse cotton at my back and Evie's weight burning down into me like a rocket, tumbling back too fast into the atmosphere. Girl sex, who said pimply girls can't have it, serene on the outside and secretary shy. No rosy limbs here, in spite of all my action adventure lately, I remained thin and sickly pale, never mind my father's health-conscious cooking. So what, it didn't matter in the heat and weight of this entanglement — anger, fury of betrayal, recognition, and perhaps also love?

Evie's unmistakable salt fish smell, my cool durian stink melding. See, there is somewhere to sink to, rapid hands and buttons still popping, down down down, hot skin against cool releases generative mist, what do you think you're doing, Catholics would have a field day, not to mention all those calm-voiced, bespectacled therapists in their carefully flowered offices.

Touch me here, where hip bone meets belly, soft and moving inward, and smooth cheek against neck, yellow teeth razor sharp, the threat of cut, of bite, sudden letting of blood from beneath the surface.

Who taught you this? Schoolyard taunts or hot fast Hollywood, too blonde for either of us, Sharon Stone pantyless recrosses her legs, or does it come from anger, this anguished eating, teeth bursting apple skin into crisp, pale flesh, and squirt of clear, sweet juice. Who taught you this, teacher, tell me, touch me, girl mouth against breast. And then something hard, a twist from fag boy personals, bulging cock, nine inches uncut, but something better, a sudden sprouting through masses of wiry down there hair, a startling peeking out of flesh, girl cock, teach me, what would you call it, red curve of traffic light, stop. Or at least take it slow, imperceptibly slow.

Tell me a dirty story, she said. Fingers moved small

circles against the hard button. On-switch, I said, a new way of lighting this dark house. I can't tell you a story when you're playing with the on-switch. She laughed, dark head against my breasts, spiky short hair prickling where the skin is less than smooth, where I knew the pepper pissy sweat stink of durian rose, not stinky, she said, sweet, like steam rising through the small hole in the rice pot's lid, pooling a thin, translucent liquid over the top, which would later dry to delicate skin. Tell me a dirty story.

So I tried. Once there a was girl cop, traffic cop (Her head slid down my belly.) . . . a girl traffic cop who stood every day at the intersection (Couldn't they just put up a traffic light?) shut up, this was a long time ago. She spent the day beckoning and holding off cars, eyeing the drivers to make sure they understood. (And?) I can't think. (Her head moved downward, laughing mouth suddenly full of wicked intent. Well? she said, her mouth too full.) I don't know, there was a truck (What kind of truck?) a red truck, a beat up one with rust on the door and a sleek, black dog in the back, and a no-hair-buddhist-nun-in-a-checkered-shirt truck driver. And the traffic cop was so mesmerized by her strange beauty that she could not let her pass, and so she held up her hand, Stop, and let the traffic keep coming and coming in the perpendicular direction, waved it on and on all the while staring at the buddhist-nun-in-the-checkered-shirt truck driver until she realized there was no more on-coming traffic to wave on. (This is not a dirty story, too tame, she complained, flicked her tongue hard and too accurately by way of punishment.) Okay, so the truck driver nun charged the intersection, opened her door and swept the traffic cop up off the street and into the truck. (She must have been very strong.) Oh yes, she was very strong because she worked out every day at the YWCA. (And then?) And then, Jesus Christ, I don't know (You taste good. Tell me.) and then the truck driver nun barrelled off down the highway while the traffic cop lapped her cunt. (Disgusting. How do you think of such things?) I don't. You made me. And quiet and quiet, and then only the sound of, the smell of, the taste of, sudden flash of water gushing and gushing and gushing.

carellin brooks

FIFTY-ONE

1 THE BOY WITH THE BLACK ARMY PANTS AND THE BEAUTI-ful mouth and eyes, and the way his father used to just walk into the room. Sorry.

2 If you write things down one way, do you lose your memory of the rest?

3 Her name was Rachel and she did have that biblical look, especially later.

4 I didn't know if I really wanted to date any French women, so what I got was a Frenchwoman who hated her own culture and told me to stop whenever I tried speaking French. She took me to the amusement park where she worked.

5 Then we got involved in a threesome with this little thing from the other university's queer discussion group who later on, in another city, started her own sex magazine.

6 Robin used to come to my house to teach me how to hurt people. We used her as a subject. My roommate, another Québécois twenty years older than me, didn't approve. My roommate's girlfriend, with the big blunt hands and break in her voice, her I liked.

7 Michele had a little silver car and she used it to show me New York. Inside and out. My grandmother always remembered how well she drove.

8 I met Lesley at the gay centre in New York. She claimed she knew me from school. After we'd already started, her on the floor at my feet, I found out she'd never done it with a woman before.

9 The first weekend I was there I caught a bus to London. I sat in a corner of the gay café reading *Polysexualité*. At eleven o'clock the lights went out for last call and the woman who'd been sitting at my table grabbed me and we necked for long minutes. I never saw her again but, oh, how I thought of her.

10 If you travel to a different place, does it count? If you don't know their name, does it count? What if you forget later?

11 Then this other little one, well, she was ginger all over, and she taught me lots of words I didn't know, and used to leave chocolates in my box at school. She was a good one.

12 Rachel was this tall, supercilious girl with a sister who looked just like her but almost better. They were practically twins. I met them first in New York when I was at a sex club breaking up with my girlfriend. I saw her again in Brixton one night, alone. She took me back to her council flat but we never did anything.

13 I still have that leather vest.

14 There were a lot of clubs and it all starts to blur. AJ met me in a bathroom. She lived in Walthamstowe.

15 There was a little butch I took back to Oxford because I didn't have anything else to do with her, and she stayed around for two days, and I had to tell her to leave, and her friends were mad at me afterwards.

16 The one from Canada sent a nice note. The next morning she was standing in front of the sink with her shirt off when the scout walked in to empty the bin. Other than that I never once got caught with anyone in my room.

17 Al and I slept in the street after she answered the butch survey. She made me come right there on the pavement.

18 I insulted Wally by asking about her flowered pants. They were camouflage.

19 Chuck won't talk to me anymore. She says I trivialized our relationship.

20 I was in love with the Canadian. It was a nice kind of pain. She'd ask me for advice about the girls she was after.

21 Katherine was a piano teacher. We broke up in a restaurant.

22 She asked if I'd ever been caned and I said no. Later, when she wanted me to go home with her I wouldn't. My friend was so in love with her even after they broke up. It was tragic.

23 My girlfriend drove me to the bar where they were holding the sex party. Later, upstairs, the two skinheads wouldn't believe me when I said I was too small.

24 I heard Jacquie's accent and jumped right into her arms. I wasn't wearing a shirt at the time, which she remembers better than I do.

25 Al and I would see each other, cock an eyebrow, go into the nearest stall, spend five minutes and come out afterwards, but we never spent the night together again.

26 Niz started sleeping with somebody else.

27 I forgot about the girl who threw her dirty socks out the window so that I found them the next morning.

28 The one in Japan who was sitting on the railing, all butched up, when we came out of Shinjuku station, and I turned to my friend as if to say, this is what you've been hiding?

29 For a while I got celibate. Then we broke up.

30 There was this woman I used to visit every time I came up, and she used to say she couldn't connect with me, because it had been two years or whatever, but in the meantime she would never answer any of my letters.

31 Nancy worked as a security guard in my building. We used the first-aid room on the fifth floor.

32 I met her at the Lesbian Avengers, where I was really interested in this punkish little mother who wouldn't even look at me. She took me back to her dorm room in Regent's Park and the next morning her new roommate asked for a transfer.

33 My friend said I should look her up when I was in Montréal so I went into her bar and said a few things to make her notice me. Later we were in a car in Scotland. She was driving and her dick hung out of her pants.

34 We went to this straight pub up the street and all the time she kept asking what I was thinking, what was in my head, and it was such a relief.

35 She had these lush, big breasts and now she says she wants to cut them off, even though she doesn't want to be a guy.

36 My ex who was also her ex decided, along with her other ex, that we should get together, so they arranged everything, and when I was already under the covers she came in and threw the dildos on the bed and we did it once.

37 She was such a tease, saying she didn't really want to, she couldn't decide. Later she died of cancer. Why hadn't I seen anything, when she was lying there and I had the speculum?

38 She took off her shirt because I asked her to. We had sex with the rest of our clothes on because I was worried about my girlfriend.

39 I forget which ones it was the first time for, whether I made them bleed, who did what to whom, stuff like that.

40 She looked good in a suit, but that was all. Once I asked if she was angry and she said no but it turned out she was.

41 I went out with her because she had the smallest hands on the planet. Neither of us seemed to like it much.

42 He was the only other boy who ever really bothered to try.

43 We had to sleep together because we had both recently published books and were equally recognizable.

44 The girl in Toronto, I thought she'd never know anyone I did, but it turned out she had roomed with my friend's girlfriend in Belfast. What are the odds?

45 She didn't want to do anything so we just lay there all night and cuddled. Later she said it was because I was such an asshole.

46 My doctor said, "No change in partners since the last time, then?"

47 She said that I was the love of her life, but just like all the other ones, she only figured that out after we broke up.

48 I really would love to run into her in the supermarket where she works.

49 She had the softest, most delicate mouth for such a caustic woman.

50 I said, "No, of course I didn't desire you, I just wanted to see what would happen." Because most of the time, it's true, I don't.

camilla gibb

ON ALL FOURS IN BROOKLYN

IT MUST HAVE BEEN OCTOBER BECAUSE I REMEMBER PUMPKINS perched on verandas and window sills, and the smell of the air changing from still to bitter. I do know that it all started the fall after the summer when no one could pronounce my name. Mid-1970-something. The fall before the winter when I decided to lock my bedroom door and write poetry in front of a window propped open with a carrot. My hands were stiff as I scratched lines of rhyme about dead cats and other roadkill. I spent hours in the bath on Saturday mornings, reading biographies of famous women writers who had sewn stones into their long skirts and thrown themselves into rivers, or given their children glasses of milk before they stuck their heads in ovens. I was just about thirteen years old.

No one could pronounce my name because I had changed it at the beginning of that summer. I was no longer Penny Hill but Oksana Vladivostok. I was the only surviving member of Russia's royal family, the great granddaughter of King What's-His-Name. I had narrowly escaped execution by hiding in the womb of an English woman called Mrs Hill. Or was I a mole? Perhaps I was to attend Eton and Cambridge and get a top secret job with MI5 working for a certain Mr Philby, but here I was thwarting the whole plan by revealing myself at almost thirteen. I was tired of being Penny Hill. I had lived in Mrs Hill's house for far too long.

The whole charade was crumbling into ruins anyway so I thought I had nothing to lose. Mr Hill had fucked off about a year earlier. Mrs Hill had screamed down the alleyway behind our building, "I should slice your stinking prick off, you bastard," and that was the last we saw of him. A moving van came a week later and cleared out all the decent furniture, leaving us with the formica table and the plastic kitchen chairs in our third-floor Brooklyn apartment. Two weeks later, an insipid American salesman named Roger moved into Mrs Hill's bedroom. I didn't have to put up with this. I was, after all, Oksana Vladivostok. If I revealed myself I could probably defect on the grounds of seeking political asylum and find a way out of this increasingly awful mess. Perhaps I could be sent to some boarding school for Russian defectors, and study Latin alongside other reformed moles, anorexic gymnasts, and closeted ballet dancers.

Mrs Hill wouldn't hear of it. Everyone else listened, though.

"Suck my cock, Vladivostok," cretinous boys in the schoolyard would taunt. "You fuckin' commie."

The *kinder*-whores with their tube tops and satin shorts preferred calling me "Princess Commie Big Shit" and, occasionally, "Lezzie."

> > >

I first got the reputation for being a lezzie after Gary Fraser, the boy I was going around with in grade eight, stuck his tongue in my mouth. Gary, who was a geek, but a cute geek, had asked me to dance the slow song with him at the end of our chaperoned junior highschool Valentine's Day party. I'd never danced a slow song before and suddenly there I was with a boy's head on my shoulder looking over at my almost-best friend Charlene Boysenberry who was dancing with Dillon and mouthing "do this" as she rubbed her hands up and down Dillon's back.

"No way," I mouthed back at her.

In the alarming glare of the gymnasium's lights after seven whole minutes of *Stairway to Heaven*, Gary said,

"Uh, thanks," and then popped the big question: "Hey, you wanna go around with me?"

"Sure, I guess so," I said, looking at my shoes.

"Well, I guess I'll be seeing you then," he said, leaning over and giving me a peck on the cheek.

"Sure, see ya," I said, not looking up.

He walked off with his hands in his pockets and Charlene came running up to me and said, "Score!"

"Charleeeeene," I protested.

"So, did he ask you to go around with him?"

"Yeah, so," I shrugged.

"I knew it!" she shrieked.

"It's no big deal," I said dismissively.

"Oh, yeah. Like Miss Snotty big tits Brenda Tailgate doesn't even have a boyfriend. She'll be so mad," Charlene said with glee. "So, is he a good kisser?"

"How should I know!" I said defensively.

"Well, didn't you?"

"No. Gross."

"Well, you're going to have to kiss him."

"What for?"

"'Else he'll think you're a lezzie," she said.

>   >   >

Ugh. So I let him be a disgusting boy. But only the once. I walked home with him after school the next Thursday and we sat in the park and I picked at my cuticles while he told me all about his drum set and the band he was going to form. He asked me if I wanted to do back-up singing at a bar mitzvah he was going to play at — told me I looked a little like Karen Carpenter — and then stumbled over his big feet as he stood up and lunged across the sand with his tongue outstretched. All I remember is the horrific feel of peanut butter over bristly taste buds as he plunged his fat purple tongue into my mouth. I thrust out my arms like an automatic weapon and pushed him and his purple peanut butter muscle about seventeen feet across the park.

I might be exaggerating a little, but I haven't been able to eat a peanut butter sandwich ever since. No, siree. I would rather eat a barbecued toad. At least that's what I told myself when Mrs Hill plopped down a plate of mushy peas and soggy fish fingers in front of me at the formica table and said, "Okay, whatever your name is. You still have to eat."

"Not as long as he's looking," I mumbled derisively at the sight of my mother's dullard boyfriend, Roger.

> > >

The story of my reaction to Gary got around school pretty quickly. If we'd had a school newspaper the headline would have run: "Commie Girl Rejects More Than Capitalism." In fact, it only took a day before even Charlene was calling me a lezzie. "I don't know if we can be almost best friends anymore," she said one day after school. "You're ruining my reputation."

What reputation? I wanted to know.

"First, you're not cool. Nobody wears jeans like that anymore. Second, people will start thinking I'm a lezzie too because I hang out with you."

"Fine," I said. "Why don't you go and be best friends with Brenda big tits, then?"

"As a matter of fact," she said, coyly, "Brenda did invite me to her party Friday night."

"I don't care."

"Well, I think I'm going to ask Gary if he'll go with me."

"I don't care what you do."

So for the next three months it was Charlene and Gary holding hands in the schoolyard and her rolling her eyes every time she saw me. Being a Princess Commie Big Shit Lezzie was at least better than being boring old Penny Hill though, even if it meant everybody hated me. It also meant an accelerated trip from normal grade eight into the special ed. class in high school, a euphemism for what everybody else in grade nine called "the retard class." We knew we were a bunch of mutants but at least we had each other. There were twelve of us, of varying degrees of lunacy, neglect, and corruption — the worst given to throwing matches at girls with peroxide blond hair. The saddest was Luke the deaf boy, whose hand I took to holding when other boys in *normal* grade nine opened their mouths and made whale noises at him. The best was Trudy, who called herself Rudy because she was a girl who believed she was a boy.

They called Trudy and I "lezzies" when we showed up to the grade nine dance together modestly drunk on rum stolen from Trudy's evil stepmonster — hot spicy liquid we had sucked through a straw in the subway station. I was glad they were calling someone else a lezzie, too, but technically, I knew they weren't right: Trudy thought she was a boy and I thought I was a Russian princess. We were a match made in some heaven other than mid-1970-something Brooklyn. Trudy Rudy with her crew-cut and army fatigues and her all-purpose jackknife chained to her studded belt. Oksana Vladivostok with her long, auburn braids, wearing a corset suffocating her thin frame under her baggy, patchworked, flared overalls. Oksana with her head on Trudy Rudy's belly reading the *S.C.U.M. Manifesto*. Trudy Rudy blowing smoke rings over Oksana's head in the heat of the late afternoon.

Mrs Hill said, "I don't know if she's quite right, what's your name," as she plopped down a plate of bangers and mash in front of me on another one of those endless nights at the formica table. Vapid Roger burped in collusion, and then me behind the locked bedroom door again, at the open window. Writing poetry again — rhyming lines less about dead cats and other roadkill than the winter before, and more about the sickness of Trudy which was churning in my stomach. I wanted to throw up every time I smelled anything resembling her. Camel Lights, burnt rubber, Carmex. I wanted to throw up. I wanted to smell her.

> > >

"Fuckin' lezzies," my ex-boyfriend Gary Fraser and his posse of pimpled pinheads shouted as I inhaled Trudy's cigarette smoke in the alley beside our school.

"Fuckwit," Trudy shouted back. "I'm not queer. I'm a guy."

"Yeah, right. Good one. Like you got a dick, right?"

"Bigger than yours, pencil prick," she snickered under her breath.

"Whaddya say, bitch?" Marco said out of his dirty, peach fuzz-covered mouth. "You're fucked, man," he said as Trudy just glared at him in mocking silence.

"A lot more often than you," jibed Trudy. "Had more girls than the whole lotta you," she boasted.

"It's true," I said in her defence. "No one's gonna put out for a limp dick like you, Marco. Rudy's a regular Don Juan."

"Yeah, well, no one else would fuck a retard like you anyway," he said, wandering off in pathetic defeat.

>　　>　　>

"Hey, thanks for standing up for me," Trudy said to me later.

"'Guy's an asshole," I said, matter-of-factly. "Got a face like a shit-covered bum."

"They're just stupid guys. They're just jealous."

"Jealous?"

"It's a dick thing."

"You mean, you really have a dick?" I asked, somewhat timidly.

"Sometimes," she shrugged.

"But how'd ya get one? I mean, were you born with it?"

"From Mrs Salerno."

"The gym teacher?"

"Yup."

"She gave you a dick?" I asked, open-mouthed.

"So I could give it to her."

"Like how?"

"Do you really want to know?" she asked me provoca-
tively.

"Well, yeah."

"By bending over on all fours in her office and showing me her ass and asking me to fuck her."

"No way."

"Yes way."

"And so did you?"

"Until last week."

"Last week?" I asked, feeling a strange jealously creeping over me.

"Till Mrs Kudagrass 'the stupid ass' walked in."

"Mrs Kudagrass walked in?"

"Yup. Wasn't too pleased. Seems their happy marriage
is on the rocks."

"What? You mean they're lezzies?" I said out of my gap-
ing mouth.

> > >

The poetry I wrote behind my closed bedroom door
stopped rhyming then. It started searing and crying and
thumping beats like erratic hearts and not altogether making sense. I could hear Roger outside my door pacing between Mrs Hill's bedroom and the bathroom. I imagined
him in his ugly beige K-Mart underwear telling Mrs Hill to
hurry up because he had to take a dump. I blocked them
out, carried away with the sickness of Trudy and the words
in her honour which made no sense. I crouched on all
fours with my tight begging ass in the air while Roger shat
himself in the hallway.

The last dance of our grade nine year, Trudy dyed her
hair black and wore a white polo shirt. She smelt like
Stetson and Carmex and my legs felt weak at the sight and
smell of her. We drank tequila from a mason jar marked
Black Currant 1975 in a phone booth at the intersection
down the road from the school.

"Look, the lezzies are here on a date," mocked a pack

of pimply boys as we walked up the stairs to the gym. Mrs Salerno was there at the door talking to a group of teachers but stopped dead at the sight of us.

"Spot check for alcohol, drugs, and weapons," she stated in military fashion. I looked alarmed. Then she grabbed Trudy, pulled her arms into the air, parted her legs, and started imitating an airport official.

"Forget it, Helen," Trudy said to Mrs Salerno under her breath. "Who do you think you're going to embarrass?"

"Think we've got one here," Mrs Salerno said, gesturing to her colleagues. "Feels like she's packing a pistol." She unzipped Trudy's pants, and out sprang seven hard inches of blue plastic.

"Oh my God," Mr Mackenzie said, stepping back in horror.

"Don't worry, it's not loaded," said Trudy, rolling her eyes.

"I don't know what that is, exactly," said Mr Mackenzie, remembering he was supposed to be an authority. "But I'm sure it's against regulations."

"I don't think the school has any rules about this," Trudy said.

"That's enough young lady, person, whatever you are," said Mr Mackenzie. "I think you and the Russian girl should just leave."

Trudy looked at Mrs Salerno with disgust then, grabbed my hand and said, "We're outta here," and jumped down the stairs three at a time.

>   >   >

We never talked about it, but whatever had just happened was enough to get Trudy Rudy chucked out of school. It's been years now but I can still feel the tight grip of her hand as we crossed the school parking lot that night, her three steps ahead of me, apologizing. I remember every footstep through air thick with the hormones of a high school dance. Moaning in my green bedroom with the air conditioning on in winter in order to muffle the sound of poetry searing through me. Writing lines on bent knees.

She didn't turn around and look at me that night. In fact, she never let me see her face again, but I've been reaching out in the dark ever since, trying to find her lips. Imagining my hand moving across her cheek, and running through her hair. The feel of her lips on mine, soft, warm fullness, the envelope of my mouth unfolding, begging. The tequila-brushed sweetness of her breath as she sighs heavily into my mouth and her tongue flutters across my lips and teeth like a butterfly dancing around the edge of a flower.

I levitate from my bed in search of her body. Float into her and gasp at the feel of her dick through her trousers, pulling her harder, closer to me. I move my pelvis, dance my pussy through the silk of my skirt, through the denim of her trousers, the cotton of her boxers, the space between my bed and ceiling and the fantasies of most of the last several years. I moan in anticipation as Trudy's hands hover over my breasts. Her fingers move in quickly and tightly to tug at my nipples and my tongue tumbles into her mouth and moves slowly, dreamily. I move in time to music I still hear echoing from a gym full of mutants where girls are choking on floundering purple tongues.

I turn around, bend over slightly, and imagine resting my palms on the trunk of the principal's car.

"Perfect," I can hear Trudy laugh as I move my ass in small circles against her. "Too sexy," she groans behind me.

I move like the poetry I have known only on pages. I reach behind me and slowly pull my skirt up over my ass to tempt her. I hear her unzip her trousers. She pushes her dick against me and I lean down further. "Do it to me now," I whisper.

"Are you sure?" she breathes into me, her lips against my ear.

"I want to know what it feels like."

"All at once, greedy girl?" Trudy laughs.

She teases, pulling her dick slowly across my clit and

through my wet pussy. Slowly over and over and then suddenly plunging deeply, her hips thrusting against me as I cry out. My mouth is wide open and I am soundless as she pours in and out of me with deep, slow, measured, determined movements. The hormones of a high school dance invade the night air and I stretch out my tongue to try and lick the windshield of the principal's car. I am bathed in blue halo from forehead to soles, radiant in the moonlight of first fuck and wanted tongue — or so, more or less, it would have, could have, should have gone, but didn't, because I wasn't, you know, whatever. At least, I didn't think I was, but here I am still, on all fours in Brooklyn, hoping, waiting.

suzette mayr

THE EDUCATION OF CARMEN

My purpose is to tell of bodies which have been transformed into shapes of a different kind.
— *Ovid,* Metamorphoses

CARMEN AND GRIFFIN BEGIN DATING THE DAY SHE TURNS eighteen, back when she is still a white girl. When she is eighteen and a half they make love for the third time under the pool table in his parents' basement; she knocks her head on the table leg, and her skull roars with pain while Griffin pumps, his eyes closed. Her eyes roll back until the whites gleam pearl, her bottom jaw drops, and when she comes to she figures she's been unconscious for about a minute and a half. Griffin takes about fifty-eight seconds. Carmen's timed him. They've timed each other. Griffin fifty-eight seconds, Carmen ten minutes — they've learned that orgasm speed relies on biology, the difference between men and women. Some of her girlfriends never have orgasms. Griffin's buddies, on the other hand, have no problem. Men and women.

They have concussive sex in the same room as the wooden inlay picture of three happy black people, Africans she supposes, with long thin necks, baskets on their heads, thick red lips and gold hoops in their ears. Under the pool table they can lie relaxed and sweaty, side by side, and look up at the picture, the only decoration on any of the walls. A souvenir, Griffin says, a souvenir his mother picked up on one of her business trips.

Where? asks Carmen.

I don't know, some place where blacks live, obviously.

His mother, Fran, doesn't like Carmen at all. Carmen is not the kind of girl Fran would choose for her son, not the kind of girl Fran wants included in her family's bloodline. Carmen doesn't talk, slides in and out of Fran's house without so much as a hello or goodbye, as though Fran were invisible or merely a servant. Fran only ever knows if Carmen is somewhere in the house from her grimy sneakers parked in the front hall, or the normally immaculate ashtrays crammed with lipsticked cigarette butts. Griffin and Carmen disappear for hours, the entire day sometimes, slam the front door or the back door or the patio door when they're back from wherever they go. 6 PM, a door slams and Griffin asks, when's supper, Mom? just like nothing's happened, and the next thing Fran knows, Griffin is stuffing an entire bowl of green salad into his mouth and Carmen's beside him at the dinner table holding out her plate as if Fran owes her food. Fran's mother would have slapped that plate out of Carmen's hand, then slapped Carmen hard in the face. The least Carmen can do is help clear up. Fran is tired of being her servant.

Have some more green salad, Carmen, Fran says, and whips the bowl of salad across the table.

Fran also disapproves of the premarital sex she knows Carmen and her son are having. Fran isn't stupid, she wasn't born yesterday. Sex is for people mature enough, financially stable enough, to handle an accident. She wouldn't put it past Carmen to get pregnant just to get her bitten nails into Griffin now, while he's still young, with so much promise. Oh yes, Fran's laid down the rules, no Carmen in the bedroom, no closed doors in the house, all the lights on the moment the sun goes down. She doesn't approve of the two of them disappearing for entire days, or Griffin arriving home at four o'clock in the morning, but she refrains from commenting because even if Fran doesn't like Carmen, at least Griffin isn't homosexual. At least he's sticking to girls, whorish and unmannered as Carmen may be.

Now if he was out until four o'clock in the morning with some strange boy, she'd certainly have something to say. Ida Sorensen down the street found out her son was homosexual, walked in on him and some young fella kissing for God's sake. God knows what would've happened if Ida'd walked in just ten minutes later. God knows. Fran would kill herself first. Carmen is a quiet and devious little tart, but maybe Carmen can learn. Be changed. Converted.

When Carmen turns twenty, Fran hints during Sunday dinner that they should be thinking about marriage. She wants to see grandchildren before she dies. St Francis, she says, is a beautiful chuch. Carmen doesn't say anything — she doesn't believe in God or St Francis or church or marriage — and Griffin chomps with his lips drawn back on the tail of his steak. He's a vegetarian when he's not in his mother's house; he doesn't become a meat-eater until he goes home at night. Fran sulks if he doesn't eat her dinners.

We were thinking maybe we'd just live together eventully, Ma. He chews the steak slowly, doesn't eat the fat, doesn't suck at the juice, doesn't let the bloody flesh touch his lips.

Oh, well, if that's what you want, says Fran, stacks the dishes loudly, one on top of the other so that long cords of fat lop down over the rims. If that's what you want, but her face says Closed For Business. If her body were a section of land, she would be surrounded by coils of barbed wire, protected by Doberman pinschers snarling. No Trespassing. No Ingrate Sons Allowed.

> > >

When Carmen and Griffin are together they are so much in love. These are the kind of dishes we'll buy, says Carmen. Brown ceramic. That's my favourite. Earthy. I just can't do porcelain.

Mine, too, he says, surprised. And I've always liked the name Italo for a boy.

Hmm, says Carmen. I won't breastfeed, so you and the baby will have a chance to bond via the feeding experience.

I could be a superior househusband, he says doubtfully. Griffin doesn't know anything about children. Neither does his mother. Fran wrinkles her nose in disgust at the masturbation stains on his bed when she changes the sheets.

Anyway, how can they live together, let alone get married; it's a great big joke what with both of them still in school and no real money to live on except from rotten summer jobs, landscaping for Griffin and waitressing for Carmen.

There is always more opportunity for sex in the summer, though, since the warm weather lets them use the car or the shelter of trees in city parks. Their bones clash rhythmically in the dark, bodies pale and pasted together, a four-legged, two-headed amoeba. Because they have no privacy, they rely on masturbatory short cuts, their uniforms clothes that fall open but stay on. Most of all, they rely on speed. Carmen scuttles for cover when headlights peer through the dripping windshield, or the beam of a flashlight skips through the trees. She is an expert at pulling her jeans up, or her skirt down, her cheeks bright red but her mouth bland and virginal, her hair, the colour of blades of wheat, falling smoothly into place. Griffin just takes a flip to his fly, lies serenely in the half-dark of the car seat, or propped against a tree trunk, arms crossed behind his head, his skin opal.

It's not like we're committing a crime, says Carmen. Next time we should just keep going. Too bad for whoever walks in on us.

One day they will live together like a real couple. Not necessarily get married, Carmen sees marriage as territorial and possessive. Why, once she tried to find a married

friend in the phone book and couldn't because she didn't
know the husband's last name.

Sometimes bits of gravel and dust on the floor of
Griffin's parents' car get stuck in her underpants. One day
she will stop lying and tell her parents she and Griffin are
spending the night together. She will just *tell* them.

Screwing in the car and getting gravel in her pants is
preferable to winter sex. Winters they have to resort to a
dangerous game of tag with Fran, grabbing sex in whatever
room of the house they're sure she's not in. If she's upstairs
they skitter downstairs to the room with the pool table, or
the laundry room. If she's downstairs they spill their juices
in his bedroom (not on the bed, for God's sake — the
springs! the springs!) or on the kitchen floor, or upright in
the dark front hallway. What can they do, they're so much
in love, the urge just takes them and they can't help themselves.

For now, since it's summer, they use Fran and
Godfrey's car floor, Carmen's parents' car, Fish Creek park,
or if they're lucky, her best friend Joan's apartment. Do it
on top of a sleeping bag on the living room floor. Carmen
gets nervous about having sex in other people's beds.
Profane somehow. Embarrassing when there's a mess.

>   >   >

Carmen works mostly the morning shifts and then leaves
for home in the middle of the afternoon. Her uniform is a
pair of navy blue cotton shorts with a white cotton shirt
and an apron she folds over and ties around her waist. She
carries menus in her left hand, swiftly pours coffee with
her right, and can carry up to six full plates of food at a
time. Most days she combs her hair into an orderly pony-
tail, barrettes the sides so the long straight strands don't
drag in the food, and sprays her bangs until they crackle.
If she wakes up early enough she can French-braid her
hair, spray it, then curl the bangs into a springy slope
across her forehead. Ringlets are her favourite, ringlets on

both sides of her face, and her back hair in a bun. She looks dynamite with ringlets, Griffin says so, the other waitresses say so, *Carmen* says so, but ringlets drag in the plates of food and by the end of the shift have transformed into long, greasy, eggy, jam-encrusted strands tucked behind her ears anyway. Bangs scraped back and a bun at the back of her head are the most sanitary way to go, but really, what is she? A nurse? Or worse, a nun? She has to feel proud of herself.

The more tables she has the more challenged she feels, the better she performs; she moves with figure-skating speed and grace as she whirls out coffee, menus, food, keeps her customers happy, and chatters in a friendly but business-like manner.

White or brown? Apple or orange? Overeasy or sunnyside up? Cash or charge?

She is, undoubtedly, the best waitress in the world. But being the best waitress isn't necessarily the best career choice.

Waitressing is the job she resigns herself to every summer. Every year she swears she'll find a job more suitable to her area of university study, a job less demeaning, a job less *high schoolish*.

We have unlimited potential! she insists to Griffin. We can do better than this!

But the wage improves every year and so does she; she has to be realistic. She will keep waitressing until she is offered a better-paying, more meaningful alternative. This year her manager, Rama, is a woman, originally from India or somewhere, and so sensitive. Rama unbalances all the waitresses, not only because she is so strict but also because she is the most beautiful woman in the world.

You know, says Luce, a waitress who's been at the restaurant even longer than Carmen, these Pakistani-types have such beautiful complexions. Smooth as babies' butts. And big brown puppy eyes to boot. Amazing.

Uh-huh, says Carmen.

Although, you know, continues Luce, my second cousin's married to a man who's black as the ace of spades and his complexion isn't the greatest, I have to say. So some of these coloured people don't have the best skin. Rama has beautiful skin. She's one of the lucky ones.

Uh-huh.

Because what else is there to say. Carmen is afraid to say anything else, she has never worked so closely with a coloured person before. Rama smells different. Spicy, or flowery, some strange brown-skin perfume. The distinctly gritty smell of armpits when Rama sweats. She's seen Rama spread hand lotion on. Standard hand lotion. It's the chemistry of a person's skin, she's heard, that can make a perfume change its smell. Rama must have a certain chemical makeup to make her body smell this way with just a bit of hand lotion. Or maybe it's what Rama eats at home, although Rama eats restaurant food just like every-one else during breaks. She's heard East Indians eat a lot of curry in their food. Is it curry? Carmen likes curry. Maybe it's just the combination of hand lotion and brown skin and sweat. Pigment transforming smell.

Carmen has known few coloured women, so Rama makes her nervous; she would never ask Rama what she eats at home or what perfume she wears. All the coloured women Carmen meets are so *angry*, not that Carmen's re-ally met any — well, she's been in the same classes as some but they don't really talk that much generally. She's seen them on television at demonstrations and riots and things in the States. Always in packs. Carmen is afraid to speak in front of Rama, afraid to say something that will offend. What if Carmen causes a riot by saying something racist? Carmen knows how different races stick together, she's seen ethnic gangs on the news.

Rama's hair, long, shiny, black hair cut so perfect and make-up matched to her skin. Carmen tells Griffin that Rama's skin is like cinnamon, or no, like cappuccino. Carmen would like a tan halfway between her own skin colour and Rama's. That would be the perfect colour.

Customers naturally ask Rama where she comes from, and Rama says CANADA like she's offended. Carmen and the other waitresses hang out in the kitchen, gossip and flirt with the prep cooks whenever Rama's out of the way. Rama's too uptight, she'll never last, they say. Is she even qualified to be a restaurant manager? Heard she's sleeping with the owner.

Get your asses back to work, yells the chef, he's a grouchy little man, and the prep cooks mutter about how they work ther asses off, work like niggers, do most of the work in fact — why's a Chinese guy cooking hamburgers anyway? Stick to egg foo yung at the Long Duck Dong.

Yeah, Long Duck Dong, Long Duck's Dong, Duck's Long Dong, echo the waitresses, and they scatter. Carmen doesn't ever say this out loud, but Duck's Long Dong is what pops into her head whenever the chef screws up an order. Long Dong Duck. Long Dong Duck.

Norm, yells Luce. I can't serve this bacon! This bacon's still squealing!

Luce skewers the bacon on a small plate with a fork, takes a bite out of it.

Maybe in China people are happy with raw meat, but welcome to the Western world!

Norm pushes a small plate of bacon towards Luce, doesn't speak, only keeps cooking, sweat dripping from his forehead, soaking into the rim of his chef's hat.

Stick to making chop suey, mutters Luce. Ching chong duck damn dong. She pops a piece of butter on her plate of food.

What did you say? says Rama.

Nothing, I didn't say anything. Just talking to Norm.

What did you say?

Nothing. Jesus.

Rama goes into her office and closes the door. Luce serves her customers their breakfasts, passes the office on the way to the coffee station.

Rama opens the door slightly and gestures to Luce with a long, shiny fingernail, the inside of her finger pink and the outside dark, coffee-flavoured brown. The office door closes behind them.

Carmen and the other waitresses do their jobs, keep their ears toward the office door in case either Luce or Rama says something loud enough to penetrate. The waitresses change ashtrays that contain only a smidgen of ash, pour coffee for their tables over and over until customers become annoyed by the excessive attention. Could I have the bill, miss, please? I don't need any more coffee.

Carmen's bangs droop and feather into her face from the nervous sweat on her forehead. She takes over Luce's tables.

Luce stays in Rama's office until the restaurant is closed. Luce's voice pierces through the door, shrill and constant. The waitresses cluster, waiting for their tips to be collected and distributed. They stand close to the office door, but not too close in case either Rama or Luce behind the door lashes out and burns them.

Luce steps out of the office and closes the door behind her. She stands facing the other waitresses, swaying a little, her face carved from wax. She stands and sways under the fluorescent lighting of the restaurant, her skin shiny from sweat and oil, her lipstick bitten off and the exposed skin on her lips chapped and raw. Luce's body suddenly shrinks, crouches as she gathers breath into her lungs. She screams. Screams and screams and screams, her face blossoming into a bright and rabid pink. She twirls around and gives Rama's door the violent middle finger of her right hand, then her left hand, then kicks the fake wooden panelling, left foot, right foot, left food, right foot.

Everyone says that, shrieks Luce between kicks, everyone does! We say it to his face, he doesn't mind, he likes it, he's used to it! What does he expect coming to this country, that he'll *fit in?* I was going to quit this job anyway! You wouldn't know how to run a fucking restaurant if your fucking life depended on it!

Luce holds a pink slip, the same colour as her face. Blood gone from her knuckles, she crumples the slip in her hand, and throws it on the floor. Rama doesn't answer, doesn't even watch Luce run out of the restaurant and down the street still in her uniform, just opens the door to her office, then sits back down behind her desk. Rama counts out the waitresses' tips into even piles of ten-, five-, two-dollar bills and loonies with her dark brown fingers, her fingernails polished and pinky-brown as sea-shells on a tropical beach. Her fingernails brush and tap the surface of her desk. The door to the office now wide open, Carmen and the other waitresses line up at Rama's desk, listen to the fine clicks of her fingernails, the snap of money in her hands. Rama counts out money, writes down numbers, lightly swivels her body in her chair as she reaches from one part of the desk to the other. The waitresses stand around the desk in a semicircle, simmering, resentful, afraid. Rama lifts her face, wrings them all dry with a *look*.

Carmen's stomach sinks whenever Rama approaches her, whenever Rama swishes past, long black hair spread fan-like across her shoulders, make-up always dark and perfect. Rama the thundercloud. She tells Carmen not to forget to water table eight, or that table one needs their ashtray changed — as if Carmen needs someone to tell her how to do her job. Carmen speaks to Rama not at all if she can get away with it.

Hi, Rama, bye, Rama. This is all she would say if she could get away with it.

The prep cooks, one by one, are replaced.

>   >   >

Not too busy today, eh, says Rama.

No. No it's not, says Carmen. She looks down to make sure her apron's on straight. She left a little note for Rama asking for tomorrow off, she hopes and prays that Rama will give her tomorrow off, tomorrow Griffin has promised to take her to the mountains.

Guess we won't be needing you tomorrow morning then. Hasn't been busy lately.

Thanks!

Carmen feels a tear-pricking surge of gratitude and fondness for Rama. Carmen wants to hug Rama until she cracks. Rama smiles.

Where do you come from Rama, Carmen ventures, feeling chummy and happy, I mean originally you know?

Well, Rama hesitates, I was born in Winnipeg. That's where my parents come from.

Rama isn't so frightening after all, maybe they could even be friends.

Winnipeg. Well. I guess I mean where does your family really come from. My boyfriend's Scottish all the way back and his dad even has a *kilt* stashed away. You speak without an accent, just like you're Canadian. You know, with Canadian parents.

The air around Rama's body glints polished slate. Carmen, unable to stop, finds herself saying: You're not like other coloured people of course. You don't *act* coloured. A lot of time I don't even notice. Your skin, I mean. Maybe it's none of my business.

Maybe it's not, answers Rama softly.

I'm sorry. But I don't understand, I don't understand what the big deal is. I mean we're all the same underneath aren't we? I would never say anything racist intentionally, but wouldn't it be better for me to know just in case I make a mistake. Why can't you just tell me why it bugs you so much when people ask you where you come from? Why are you so angry all the time? What d'you have against white people anyway? This isn't a racist town, it's not like the KKK goes galloping up and down the streets or something. You've got a good job. I don't know why people have to be sensitive all the time. Why not just integrate? Why try to stick out all the time? People don't mean to be mean. Surely you understand *that*. Don't set yourself up as a target — be more casual.

The sound of her own voice sounds off-key to Carmen, too high or too low, strings snapped from a violin under a rigidly-applied bow. The words that come from her mouth don't belong to anyone she knows. Belong to the other, another Carmen.

Carmen sees Rama's hands start to shake, the blood rush to Rama's face, Rama's mouth about to say something, but her voice is eclipsed by Carmen's questions. Carmen sounds like a drunk person, slurs her words in a tipsy monologue.

Educate me, says Carmen. Show me where all this racism is, why you're so angry and bitchy all the time. Show me. If I cut you you bleed, if I cut me I bleed, we're all the same underneath. Show me the difference. Show me the difference!

Carmen's lips can't stop stretching and singing: Luce calling Norm Long Duck Dong is the same as you calling us Canucks. Being called a Canuck may hurt my feelings but I don't let it get to me. I have more important problems.

Carmen flinches at the backfire crack in Rama's back, Carmen having laid on the last precious straw and at last, Carmen is going to lose her job, she's going to end up like Luce, broke and with no reference and her work history ruined. Now she won't be able to pay for school and she'll have to ask her parents for money and they'll want to know why and what if they don't have enough money to put her through school this year? She'll have to take out a loan, she knows all about loans, her cousin Josepha got a loan and she's *still* paying for it, $25,000 in debt and only twenty-six years old. Carmen closes her eyes. I am not going to cry I am not going to cry dear God please don't let me cry, dear God please don't let me lose this job I'll do anything, and she prays oh she prays even though she doesn't believe in God, up until now she hasn't believed in anything anything anything. Her mouth opens and closes, opens and closes, her instrument wound to the breaking point.

Three veins in Rama's forehead stretch upward in the shape of a trident. She gives Carmen a *look*, but this time the look pulls apart Carmen's face, peels off Carmen's skin. *I cut you you bleed I cut me I bleed*, burrows through the layer of subcutaneous fat and splays out her veins and nerves, frayed electrical wires, snaps apart Carmen's muscles and scrapes Carmen's bones, digs and gouges away Carmen's life.

The colour of Carmen's pink and freckled fingers and forearms deepens, darkens to freckled chocolate brown and beige pink on the palms of her hands. Her hair curls and frizzes, shortens. Hairs dropped into a frying pan kink up around her face, curl into tight balls on the back of her neck. Her skin, covered in a thin layer of dry skin, flakes from where she missed with the skin lotion this morning. Her hair is drier, finer; irises freshly dipped in dark brown cradle her pupils. And her scars, old knotted scars from childhood, from last year, from last week when she touched the hot oven wth the back of her hand, open their eyes and glare pale against her skin. Her history is etched out in negative.

The hot slab of granite that is Rama's face dissolves as Carmen changes and Rama suddenly laughs. Laughs and says, Yeah, some of my best friends are coloured people too. I even know some okay white people. And Carmen lets out a breath.

Carmen, now a brown girl, keeps her job *and* gets tomorrow off to go to the mountains with her one true love.

Carmen also starts to laugh, the bridges of the two women's noses wrinkle meanly as they laugh, and Carmen goes back to her station. Waters the customers and fetches more buns and whipped butter from the kitchen to stop the rumble of hunger, the questions: Where do you come from? How long have you been in Canada? Is the seafood here fresh?

Part of the job, part of the job, the customer is always right.

One of these days, I swear Rama, Carmen says, I'm going to give these dumb white people what-for.

> > >

This is how metamorphoses work. They happen all the time. Women turn into trees, birds, flowers, disembodied voices at the moment of crisis, just before anger, grief, desperation eats them alive. Daphne twists and stumbles before Apollo until she gnarls into a tree, her smooth skin rough and impenetrable, forever a virgin. Echo's love unrequited, she withers into her name. Loses herself to love instead of cutting her losses and finding a new lover. Other fish in the sea — she should have asked to be a trout instead. Women who've lost their mothers grow poplar bark and weep sap, as though tears of sugar instead of salt make the sadness less. Or attractively more. The more charming you are in your sadness the more likely you are to be saved. The more desperate the more likely you will be saved. Take a second look and become a pillar of salt.

At the most terrible moment bodies transform into bears, nightingales, bats. But which bodies? Who's so lucky? White girls in a blasted moment grow the bark and flow with the sap of coloured girls. But this is only one moment.

> > >

I've never seen lips on a vagina so brown, says Griffin. I've never touched black hair, can I touch it? So soft.

Stupid question, Carmen says. What a stupid question.

Well, you know what they say, says Griffin, as he strokes her black hair, pushes in her dark brown nipples. Once you sleep with black, you never go back. Something like that.

Carmen and Griffin cover their mouths with their hands, giggle at his naughtiness.

I've always wanted to sleep with a black woman.

Oh, yeah? Why's that?

But she is more concerned that he is leaving, going to Europe, than she is about her new *pelt*, as Griffin calls it.

Her *pelt*, he says and strokes the skin all over her body. She knows Griffin has always wanted to travel to Europe, *has* to. It's his dream, he's planned to go all his life, still it's hard not to want him to stay with her, it's hard to give him up for so long. She thought of going, long ago when he first mentioned Europe, but he never *asked* her.

Of course she never asked him to ask her. Her priorities are different. What's the big deal anyway, meet more people, meet more problems. She works in the public service field — she knows. And money. What about the money? She wants to finish school first, she's not a stupid girl. Europe is all fine and dandy but afterwards, then what?

It's the experience, Griffin says. I want to see other places, other people. Get a better sense of how I fit in the world. See Buckingham Palace before I settle down.

One of them has to be practical, experience won't pay the rent, won't free them from living in their parents' houses. She doesn't mind being the practical one. If they both went to Europe they couldn't afford to move in together until they were both in their fifties! She loves Griffin, but sometimes he can be so unmotivated, so shortsighted, so live-for-the-moment.

Don't spend all your money over there, she pleads, Save some for when you get back, remember our moving-in-together fund!

Maybe his spontaneity is why she loves him, so different from herself. She'll miss him so much, like having roots ripped out of her soil.

Do you love me? she asks.

Of course.

If you love me then why are you going to Europe?

Umm. Uhh.

She sees the sweat spring out on to his forehead as he scampers in his little brain for an answer. Poor sweet thing.

I'm just kidding, she says. Just testing.

They walk in the park together. She admires her long brown legs in the sun, smells the lemon-scented laundry detergent of her clean cotton t-shirt. She puts her arm around his waist. A beautiful day. *They* are not as beautiful as usual, though, she isn't wearing make-up today. Hasn't worn make-up for almost two weeks, her make-up from before no longer fits her brown skin. She never realized how vital make-up is to making a girl feel good about herself. Just a little something to brighten up her face, her heart. She even catches herself avoiding mirrors now. But at least she has Griffin, and Griffin doesn't seem to mind her naked face. Griffin thinks she's beautiful no matter what. He is wearing the nice blue shirt she bought him last Christmas, 100 percent cotton. She slides her hand under the shirt, feels the indented small of his back, the shifting muscles with each step. Notices how people stare.

Haven't you noticed? she asks. Strange, isn't it?

I guess that's because we're a mixed couple now, he says. Just like John Lennon and Yoko Ono. He squeezes her hand. He's so smart.

I guess we'll have cocoa babies, he says, and Carmen smiles. She has always liked the look and smell of cocoa. Hot chocolate is her favourite drink. Hot chocolate in winter, chocolate milk in summer. Small brown babies, hers and Griffin's. Maybe if they have a boy, the baby's middle name could be Italo.

Pushing her little chocolate Italo in a carriage through a park.

erin soros

STROKE

WHEN DOLLY WALKS INTO THE ROOM, EVERYTHING LOOKS AT her. The uncurtained window, the dark wooden floor with wide eyes in the grain. Deer eyes, their unblinking rounds watch as she scurries over them trying not to make a sound, quick scuff of soles then a silent, slow, heel-to-toe creep.

A wooden cabinet perches by his bed, squat, a shade lighter than the floors, as if bleached by the ammonia hanging in the air, thick and acrid as urine. Through the cabinet's glass door she sees pill bottles, one spilled open. White pills, white sheets, white walls. His white hands hold down the sheets. His white face is blue-white, metallic like the railing that cages his bed. A crib, she thinks, he's in a crib, he can't get out.

The bedpan lies on its side on the floor. She wonders how he uses it, since he can't get it for himself. A nurse would have to move his body, shove it to the side like furniture, nudge the bedpan underneath, plunk his ass on top of the cold rim. She'd stand with her hands held away from her sides as if letting nail polish dry, glancing at her watch and staring at the wall until the hollow sound of pee hit the metal chamber. Or maybe she wouldn't come right away, couldn't hear his incoherent moans for help. His words and urine trapped inside.

She nudges the bed pan with the toe of her shoe. It tips over with a clang. Empty.

"Well, I've come to see you," she says, smiling at how her words seem to emerge from the pan, dry metal ringing

as it rocks back and forth on the floor. "What are you doing in here? Nothing much to keep a body company, is
there? I should have brought your spoons." He can't play
them now or even eat with them. The nurse would have
to feed him. No, her mother, she was the one who did it.
Repulsion had flickered across her mother's face when she
described how she had to pry the spoon against his tongue,
then scrape it across his chin to catch what escaped from
his lips. He's a child now, and her mother never liked feeding children. She's always wanting a person she can talk
to, someone up for a bit of fun. She's a woman who wants
to laugh.

"Does Mom bring things in? Her biscuits — you'd miss
those — a bite of potato stew? Or do you have a special diet?
Bet you have to eat like I did, remember, when I was what,
going on ten, and they wouldn't even let me have a cookie
or a carrot, nothing but white mush." She looks at the white
of the walls and the sheets and his skin. "It was a mystery,
I could never say what it was. They could have sneaked
anything inside. I know how it feels. You don't want something soft, do you now? You want something hard. Want to
chew it, get your teeth into it right good." She pauses to
search his heavy expressionless eyes, nods as if he has spoken. "Yes, that's just how I felt. And then someone brought
me an orange. Was it you? No, no. You'd keep track of what
I couldn't have. I knew it too, sure I knew it, but the smell
of that orange, oh, the smell of it, Christmas and high summer all rolled into one. The whole thing to myself. I was
eating colour, I tell you, my fingers and my palms even,
they were orange, all orange, bits of the peel under my
nails, and I ate faster than you could sneeze, faster than
someone could grab it away, the skin and all. Imagine. I
ate the skin. I could smell it even after it was gone."

She examines the brown spots on his hands and face,
more noticeable now against the sheets. His skin mottled,
brown on grey on white. The room stealing his flesh into
itself.

"That's when the convulsions started. No one knew why till they saw my fingers." She waits for his interruption then remembers he can't speak. His flesh is wordless, slipping away from her as if language was all that tied his body to her own. Silence unmooring him like the eye of a storm. "Almost killed me. Didn't it now. The convulsions?" Her words fill the room. They press his body further into the bed. "I bet you would have beat me for it good, right hard, too, if I wasn't so sick. And people around and all. I should have known, that's what you said, I was grown and I should have known better. So when the uncles and aunts, when they came and told me to get better soon, I thought it meant the same thing, know better and get better, I thought you'd gone and told them all how it happened, how it was my own fault."

He can't chastise her, can mouth no warnings or commands, not even the guttural outbursts — *slippers, dinner* — after a day working a farm, hours spent following behind another man's plow. Slam of front door. Thud of boots. His orders to her condensed into one word as if she were unworthy of grammar. *Eat*, he'd say when she tried to talk. *Quiet*. His control over his family held in even the smallest particle of speech. But the brevity lasted only until he'd gotten a meal into himself. Then his words stretched with his stomach, limericks, and political rants and complaints tumbling out to fill the kitchen. Her mother laughed, her mother nodded, lips open as if she could hear through her mouth. *I'm telling you*, he said, *you listen to me*.

Dolly turns to unbutton her cardigan, her back to him. The mauve wool is too bright in this room. She folds it small, the arms twisted around the back. Sets it on the chair and then waits, watching, expecting it to twitch or fall off. Her breasts pull tight the buttons of her blouse. One nipple rubs a moist spot where milk has leaked through. She slows her breathing. Glances back to the eyes that follow her, pupils thick with cataracts. Two listless stones. Once blue. Years ago, her disappointment at how the sparkle of a beach pebble would fade when it dried. A dull grey in her hand, the sea's betrayal. She'd slip the stone inside her mouth so her tongue could paint the cool dead surface, but she could never make the colour last.

The cataracts veil her father's thoughts, his gaze flat as it follows her movements. He can still see her, her body like a shadow, she knows this. Her bloated breasts. She wishes she could cup each breast in a palm, lift them up to keep anything else from leaking out.

"Mom is worried sick. Mom is worried something awful, you in here and all. Something could happen. Do you know what you're supposed to eat, what if you went and ate an orange or worse? We'd never hear tell of you again."

She glances back to the floor. Not a mark on its wax-slick surface. It took hours to get a floor looking like that and then someone would just come in and walk on it. At home she keeps the linoleum covered with newspapers, rows of type that slip underfoot. *Young ladies line up to enlist. Hoodlums steal food from the mess hall. From now on, when we say pre-war we have to say pre-which war*. There it was, spread out for anyone to see, all of it happening again. The war, the war. A word so singular torn in two. Her husband kicking at the pages with his muddy boots, cursing this text she'd spread underneath him.

> > >

"I guess you couldn't do that, though, eat what you're not allowed, on your own. But something could happen, all the same, something in the night and you couldn't get help, you couldn't even call someone, there'd be no one to hear. No one can understand a word of you." She shouldn't tell a thing like that, really, but she can't help it. She wants him to see that she knows. All of it, what has happened to his body, what her mother kept muttering as she swirled the leaves of her tea. *Our Patrick can't speak. He can't talk. He can't feed himself.* There were things her mother didn't say, but Dolly knows those, too. She runs her tongue along the inside of her mouth, each tooth a mark of something her father can no longer do.

"She'd like to be the one, really, Mom would, she'd like to stay with you all the time, but they won't let her. And she can't be doing all of it, can she now? She can't be everywhere at once. That's what she used to say when I called her. Could never keep up with me, Mom couldn't, what with a whole house to feed."

Her father is in the only private room. In this small, cramped hospital, wards packed with the sick. His repeated stuttered demand before he lost his speech, when the first stroke met its echo. He was not a man to be seen lying down. Her mother would have to pay for it. Somehow, cleaning house again, taking in laundry or sewing clothes, but even that wouldn't be enough. The pawn shop then, if her mother could find a thing to sell. The room sucking everything pale.

She'll be taking in boarders if this goes on. Some stranger sleeping in the girls' old bed.

Dolly had already given her a bit. Slipped her mother cash from one of the jobs her father found her. All those ladies and their instructions. *Wipe the windows with newspaper or you'll leave streaks. Use this milk on the hardwood.* The Wednesday bowl on the counter; the note on how to feed the floor. Milk, then a rinse of water, another rinse of water. Dolly rubbing against the slight sour smell that remained from the previous week, how she could never rinse the milk fast enough before it seeped into the grooves. Her angry clicking bones. On each knee a permanent bruise.

"I used to think Mom really had to do that, feeding the house, at night I mean, that's what she was doing, why she was always so tired in the morning. The rooms got right hungry." She laughs then, suddenly. "You probably think I should have come long before now."

She walks toward the window that holds the room. The

bed, the cabinet, her reflection, holes where her eyes should be, a glow around her hair, the light bulb hanging naked from a cord. Her husband Phil had smashed one like that, just before the baby. Glass exploding with his fist. A room punched into darkness. He had wanted her to tell him something that time, but she couldn't remember what it was. Or did he want her to shut up? Men were always wanting her to talk or wanting her to shut up. Talk or shut up, off and on like a light. Her high-pitched voice. She could talk and talk without telling a thing.

Now you shut your trap.

The light bulb rocks her face small then big against the window. Wind and rain moan through the walls.

"She's keeping Pearl for me, now that Phil's gone off again. So I can see you. Children aren't allowed."

A closet, she didn't notice that at first, narrow, white, like the kind meant to hide an ironing board, just the door-knob and the shadow around the edge to distinguish it from the wall. She can feel him watch her as she opens the door, fingers his coats, his slick silky pockets, lint and sand and crumpled tissue at the bottom. She finds coins. If only she had brought her purse, that messy hungry sac she could push anything into, snapping it shut. Or her coat, she could slip things from his pockets to hers, rattling as she walks away down the hospital corridor. All she has now are her hands.

Daddy. She doesn't say it. The word breathes in a cor-ner of the room.

Why doesn't he move? Just his eyes following her as she walks the perimeter sifting coins, sliding them be-tween her fingers.

"I shouldn't have left Pearl. You'd like to see her. I could have sneaked her in."

She lifts his bathrobe from the end of the bed and folds it, the brown flannel wool as worn and rough as fallen leaves. The robe won't fit in the bottom drawer. She jams it in, forcing the drawer closed, flannel sticking out half-eaten.

"Daddy?" She says the word tentatively, unsure whether it will attach itself to this strange slack skin. Whispers it again and again, fixing it to his mouth, his nose, his eyes. At the cabinet she scoops the pills against the lip of the bottle, orders each bottle in a line, labels facing forward so no one will mix them up.

His eyes. Their milky thickness slides toward her. The left side of his mouth lifts, twitching, as if only half of him wants to smile.

A stroke is brown and grey and white.

"I know just what it's like. Arms and legs and tongue all splintered into pieces, into shreds, but stuck in your body all the same. I think about it at night. It's like when you dream you want to move and you can't, you've still got your body, but it's not yours."

He can hear you. He just can't respond.

When her mother spoke to her yesterday, her hushed rasp kept fading in the kitchen. Dolly leaned toward her, watched how the curve of her fingers and thumbs perfectly covered the rim of her cup so that none of it showed through. Her mother rocked her tea, just slightly, twirling the leaves without reading them.

He can feel things.

"I bet you'd give anything to have your body back." As a child she thought that losing your virginity meant a piece of your body would fall off, disappear into a crevice or roll down an alley. Girls wandering up and down, walking the streets, searching for what they had lost. Gone to the gutter. Some girls, her mother said, just gave theirs away. Dolly worried hers would go missing before she'd got a good look at it.

She rubs the coins, counts them. Enough for a pair of stockings or maybe ribbons for Pearl's hair. She adds again, a different total. Again, still different. It doesn't matter. It's enough. She can get something with it.

A stroke of luck.

At Charlottetown's summer fair, the magician had

birthed gifts from his sleeves. He spotted her, five and a half and nervous in the crowd, gripping her father's hand. The magician found money behind her ear. Her eyes wide as the coins when he tucked the shining silver into her palm and folded her fingers around it.

He can move parts of his body.

"You got mad at me for that. You hit my ear, the magic one with the coins inside. You said I wasn't supposed to take a thing from strangers. Lord, I cried something awful. I kept telling you it was from my ear, I didn't take it, he took it from me, it was mine all along." A trickle of milk slips down her breast. "It wasn't even real. The money. You went and stole it from me and you couldn't use it for a thing."

You won't get him all excited, when you visit him, will you now? Don't go carrying on like you do. All your antics. It could bring on another stroke. We're lucky to have him, really we are. We're lucky he's not dead.

Dead. Dad. Daddy.

A stroke is a hand brushed against skin.

He coughs. Phlegm caught in his throat. Spits it out, a dribbling liquid word. She doesn't wipe him off. She looks down at her hands where death spots will grow as she ages, some disease passed from his hands to hers. Her fingernails are bitten to the skin. At thirteen she let the nails grow, refused to cut them for months, extending all her fingers by five or six inches. Each thumbnail a branch thick and twisted. Visible bone. She'd scare her sister, make shadows on the wall. Nails long enough that when she ran for the streetcar the hard tips hit the pole before she could grasp it with her hands, the shock of contact jamming the nails back into her skin as if the body could withdraw what it had let out. Her father swore against them. The click click when she picked up a pot or an iron, how she finally had to stop using her fingers at all. Fumbling flat-palmed, dropping bowls, the shards of china on the floor, slivers scattered like nail clippings.

That was the year her body changed. Blood on white, her body's punctuation. The bee-sting swell of breasts. Her nails hard as her breasts were soft.

Her father told her she was finished with school. She would have to stay home, her mother couldn't be doing it all herself. No more history lessons, chalk clouds from blackboard brushes, yellowed pages of books. Her fingers grew with all the words she couldn't write.

Now he can't make her do a thing. He shifts, spits, sighs, tries to slip his thoughts into her, unintelligible syllables sliding from his slack mouth. She braces her body to keep them out, runs her thumb along the edge of a coin, pressing into it until it leaves a narrow white line across her skin.

"You were the one who called me Dolly. I wasn't born with it. When did it start, Dolly? You said I was your little Doll."

She looks up, smiles with recognition as if someone has just entered the room. "Look, Daddy, on this page, a taffeta frock, look at the puffed sleeves, isn't it beautiful? Sears, or no — this one's Eaton's. Remember? It's what I always looked at before I went to sleep."

Crouched over catalogues spread on the kitchen table she'd cut up pictures to make clothes for cardboard dolls, dressing and undressing them until the cardboard wore out and the dolls lost arms or tore in two at the waist. At night she'd open the catalogues in her mind, flip from page to memorized page, adding colour to the black and white. She'd choose what her father would buy her one day if he got rich, if she was good, helped her mother, made him happy. She wrapped herself in imaginary layers, velvet like rabbit fur, collars that tickled her neck, stockings that scratched her legs. The dank reek of wool, the musty smell of skin. Leather gloves soft around sleeping fists.

>   >   >

By the time she could earn her own money, she was tired

of trying things on. She marched her sister into stores, then sat down and watched as the younger girl modeled whatever Dolly desired. Their matching frail frames obscured their different temperaments, one meek and one stubborn, Nunny begrudgingly obedient to these sibling orchestrations. "This dress, no, slip into this one here," Dolly holding up the next outfit as her sister trundled tired and overwarm in and out of the waiting room. Filling each limp form until Dolly decided.

Nunny had grown up in Dolly's hand-me-downs. Their father would return from Labrador with cash in his pocket, fingers itching to spend it before his wife took it for the house. Dolly passing on to Nunny what she would no longer need. Gifts by proxy. A sweater with that warm smell of sister. The two girls shuffling home through a snowstorm and Dolly deciding she wanted it back, immediately, whatever she had given away. Everything was still hers, her old sweater, her old coat. "But you're wearing a brand *new* sweater and a brand *new* coat," her sister whined, her fingers already working the buttons. Left to hurry home with hands in her armpits, feet fast behind the fat woolen layers of Dolly.

"And on this page there's a pill-box hat as black as stone, like ink, Daddy, black for dress-up or a funeral, only I'd not be saving it for funerals, I'd have it on all the time."

She speaks excitedly, but her voice is flat, stammering slightly and trailing away at the end of each sentence. The coins are moist in her palm. His arms and legs are rigid behind her, but she can't see his body. She sees only the paper, the pictures.

"It's the heaviest one yet, isn't it, Daddy?" The catalogues this fall were thick with denial — claims that everything was cheaper than the year before, everything just as well-made. As if time could turn backward, war-time substitutes replacing the real thing. Pictures more abundant while the merchandise shrunk away. *Feels and looks just like genuine silk. A quality shipment purchased before our troubled times.* The print promised stockings, though the last pair had been gone for months. Dolly inking a line down her leg to mimic a seam. "The catalogue for last winter wasn't near as nice. We're going to cut it up. We're going to dress our dolls in pictures. We're going to give them the nicest things. They'll be so warm this winter. We'll cover them in clothes, in pictures. We'll smother them."

Her father's eyes dart back and forth, searching for the pages she turns with her words. Her hands are cupped in her lap. Her hands thumb the coins. There is no catalogue. She is staring straight ahead, eyes fixed on nothing.

"Spoons and forks," she continues, rubbing the coins across her knees. "Spoons like the ones you played, smacked between your leg and your hand, remember Daddy, how you'd do it, the rhythm all rat-a-tat all night? Couldn't tell whether it was the metal or your bones making that noise. Rat-a-tat trapped between your leg and your hand, back and forth, rat-a-tat."

"We could buy new ones. Look here, Daddy, those with flowers on the handle. Is that a rose, you think? I can't tell. A flower of some sort. I remember when I found out how my name — I mean my birth name — was Florence. Not Dolly at all. I'm the only one in the family to have that kind of a name. Florence, so pretty. We learned in school there's a city called Florence with all kinds of sculpture and paintings like the ones in the Confederation Building or the funeral parlour. I liked that, there's a city in my name, I carried it inside me, that foreign place, all those beautiful things. Flowers and pictures. But nobody called me Florence."

She pats the sheet, pats his leg, small steady gestures like those a parent gives a startled child. "I can't remember when I wasn't Doll. Do you remember, Daddy, when you first called me Doll? How was . . . I mean, how old was I then?" She squints to remember the next image. "Oh Daddy, look, look at this page, just look at the velvet dress. And the satin one right down to the floor. It comes in royal blue or emerald green or amethyst, only I wouldn't know what to choose. I'd like to wrap myself in all those colours. You'd like that too, wouldn't you, Daddy? Your Dolly all wrapped in paper. But the paper's so thin. And shiny, look. That ruffled one's real silk I bet. Almost feel like you got it already, don't you now, just looking at it? But it's not there. It's not real at all."

She remembers the struggle over blankets, how she and her sister competed for cover. She'd wake with the dark air nipping at her nightgown and catch Nunny nestled in the quilt they were supposed to share. Or find her sleeping horizontal at the bottom of the bed, all rolled in wool, her tight fist of a body a child-pillow for Dolly's feet.

It was Dolly who would be lifted awake by her father. He'd come with the quilt from his own bed, outstretched, an open patchwork mouth. Dolly wondered what was left to keep her mother warm, thick legs sprawled and naked as she slept off the bottled songs of the night before. He sneaked into the girls' room only in the early morning when he hadn't gone to sleep at all, cursed by a manic insomnia after a night out or a night in, when he'd prowl the house cussing or singing or playing his spoons, waiting in the dark for his wife to wake up. He'd creep on tender feet inside the girls' room and swoop Dolly up inside the quilt, her surprised smallness curled like a larva. Her giggle, her confusion between dreams and awake. Carried her downstairs. Humming, whistling, he paused on each step, her body rocking inside the hammock. He sat her beside the stove and dressed her. The first squint of morning light a line widening across her shoulders. He dressed her piece by piece and then wrapped her again inside the quilt, her eyes dreamy but expectant, her gaze transfixed by his, he slipped her out of her nightgown and into her clothes. Stockings, blouse, skirt, sweater, each layer of fabric a little sturdier than the next. If she moved, even twitched, he'd stop, the remaining clothes clenched in his hands, the cold air of the kitchen free to lick her back. She had to stay completely still. Her limbs limp, flutter of breath in her chest as he held leg-holes open and slid each foot through her panties so she didn't have to stand up to pull them on herself.

He'd talk. The party the night before or stories about his first job or just lists of things he liked, dumplings and frost on windows and the smell of her hair. She nodded and smiled as he wrapped her in words.

Once she was dressed, if her mother still hadn't moved, he'd feed her. Overcooked porridge, her mouth spooned full of the sweet steaming sludge. Always porridge, never a piece of toast or codcake, never anything crisp or hard, just this beige softness she didn't need to chew. Porridge stirred and stirred and thinned translucent with milk — an infant's first feeding, as if he didn't believe she had grown teeth. Sometimes he'd use his hands to prod the sludge inside, not feeding her really, just giving her the taste, her tongue quivering to meet his finger. She knew her mother didn't like it, him in these moods. But Dolly was warming, Dolly was warmer than she'd ever been before, inside her clothes, inside her father's quilt, her lips closing around a milk-sweet thumb.

"The dress on this page has heart-shaped buttons like the candies you bought us on Saturdays, our hands all sticky. Only look at the pleats, they'd take an age to iron, keeping all those lines from getting crooked. What I would like is a suit. Here it is, now doesn't she look smart? I want one just like that, real modern. Man-style. I seen it in movies. A wool skirt pencil-straight and a jacket with tricky pockets and padded shoulders and all in pin-stripes, Daddy, banker's grey, I tell you I'd be the only one. Could look the whole island over you won't find another girl in a suit like mine." A flickering grin as her eyes dart between the image and his face. "I pretend I already own it, that's what I do. All those pretty things I can't have."

She rubs the sheet as if it were the page she describes. Slips her hand under the folds.

"Paper can cut you, though, all the same, if you're not careful, it can get you right bad."

Don't you go carrying on like you do. He's had enough of you, Lord knows.

Her fingers brushing against his shin, the skin dry and tight to the bone, hairs like slivers. Feel of the sheet on her hand on his leg. She slides her palm up past his knee along the paper skin of his inner thigh.

You don't do anything sudden now, you hear me? You be good. Don't be getting him all riled up.

She touches the flesh between his legs, as shriveled as her fingers after a bath.

Both his hands lie on top of the sheets, palms down like bad boys ordered to keep theirs outside the covers. His skin is softer than her fingers. She folds her hand around the floppy flaccid curl. She begins to pet it, coax it, an eyeless animal.

She thinks of children who wet the bed. The release and shame of it, warmth wrapping genitals as a young boy spoons his brother's back. The stain growing cold. The sudden shouts and shoves, name-calling. Or maybe hiding it all night, lying stiff over the wet spot. Fighting the pull of sleep. Then waking quick to dread. Small hands trying to wring yellow out of white.

Her fingers in a ring around the base, she pulls slowly, gently, to the tip. Like kneading bread, she thinks, like waiting for dough to rise.

She hasn't tried this with her husband. He likes to feel himself on top of her. The papist, her father called him, angry that his eldest daughter would marry a man who eats his god. Dolly, trapped by this unexpected virulence against the church, pushing her dinner around her plate while she tried to convince her father that Phil was like anyone else, that he was the same man her father was. They couldn't be left alone together, Phil and Patrick, the young man burly and threatening in his silence, the older in his noise. She hovered over their one-sided conversations, dragged her mother and sister into the room in the hope that an audience would encourage Phil to mutter more than one or two words, that her father would let someone else talk. His mouth full of food as he pointed his fork at her sister and lectured Phil on how the younger girl had been the one to pine after the Catholic church, how she was the saint, the good daughter. The nun. Nunny. With each visit from Phil he'd point her out, her weak awkward smile, and ask why a papist wouldn't want a nun instead.

The afternoon of the wedding, he sat at home yelling at the radio as if the hitter could hear his advice. His words one move ahead of another man's arm. Other than these orders to a box barking static and scores, he didn't say a thing. Dolly in white, walking alone down the aisle. He never gave her away.

Dolly jumps as a sound twists on his tongue and oozes down his chin. He begins to rock and flap, struggling to sit up.

Her hand fills with hard dry flesh. A tiny leg.

He moans. She glances at him, then turns back to her catalogue. Pearl is safe at home, screaming and kicking off diapers. The light bulb flickers dim then bright. A slight smell of burning as if a ghost had walked into the room and lit a match.

She smiles at the smell. The spring before she started scrubbing floors, bringing her own cash back home, her father had refused to give her the money for a perm. All those picture-shows, he said, had gone to her head. Her going out dancing at night. No daughter of his. So she laid the curling iron inside the embers of the stove. She wound the scorching metal around strands of hair, holding the clamp in place until she saw smoke. Her complacent curiosity at how a single hair would coil and spin to escape the heat, how a whole lock would melt. The spitting like a final angry snap at life. Night after night she did this, the clumps falling from her scalp to the floor, her face framed by scorched claws of curls. *What has gotten into that child,* her mother asked while the house filled with the acrid stink of burning hair.

Her father ranted up the stairs, the stench thickening in his throat, smell and noise reaching a crescendo. Her steady jaw dared him to hit her. She stared unflinching like she did the morning of the last feeding, when she refused to open her mouth and he jammed the spoon through her lips, his face twisted with rage and shame as the metal scraped the fence of her teeth.

Wearing her helmet of scorched curls she held out the rod. His hands were awkward. He swayed in place, unsure whether he should knock the iron away or accept it. She waited. She lifted it up toward his body. He could use it against her. Here it is, it's yours, take it. Her burning cheeks. His blinking and blinking, Adam's apple thrust out with each swallow. Both of them flinching when the clock struck the hour.

The next morning, on the kitchen table, a puddle of coins.

Now she twirls her fingers around his cock like so many strands of hair. She locks his flesh in her hand. His eyes draw triangles from her arm to her face to the door. Another grunt escapes. He tries to throw words, his lips a crooked grimace, one arm tapping spastically at her like a branch breaking from a wind-whipped tree.

Your father can only move parts of himself. You'll have to help him.

The stains on her blouse dark blue over her nipples.

"On this page all you've got is men's clothing. Just look at the handsome trousers. Wool herringbone, a permanent crease running right down each leg, you'd look a man in those, Daddy, I'd buy them for you if I could."

He drags his eyes along her body. His left hand spasms into a fist, then opens. A voice echoes bright and metallic down the hall. The voice comes closer. He stops his sounds. He breathes. The room is quiet except for the rustle of sheets above her hand, the drag and thud of his breath. Something rolls by the door. Footsteps pass, recede.

"They've got a lot of nice things for Mama. Imitation pearls, all milky white. You shouldn't forget Mama. She'd like something from you. Why don't you buy her a choker? She'd be so surprised. You shouldn't be giving it all to me. It's not fair to her, now, is it?"

His face fades like the pictures. His mouth squeezed into a tight O.

He can't do a thing for himself.

His neck arches, driving his head deep into the pillow. His pupils roll up to leave naked the white of his eyes. She glances down at the lump in the middle of the bed, how the sheets rise and fall with her hand. Milk collects in the cups of her bra.

A shiver under her fingers. She begins to thrust faster, her hand up and down, up and down.

He can't do a thing.

And here it comes. Yes, she can tell now. Her fist pulses it out, the slick sticky release. Squirt and sputter, dribble of father. Eyes fluttering shut. Old man captured by sudden sleep like an infant, the sheets quiet over his spent flesh.

She listens to his breath. It catches, stops, then continues, a slow, even rasp. His sap runs between her fingers. She lifts her hand free, takes it back into her lap, rubs the coins, her spine straight and stiff as if she were posing for a picture. On her blouse, two wet eyes widen.

tamas dobozy

KEEPING THE MEASURE

The one-eyed man said softly, "Think — somebody'd like — me?"
"Why, sure," said Tom. "Tell 'em ya dong's growed sence
you los' your eye."
— John Steinbeck

DOCTOR INGMAR ANDERSSEN'S LAYING ON THE BED WITH A sheet wrapped around his legs. He's staring out the window, thinking of all the satellites spinning in orbit overhead, scanning him and his neighbourhood for information. He kicks off the sheet and tries to imagine how great it would feel to be transformed into a digital signal, to be stored up there in a memory bank with all the other zeroes and ones. Maybe then the satellites could beam him down into the body of some guy — who knows, a construction worker maybe — someone who doesn't sit in bed all morning staring out the window, but is, well, getting yelled at by his wife for sleeping in and missing work. God, if only I could get yelled at, Ingmar thinks; it would be so intimate.

But he gets up, and there's still plenty of time before his interview. He goes to the bathroom, runs lukewarm water over his long, spidery, surgeon's fingers, and pads around the apartment flexing them, a routine exercise he does first thing every morning, back and forth in front of the discoloured squares on the wall, where once hung three mounted diplomas, four awards for performance, a citation for excellence of conduct, plus two framed letters from kids whose faces he'd reconstructed.

Where are the friends they promised? I've got an ava-
lanche of cash bearing down on me. I've got status. I've
given to charities, anonymously and in person. I've
worked *pro bono*. I've given of my time to research and
symposiums. And what do I get? A deluge of brown-nosers!
Day after day after day. The thought of them makes him
glance down at his groin, but then he shakes his head no
— no, no, not that part of my body.

Coming out of the elevator, Ingmar lets the doors slide
open without stepping out, peeks around the corner past
the potted fern and the ashcans, over the shoulder of Mrs
McKinley's maid, herself towing a two-wheeled shopping
cart full of groceries to one of the other elevators, peeks
past her towards the lobby and the front doors, looking out
for Frank, the doorman, whom Ingmar thinks is on the
telephone, out of sight around the corner. Risking it,
Ingmar runs for the front door, leather soles skidding on
carpet, and is between the bank of elevators and the entrance when he hears the maid squeal. She's caught between the sliding doors, a wheel of the cart in the crack
where elevator meets floor, cans of soup and tuna tipping
out.

Taking a last look at the door he might have opened
for himself, Ingmar goes back, reaches down, piles the
cans back into the cart, jerks the wheel free and lifts it inside. "Oh, Doctor Anderssen, thank you so much. Thank
you. You're such a gentlem —" The closing elevator cuts
her off.

Ingmar turns and there's Frank, already holding the
door. "Thanks for helping out, Doctor. I've rung Alex to
bring your car around. Anything else?"

"No, no thank you, Frank," says Ingmar, shoulders
slumping as he walks out.

On the drive to the Institute, Ingmar thinks how he
should greet Frank with a big "Fuck You" the next time the
man holds the door for him; but he's tried being mean

before, and it only makes people like Frank that much more ass-tighteningly officious.

> > >

A half-hour commute later, Ingmar's sitting ten floors above the street, in the interview room of the Institute. In front of him, under the fluorescent lights, sit five men in immaculate, white lab coats and wire-rim spectacles, in a faint V-formation behind the Chief of Staff, a thin, bald man of six-foot-six, one-sixty or one-seventy pounds, his face so tightly wired by wrinkles you get a definite impression of the skull just underneath.

When the Chief of Staff stands, the two doctors to either side of him look up from left and right, the slope of their heads forming a triangle whose apex is the Chief of Staff's shiny scalp. "Doctor Anderssen," he begins, twin, circular lenses glinting. "Doctor Anderssen, not many men get to the final stage of the interview. Your CV, your references . . . are impressive. But this is a unique operation. And even surgeons as highly qualified as yourself often do not find themselves adequate to the environment." He twists his head to the surgeons on either side, like a camera eye tracking left and right, before bearing on Ingmar again. "Nevertheless, we are impressed with you, Doctor Anderssen." On Ingmar's patronymic, the air-conditioning cuts out, leaving the room so quiet he can hear his eyelids flick. "As you know, we do not treat the penis. That would be too clinical. Nor the cock. Too slangy. Nor the wiener. Too metaphoric. And Dick is a man's name. For this, and for other reasons, policy holds that insofar as clients are concerned, the Institute treats . . . the dink. Can you understand me, Doctor Anderssen? Without laughing? This is essential. We must present just the right attitude to the men who come to us — serious, but not without a certain sense of unacknowledged humour. The word dink fits. It fits perfectly, Doctor Anderssen."

Ingmar lays his hands on the table as a way of saying

yes without saying it. "Good," the Chief of Staff asserts, "then we'll start." The other doctors click their pens in readiness. "Tell us, if you will, Doctor Anderssen, do you like your dink?"

"Yes, I like my dink."

"Is it a nice dink?"

"In the dictionary definition of the word, yes."

"Do other people like your dink?"

"As far as I've ascertained. Criticism tends to concentrate more on how I utilize my dink — to what end it's put — than its intrinsic qualities."

"If you could trade dinks with anyone in the world, who would you trade dinks with?"

"I would not trade my dink."

The surgeons to either side stroke tics into the appropriate boxes on the forms; Ingmar's happy to think of them as oil-jacks working in unison over some sterile stretch of prairie, while the Chief of Staff waits for them to catch up to the interview. Then, with a sharp, collective inhale the four surgeons tilt forward, following the lead of their superior, as he asks the question to end all questions, "Doctor Anderssen, how big. . . ?"

But Ingmar's on it before the Chief of Staff has finished. "My dink is medium-sized."

The Chief of Staff's face almost cracks and flakes off as he says, "Welcome, Doctor Anderssen, to the Institute."

>   >   >

As always, Ingmar's name, no matter how small he prints, multiplies the minute he signs it, replicating by itself like some single-celled organism — from *Doctor Ingmar Anderssen* mounted on his door, then desk, then security pass, then parking sticker, and so on, and so on, until he's wrapped in his name like a sleeping bag of pink insulation.

For weeks Ingmar walks, talks and toils in the examination and visiting rooms of the Institute, waiting for the change, for his isolation to melt away and the friends to come pouring in. But the patients still defer to him, already so ashamed of their dinkiness (a word the Chief of Staff has forbidden in the Institute, on pain of "de-hiring"). On the phone his stockbroker and accountant are still so polite Ingmar can just bet, just bet, they're wearing those shit-eating grins. At the club they still have that seat reserved for him, whether or not he turns up at six, the usual whiskey sour waiting beside the fresh copy of the *Globe and Mail.* Charities treat him with the respect due a long-standing benefactor. And so, after four weeks of working at the Institute, Ingmar's still sitting up in bed in the morning, huddled in sheets and hoping to attract the attention of at least one, lone satellite.

In the operating room he tries for sarcasm and levity as a change from whistling Beethoven's *Fifth,* which is what he used to do while remodelling the faces of accident victims. He checks the complicated arrangement of ridges requested by the patient (often drawn, in a not quite reasonable facsimile, on the back of a bar coaster) and whistles: "How rococo!" then sucks fat from a patient's stomach and ass and injects it, subcutaneously, into his dink, increasing the diameter and laying down an intricate grid of bumps and rings along the shaft, crafting — as the Chief of Staff put it during the last briefing — a French-tickler *au naturel.* "And so it becomes unique," Ingmar says to Nurse Strindberg. "And more so because it's temporary. It may not happen in weeks, or even months, but eventually the body metabolises the fat and they're back, ready to improve on the design!"

"I know, Doctor Anderssen."

"Can't anyone call me Ingmar, ever?"

They wheel out, they wheel in. Ingmar calls for a fresh syringe.

> > >

Each month has its catalogue of traits: for instance, Ingmar could never mistake October, as the last of the red leaves fall and the stores stock up with Halloween treats and leering rubber masks of the Mummy and Batman. And who wouldn't place November, its satellite photographs swirling like a fingerprint? And then there's winter fuelling February's coolness until it sits in the hollow of your throat. So Ingmar navigates the months at the Institute, thrilled by their year-to-year consistency, their total indifference.

But suddenly May turns into a month of worry, mainly because CBC's *Comic Documentaries* decides to do a story on the Institute, sending out their sarcastic ace — Claire Braxton — to skulk around the Institute's front door with her cameraman, harassing doctors and patients. For one thing, Claire's CBC uniform violates the season with improper colours: black, orange, rust. For another, her microphone — shaped out of plastic and foam rubber to look like a big rigid dick — really violates May, probably the least masculine and phallic month of all.

From his open office window, Ingmar uses binoculars to spy on the investigative team as they hide behind trees, parked cars, the corner of the building, and then jump out to heckle patients (usually disguised in sunglasses) running from the Institute to their cars. There's a patient coming out right now, and Claire and the cameraman are right behind him, hips flaring like three penguins as they speed-walk towards the parking lot, jolting the camera so much it's bound to make the viewing audience seasick.

"We're from *Comic Documentaries*. Mind if we ask a few questions?" The empty parking lot leaves few escape routes. "Did you just get the operation?" The cameraman sashays into position as the patient mumbles. "It's not really an extension, is it?" Claire continues.

"They make it, uh, thicker."

"I'm sorry, I can't hear you."

"Thicker," he speaks up. "They make it thicker. Hey, I don't want to be on no camera."

"Don't worry. We'll digitize your face and remix your voice."

"Well, but still. . . ."

"Does it hurt where they took the fat from?"

"No. No, not really."

"Was it really small before?"

"Small," the patient says, too low to record.

"How small?"

"Like . . . a little pickle." The patient's voice fades to zero on "pickle."

"Uh, I didn't quite catch that. Did you say it was the size of a gherkin?"

"Yeah. . . ."

"It was the size of a gherkin?"

"Yes! Now, leave me. . . ."

"You had a penis the size of a gherkin?"

"Look, shut the fuck up, lady. . . ."

"So what is it now, a fat gherkin?"

"Fuck off!"

"Gherkin man! Gherkin man!"

The patient lunges forward, claws the camera out of the cameraman's grasp and smashes it to the ground, kicking in the lens and then putting a headlock on Claire. The cameraman circles, scared to strike. Finally, a security guard rushes in and rips them apart.

Ingmar lowers the binoculars, turns, and his skeleton nearly leaps out of his skin and runs off, tailbone tucked between its legs, to find that the Chief of Staff's been standing there the whole time, right there behind him, and so quiet Ingmar can't tell whether the man's breathing.

"Trouble," the Chief of Staff says, his lips barely moving, his face not at all. "I'd like you to do something about it. Consider this a test of your loyalty, Doctor . . . Ingmar." The Chief of Staff's head pivots slowly and slightly to face him, then the body of the man turns without feet lifting from the floor, as if it were spinning on a turntable.

Ingmar calls Channel Twelve and agrees to sign an interview waiver.

>   >   >

Claire Braxton accepts a cigar and even lets Ingmar clip the end; she cradles the phallic microphone in the crook of her arm as the two of them release competing puffs of smoke. "Do you play golf as well?" she asks, extending forward the cigar to show she's talking about stereotypical surgeon hobbies. Ingmar nods and jots a mental note to take it up. "Do you like handling men's organs?" Ingmar shrugs. She continues probing: "How about your job?"

"It's a job," he says.

"Well, no kidding! Hey," she looks to her cameraman, who's busy fanning cigar smoke from the lens, "we've got a real master of subtlety here," then turns back to Ingmar. "But you never answered me. We've done our research on you, Doctor Ingmar Anderssen. Reconstructive surgeon. Degrees, honours. A successful practice doing surgery on accident victims. You live in a tiny apartment, don't drive a fancy car, donate big sums to the charities. A real pillar of the community. Then, one day, you have a nervous breakdown, grab some patient's member in the operating room. Next thing we know, you've quit that and joined up with this outfit. So what's the story? You like working with men? Is that it?"

"As much as any prostitute."

"What's that supposed to mean?"

"Do you like your penis-shaped microphone?"

"Hey, I'm asking the questions here," she shouts. Ingmar remains still. Claire continues: "Have you ever been tempted to operate on yourself?" Ingmar stands, unbuckles his belt, drops his pants and undies and steps up onto his desk, one foot up on a stack of files, standing there like Tarzan over the body of a lion, his unexceptional dink swinging, and begins to yodel. "Stop it! Stop it!" Claire yells. "You can't do that on TV!" But Ingmar continues yodelling and swinging until the CBC unit scrams.

>   >   >

Ingmar decides to decline the bonus offered by the Chief

of Staff for the performance, not only because he doesn't need the money but because he doesn't want to add professional jealousy to the fear already creeping its way through the other members of the surgical staff — a fear that principally radiates from the tight crotch of Doctor Yngwie Sundquist's trousers. "Yngwie's really pushing the envelope," they whisper in the scrubbing room, nodding towards the bulge between their colleague's legs, from which a thick tube worms its way halfway across a thigh under the tight fabric.

"I can't help it if I'm special," says Yngwie when the other doctors express their concern, "anymore than I can help it that the Chief of Staff has a small dick."

"Tut, tut," the Chief of Staff says when Ingmar, as requested, reports this conversation.

Yngwie gets his pink slip the next Monday. On Tuesday, the surgeons silently watch the Chief of Staff as he moves towards the cork bulletin board — the guy doesn't walk, he hovers — and pins a fresh printout of the Institute's rules and regulations onto the bulletin board, which declares: SINCE TIGHT PANTS ON THE WELL-ENDOWED MAY ENGENDER FEELINGS OF INADEQUACY AMONG STAFF AND — MOST IMPORTANTLY — PATIENTS, SURGEONS SHALL RESTRICT THEIR DRESS TO LOOSE-FITTING CLOTHES AT ALL TIMES.

On Wednesday, technicians arrive and install security cameras in the hallways, operating rooms, and even the toilets, to track the surgeons going back and forth, cameras that seem, to Ingmar, to be monitoring his time, taking possession of moments he's happy to contribute.

On Thursday, Yngwie, in the midst of clearing out his desk, rushes out into the hall, file-folders falling out from under his armpits, grabs Ingmar by the elbow and hisses: "The Chief of Staff . . . he's afraid of the world ending. That's what tight pants mean to him: apocalypse."

Ingmar responds: "No. It's your arrogance. It's your calling attention to yourself!"

On Friday, the Chief of Staff brings in a plate of gravlax for everyone except Yngwie, who's so insulted he storms out of the Institute well in advance of his last "official" workday; hardly anybody notices him go, though, surprised as they are to discover that the food's been prepared by the Chief of Staff's wife (nobody, except Ingmar, suspected he had one).

> > >

Ingmar's standing outside the staff toilet after ten hours and twenty-five dinks in the operating room. The Chief of Staff glides out of the door — now it's his turn to be surprised at finding Ingmar standing there — and flashes his junior colleague a tight, embarrassed smile. "Evening, Ingmar," he says. Ingmar returns a smile just as crisp, enters the bathroom and, turning to pull out a fresh seat cover, notices words written above the toilet roll, the ink still wet:

> Please complete these sentences:
>   1) Dinosaurs await me where I go repeat
>   2) Clearing from my mind the image of
>   pterodactyls with blunder
>   3) Dream of dodos in open graves to cut
>   4) When I realize sabre-tooth tigers I realize
>   as about

Ingmar pumps a bit of hand-soap onto a wad of toilet paper and scrubs off the ink before it sets.

The next day, the Chief of Staff thanks Ingmar for his quick thinking: "You did me a great favour. Yes, a great favour indeed."

Ingmar can hear a lidded pot buzzing with flies whenever the Chief of Staff opens his mouth, and cuts off the older man before he can continue, already so grateful for the amount of time the Chief of Staff has spent patronizing him. "It's nothing, nothing at all."

A bit later that day, the Chief of Staff again glides into the lunchroom with a new regulation for the bulletin board: ALL SURGEONS SHALL REPORT TO NURSE STRINDBERG FOR IMMEDIATE DINK MEASUREMENTS.

"That's going too goddamn far," Sven yells at the Chief of Staff, who raises an expressionless face (from this angle Ingmar can tell that the man has no eyebrows behind the rims of his glasses) to the junior surgeon. "There's no need for that. You just want to have the biggest dick on the block!"

"What's wrong, Sven?" Ingmar cuts in. "Are you afraid of having the smallest?" The skin on the Chief of Staff's neck develops perfect, army-cot creases as he turns towards Ingmar, the corners of his lips twisting up into little curlicues.

"Yes. Highly amusing, Ingmar. Highly amusing." The curlicues flatten out. It's the first time Ingmar's seen the man's facial muscles try to cope with a smile.

But Sven's missed it, and he scowls: "I won't do it. I refuse."

"Then, Doctor Bjornson, you may consider yourself terminated."

"Gladly, you little megalomaniac!"

And then there are two.

Ingmar turns right out of the lunchroom, strides down the hall, and stands in front of Nurse Strindberg's desk. She looks up at him. He reaches down, pulls a metric ruler out of his pocket and hands it to her.

She feels uncomfortable with the procedure — which is weird, he thinks, considering all the dinks she's handled — and asks Ingmar to do the measuring himself, which, feeling sorry for her, he does. But when she starts quibbling over whether to put in the millimetres or round up to the nearest centimetre, he grows impatient and tells her to just stop worrying about insulting him and include the fractions, since the Chief of Staff is a bit of a precisionist anyhow.

After surgeon Gustavus Branting measures up, the Chief of Staff shakes both his colleagues' hands and compliments them: "Both of you gentlemen always struck me as gentlemen," he says. "Not like the other gentlemen."

A week later, Ingmar pulls an envelope from his office mailbox with *Measurement Bonus* written on it. He spends the money on a new coffee machine for the staff room and an oak-grain filing cabinet to fit all the caseloads he and Gustavus inherited from Yngwie and Sven.

"Very nice," says the Chief of Staff, running his fingers over the new cabinet, then snaps the fingers up off the metal and slides them back into the pocket of his labcoat. "We have some vacancies on staff, Ingmar. Either you or Doctor Branting will become Assistant Chief of Staff. Doctor Branting is senior, but you have proved very committed. The matter is by no means closed. By no means mastodon. . . ." The Chief of Staff trails off, raising an eyebrow muscle under the veiny skin of his forehead, but Ingmar refuses to complete the sentence, and then the two men smile at each other — flashing their over-large teeth — while clouds, reflected from an open window, stream across the Chief of Staff's oval eyeglasses.

> > >

Sure, Ingmar dabbles in the animal life, too, taking time out for some instinctive behaviour, such as the night of the staff Christmas party, when he and Nurse Strindberg have risky sex on his office couch, not caring about the spilled drinks, or if they'll be missed by the other office members, or, hell, even if tomorrow they'll remember doing it; and the spiked punch does cost them the memory of the sex. Nurse Strindberg knows something happened, but not what, and for a few days she's awkward around Ingmar, then normal again, then back to awkward when she misses her period. She marches into Ingmar's office, not bothering to knock first, a test-tube of blue urine in her fist.

After deciphering her breathless delivery — which

goes, "Baby . . . me . . . turned blue . . . at the Christmas party" — Ingmar counters with "Let's see," and together they examine the couch, neither touched nor sat upon since that night (most patients, being nervous and embarrassed and wearing sunglasses, prefer to stand). There are enough stains and sickle-shaped hairs under the slip-cover to trigger both their memories. "Wow!" The net descends so heavily they sit, side by side. "None of the other surgeons have kids."

"What has that got to do with us?" she asks.

"What about the Chief of Staff," he wonders. "If he has a wife he must have kids."

"Ingmar, what are we going to do?"

Ingmar rubs his arms, then itches; it feels as if someone's taking the slack out of his skin, like his skin's tightening up on his bones, going from a few sizes too big to a size just right.

It's at this moment that the Chief of Staff knocks on the door and walks in, surprising Nurse Strindberg and Ingmar, who jump up off the couch and brush themselves off, saying "Yes, yes. Well, well," then adjusting their hair and glasses in a little game of patty cake. The Chief of Staff glances from one to the other, his glasses as clear as gin.

On his way out that evening, Ingmar, too excited to bother to check whether the security cameras are pointing at him, drops a note on Nurse Strindberg's desk, inviting her for dinner.

The Chief of Staff follows the surgeon's every stumble and turn, from his office to the parking lot, on a bank of security monitors installed in his office; Doctor Branting stands off to one side with an I-told-you-so look on his face.

>   >   >

She walks around his apartment, and rather than overturning various knick-knacks, or peeking into closets, she tries to imagine the knick-knacks that might stand, one

day, on the empty shelves, the pictures that might hang
on the walls, the clothes that could take up the two-thirds
of empty closet-space. Ingmar's apartment rings with a
Spartan emptiness. Such a small place for a baby, Nurse
Strindberg thinks.

"Why don't you take off your jacket, Helga," Ingmar
says, uncorking a bottle of de-alcoholized wine.

"You live here?"

"Yes, I do."

"But it's —"

"Perfect," he says, the cork sliding out with a pop. "It's
small, contained, no frills. You'd never know a thing about
me, seeing this place."

"But you could have so much!" She takes off her coat
and puts it on the couch. "And you gave up a famous practice . . . to work with dinks!"

He pushes his finger into the bottle, tilts it to get a bit
of red wine on the tip and then places the finger inside his
mouth. Exiting the mouth, his finger pulls out the following words: "It was the most ludicrous thing I could do."
Ingmar puts the bottle down on the table, beside the candles, and walks to the window, laying his hands flat against
the cold glass. "I was such a normal child. I used to wake
up in the morning, and it was . . . it was like. . . . So, it took
me hours to separate myself from the surroundings. No, it
wasn't like that. It's that I wasn't thinking about it, and so
I didn't realize there was any division between me and my
parents and my friends. We were all occupying the same
space. Phased together.

"When they found out about me I was sixteen. It was
my hands. I tried telling them that even though my hands
were exceptional it didn't mean I was. It didn't matter, my
parents . . . they were interested in this special school. So
I went. Academics. Heavy on the sciences. Piano lessons.
All geared towards taking me into surgery.

"Now, I'm not big on erections. Never was. But I was a
kid . . . you know. All kids diddle. I remember waking up

in the dormitory, morning after morning, and everything was in stark relief, so distant. I'd quickly start masturbating. Pretty normal behaviour for a kid under the circumstances, right? But instead of bringing me pleasure it was like every stroke of my hands was making my dink longer and longer, like there was no end to it, and with each stroke and each elongation the things in the room, the furniture, the people, everything, were getting farther and farther from me, moving away into the distance.

"Well, it didn't take me long to figure out it was my hands. They were doing it. My stupid hands. They were at fault. They'd brought me here.

"I tried masturbating without my hands after that, sort of rubbing myself against pieces of furniture and bedsheets, but, you know, Helga, it was just such a job! Finally, I stopped. I mean, that's normal, right? That much effort — anybody would stop. Teenagers are lazy. I suppose I don't need to tell you that. I did have sex after that, but only with a woman, and it still wasn't much satisfying because they were fucking me for my hands. Don't take this the wrong way.

"So I became a surgeon. Of course, things with my surroundings just got worse and worse. Invitations to be a keynote speaker at conferences, to be a co-ordinator for life-saving research, emcee charitable functions. And beside the society business, there's the sycophancy of nurses and interns and patients. You can't believe the ass-kissing a person like me endures. Like my rear-end's been dipped in saliva. You go into a room and tell a joke and nobody knows how to react, as if they're not sure whether it's okay to laugh in your presence; or the person telling the joke stops in the middle of it. Every time you walk into a room it's like you're some feared principal walking into a noisy classroom. Sudden silence. And the people are looking at the floor. Of course, there are always those, colleagues or whoever, who feel threatened by my success; their jokes are pointed, sarcastic, rigged for my humiliation (which

wouldn't be bad if someone laughed). On top of it all,
you've got this schedule of eighteen-hour operations. The
beeper I couldn't bring myself to turn off. The diet of coffee, once in a while some benzedrine. Subsisting on
snatches of sleep. This money I've no use for, that takes
up as much time managing as accumulating it does.

"So it's no surprise, I suppose, when one day things go
a bit crazy in the operating room."

"I heard," says Helga, quietly.

But Ingmar continues, happy there's someone he can
get all of this out to. "Some guy. Brain cancer. We'd sawed
off the top of his head and I was in there, trying to get at
the tumour. We were in the part of the brain responsible
for certain motor functions, and I probably glanced the
nerve. Something. I was tired. But anyway, the patient,
who was anaesthetized but awake, started getting this
enormous erection. And that's when all hell broke loose.
Once again, it was my hands that were causing this thing
to happen. The room starts bending in and out. Warping.
And then, when I dropped the scalpel, things just started
to race away from me. I mean zooming away, Helga. In all
directions. Such speed," Ingmar shakes his head.
"Everything was breaking apart, like an image on water.
Even my skin felt like it was unravelling. The nurses were
trying to get to me, reaching out, but they couldn't keep
up to the rate they were moving away. And me, I did the
only thing I could do. I lunged for that hard-on before it
too went beyond my reach, and grabbed it, one hand
around the base, the other pressing down on the head, trying to keep that erection from growing. God, it was like trying to push a champagne cork back into a bottle that wants
nothing more than to explode. But I had to do it, you see?
I had no other choice. It was that or be forced into some
corner of the universe, with the things I wanted forever
out of reach. Lost in this vastness. It was then and there,
Helga, then and there that I knew that the sole purpose of
that erection was to destroy me!"

Helga sits, gathers her skirt in her lap, and looks back at his sweaty face.

Ingmar pours two glasses of wine and carries one over, then takes a seat across the coffee table. "After that, after I quit, was asked to quit, my practice, the feeling of separateness lessened. And the Institute has helped. Such a stupid place. It makes me feel idiotic, unimportant," he giggles. "You can't imagine the professional respect I've lost since I joined up!"

"I will have this baby."

"Of course. But, listen, I should be the one to tell the Chief of Staff."

"Absolutely not."

"But I know exactly what he wants to hear!"

> > >

Ingmar rises in the glass elevator, past floors and floors in the circular, bubble-shaped building of the Institute, past access doors open to all, and then, with the turn of a key left in his mailbox this morning, beyond, to the penthouse few employees ever see. The shadow of a bird passes through a high window, drifts from bare wall to bare wall and then up and out again.

At the end of a pale hallway, light shooting through glass walls to either side, he enters the white room where they held his interview. The Chief of Staff sits behind a circular and vacant desktop, surgeon Branting slightly behind and to the right of him. Ingmar follows the Chief of Staff's motion to a straight-backed chair in front of a desk, where he sits down, his knee knocking on a hollow desk drawer.

"Let me ask you, Doctor Anderssen?" Ah, it's back to Doctor Anderssen, then, is it? Oh well, Ingmar gives himself a silent pep talk and nods. "Please," the Chief of Staff continues, "tell Doctor Branting and I, if you would, what it is, exactly, that this Institute does for its patients?"

Branting's eye winks or falls under a shadow. Ingmar begins carefully, like a man testing a minefield with his big

toe. "Chief of Staff, Gustavus, I no longer feel comfortable
with question and answer. Having been at the Institute for
over a year, I feel the very nature of our work is a rebuttal
— a complete refutation if you will — of catechismal information." The Chief of Staff's lenses opaquely reflect the
light of the setting sun streaming in from the corridor. "I
say this in order to clarify that I will henceforth provide
no specified answers, and will proceed uncategorically."
Rays of orange and red shimmer across the walls. "Every
day in the operating room, I ask myself: 'How many of the
dinks are average rather than undersized?' Probably eighty
percent, or more."

The Chief of Staff falls into immobility, while Doctor
Branting's face grows so long and black it seems to be swallowing itself. Ingmar continues: "These are men to whom
the words 'small' or, worse, 'average' are anathema. They
have a fear of erasure, not so much physical as statistical.
They want an identity outside, or above, standard classifi-
cation. And, therefore, what we alter is not anatomy but
their portion of words." Ingmar has guessed, exactly, what
it is the Institute sells.

"But in making them exceptional, we humble ourselves," he continues, "humble ourselves by conforming to
the average itself, by not displaying anything unique or
characteristic in ourselves — by wearing, if you will, baggy
pants. The word 'dink,' Chief of Staff, neatly summarizes
for me the power of ugliness, an ugliness that attracted me
to the Institute in the first place; it's the power of uniting
under a number, of belonging to the mass that outnumbers
the exceptions, of being bland, nondescript. This is the
power patients relinquish in paying us to wear these loose-
fitting uniforms!"

Because the Chief of Staff has gone immobile, like a
silent machine flickering with the fading colours of the
sunset, it's Doctor Branting who must answer Helga's rap-
ping on the glass wall where the corridor meets the interview room. "Come in," Doctor Branting hollers, then barks

at Ingmar, "Give her your place."

"I can't believe you came up here without me," she says, out of breath and sliding into the seat Ingmar's vacated.

"Now!" the Chief of Staff bursts out, all of a sudden, "maybe, Ingmar, you would like to tell us a little about procreation." Doctor Branting folds his arms and snorts, but even he has noticed the shift in the Chief of Staff's address, from Doctor Anderssen back to Ingmar.

"In that case, Chief of Staff, I will tell you how we are con artists." And Ingmar begins talking about the men who measure from point A to point B, who call the fifty-metre sprint a cosmic law, a test for who's best and who's, uh, the rest. "But they miss the range of our operation. If all the Institute did was extend the dink, I wouldn't have stayed. But 'expand' is another thing. Extend is straight; expand is circular. Do you realize what the logical end of our procedure is?"

Doctor Branting turns slightly towards the Chief of Staff, uncertain, deferring to age, but the older man also turns, so that they're both slightly askance from Ingmar. "Think about it, gentlemen." Since neither of his colleagues can look any further aside without conceding the argument, they both decide to stare back at Ingmar, which makes him feel merciful: "If expansion were our business — and it is — a man coming in here with a one-inch dink wanting an additional ten inches would get what, in the end?"

"A penis like a pancake!" Helga yelps.

The Chief of Staff emits one laugh.

"Exactly!" Ingmar can already see his contribution to Institute rules and regulations: WE DON'T STUFF SAUSAGES, WE POUR FLAPJACKS. "We take the dink in all directions, gentlemen. Our operation is essentially moral." Ingmar lays his hand on Helga's shoulder and she reaches up to cover it with her own.

"No! You're not going to do this to me!" yells Doctor

Branting. "It's my promotion, goddammit, mine!" The Chief of Staff slowly unscrolls a long, thin finger and presses it to his lips, attempting to silence the man's hysteria. "Tell him he's fired. Tell him!"

"Ingmar," begins the Chief of Staff, his sharp voice piercing Branting's shouts, each word less a torpedo than a fast moving molecule, "I think I speak for the Institute in saying we would be pleased if you'd accept promotion to Assistant Chief of Staff. Provided, of course, you understand our view of marriage as the most appropriate in this case. And as for you," his neck nearly creaks as he turns to the other doctor, "you may clear your desk."

But Ingmar jumps up. "Please, Chief of Staff. I am glad to cede the position to Gustavus. His skills, his experience, his time with the Institute, they will prove an asset." And with that last bit of forgiveness Ingmar feels his skin fully reattach itself; so he aims his grin at everything, anticipating the day he, Gustavus, and the Chief of Staff — like the foetus, Strindberg, and himself — will be fully integrated, three persons in one.

anne stone

RULE OF NINES

LEAVING CALGARY, I WANTED NOTHING MORE THAN TO SLEEP. I got off the airplane wearing a pair of old woolen underwear my grandmother had given me before she died and one of my uncle's undershirts. I was wearing other things over top, I suppose. It hardly matters. In the airport bathroom, I noticed that my pubic hair was beginning to grow back. It looked blunter and much thicker.

H was still in hospital.

I went to see him immediately. He was asleep. They'd given him morphine, so when he spoke to me his voice sounded very sad and very young. It didn't seem to issue from his body so much as from a very distant room, one with excellent acoustics, located in the bowels of the building or an unused wing, perhaps. I kept looking at the ceiling and the corners of the room, certain his sad and hollow voice was coming from the vents. The drugs were a good thing, and I knew it. There would be no painful questions about my absence. I'd simply tell him I'd only been gone long enough to pee. I knew I would have to come up with a longer and more tragic excuse for the nurses. One that even H would buy if it happened to get back to him. I sincerely hoped it wouldn't.

I came under the spigot in the tub they fill with saline to ease the wounds of burn victims, knowing it would blot me out, so I could sleep. It's cold to cum in a bathroom with white plaster walls, a bare light bulb. I could see each hair on my legs, the blunt ends of my clipped pubes, all of it in stark relief. It was a lonely performance, sad even, without any gaze but my own, which, after Calgary, was pretty disinterested. I don't want to tell you everything I thought in those moments, but suffice it to say my feet were pressed up against the tiled wall and it was a very awkward position. The room smelled of disinfectant. Underneath the antiseptic hush, another more disturbing smell lingered. It smelt like Tuesday at my mother's house, which is not to say it smelled of cheese and macaroni, but of the faintest hint of the previous Sunday's roast beef. I came as efficiently as possible, and then lay on the single bed next to H's, hoping sleep would swallow me whole and not bother to spit out the bones.

>   >   >

The object of desire (before Calgary):
    This lovely blank.

>   >   >

Everything I thought in those moments:
    As I said, I wanted nothing more than to sleep. I was wearing a defeated pair of Levis and a second-hand sweater. I folded them neatly and placed them on the belt they used to hoist whatever remains they'd managed to re-trieve from the still-warm ashes of somebody else's life. Yes, somebody else's life. Next, the stained undershirt and woolen underwear. They too were folded precisely and slipped into the pile, forming a layer between the denim and the poly-synthetic-wool blend. I eased my body into the tub and examined the knobs and sprockets. The last thing I wanted to do was bathe in placental ruins, as com-forting and womb-like as a saline bath might be. One of the nurses had explained the contraption to me when they'd first brought H in. I found the two knobs I needed and turned them on.
    I remember it like this:
    Thighs cramped up. A pretty awkward position. I have to lift my thighs to where the water slathers out, there's no

spout really, just a large mouth. I bend my legs, pressing the soles of my feet against the wall. Hooking one calf over the handrail, I heft my hips up to the spigot. One arm behind me, for balance, the other spreading my labia wide and adjusting my clit, so the water rushes there. I have a perfect view, as I'm in this horizontal limbo, of breasts flattened against my ribcage, nipples flaccid, the fat that's accumulated on my hips with age.

Soon, I will slip into a blue cotton robe and walk to the geriatric ward to find a mirror. In the burn unit, all reflective surfaces, including the paper-towel dispenser, are painted over. So, I will have to look into a palliative mirror to affix myself to this place. When I do so, I will think: Yes, even if H doesn't think so anymore, and tells me he doesn't think so, I am beautiful. Even if my hips are fattish and my breasts are a little flat. Yes, I will shed the hospital-issue robe before I do this.

Just now, I haven't yet walked past the bewildered octogenarian, his flaccid tube in his hands like a terrible compromise he'd forgotten he'd made. No, I am in the tub they will submerse the remains of my life in, getting tired. I switch arms from time to time, because it takes a very long time to make yourself cum while thinking of nothing at all except a clumsy act of balance, the white of the room, and the shitty job they made of the walls, too, leaving gaps now filled in with larval accumulations of silicone gel. So I look at the gaps, and at the abandoned IV rack in the corner, and the tubing itself, which dangles from the rack by a plastic wire. And coldly, intellectually, I think about things I could cum to. Try to work my way up to it. I think about the VCR, for instance, and how sometimes, when H is having a shower, I hit play on the VCR and take a measure of his latest porn tape. The morning of the day before the fire it was an older woman, she might have been forty-five. She was coming down on this fat cock, her lips spread open with one hand for the camera. The man she was riding must have been only part way on the bed. He had to have

let his head and shoulders fall in a slump towards the carpet because the camera's POV came from where his head
should have been. Unless they amputated it for the shot.
At any rate, the woman leaned back, holding herself open
and sliding up and down on this quite possibly headless
man's cock. She was wearing a half-bra, pressing breasts
into the shape of worn tennis balls, all of the peach-fuzz
scuffed bare. Her skin an aged brown, as if she had tanned
for ten or twelve winters in Florida before losing her
condo, though something of her winters in the sun has permanently stained her skin. Light mousy brown hair.
Strawish. As though it, too, had been dried in the sun. Her
whole body was a faded brown, except for her vagina,
which she spread open to reveal tissue the pinkish colour
of a baby's lungs.

The woman talked to the camera. She talked to the
camera, asking H, who is in the can, if he likes what he is
seeing.

She said, "Do you like it?"

I was surprised she thought he would, since I'm a lot
younger than she is and still, he keeps his eyes closed.
Later, I started to get off on it too. I don't know if it was
how self-possessed she was or the way she opened herself,
displaying that shock of intestinal pink.

At the time, I really did think it was H she was talking
to. Which is odd, because she was looking directly at me.

And then something stranger happened. Precariously
balanced in a backward squat, legs splayed, an antiseptic
film working itself into the reddened palm of my left hand,
I pictured the man I had gone to meet in Calgary. Lately,
when I remembered him, his eyes were very blue, though
if memory serves, they were black. On this day, his eyes
were brown. I leaned into my palm and pictured time
slowly collecting in the folds of skin under his eyes. I
thought of how his skin would have looked when he was a
child, seamless and tight. Or when he was a little older and
scuffed his chin pink, red spots erupting on skin unused to

the rough scrape of a razor. The way time pleated the flesh around his eyes, a little. Gathering it up, just here. His age could only be traced in the lines around his mouth when he was tired, very tired, but it always showed in the shot-silk folds under his eyes. I'd often thought I would like to kiss that place, as our bodies moved in a rickshaw motion. I don't know if I ever did.

I pictured him so vividly, I could almost see him sitting on the edge of the saline bath, his long face turned towards the spigot with an air of contented distraction. His lips were open, though not in a smile. Just open. Enough so I could see a single crooked incisor, slightly discoloured. His skin was very pale, and the brownish spots on his gaunt hands had become more pronounced. He clutched the edge of the bath, his fingers stiffly avian. The skin on his hands was almost translucent. I could trace bluish veins from the tips of his fingers up the back of his hand to his elbow, where the skin disappeared into a over-large t-shirt, washed so many times it had the consistency of gauze. He wore nothing else. The lump under the shirt was unmistakable. I asked him to take it off, and yes, I imagined him smiling then. I've always preferred the naked truth to a rumorous lump. Everything about this man was permissive, a little edgy, but an easy edginess, more unsettled than uninhabitable.

Still, I hadn't a thing to say to him. What could either of us say in the face of that disinfectant smell? I wasn't even in the mood to kiss this man, which was a first. I didn't want to speak, but there his spectre was, regarding my reflection in the spigot with a distracted ease. I told him I couldn't talk to him, just now. I suggested we could eat a meal, though I wasn't particularly hungry, or else, he could stick it in. At the time, I thought it would give me closure. I was surprised he went along with it. It was utterly unlike him. I recoiled from his ascent, but he'd already assumed the position of the drywall, and pressing his stainless steel cock against my pubis, slathered a stream of something warm and wet over my clit. Ghostly, I could make out his tapered penis, half-limp, human atoms interspersed with the plumbing. So yes, in an utterly resigned manner I lay back, like the good missionary's daughter I was in the days following the fire, and was fucked by his apparition — or its proxy, at any rate — an alloy protuberance that ejaculated fluids collected in a massive vat hidden deep in the hospital's architecture. It felt like a funeral. H's funeral, to be exact. And yes, the thought of that made me cum. I leaked something with the consistency of grief for three or four seconds, as his body solidified into the series of by now familiar medical sprockets, and then I reached for a towel. There were stains on the towel. I'm not sure what all of them were. Something rust-coloured. A bit of blood, perhaps. Some make-up, too, I think. It was a stain the colour of foundation. The colour of the stuff leaking up from under H's scab-encrusted skin.

>   >   >

I am not in the hospital. I am nowhere near it in time or place. H has scarred nicely and I am sitting in a dental chair, merely discomfited by the vaguely clinical scent that persists under the stink of rotting milk. Just thinking about hospital sheets is a little much for me. Enough to send me running to the lions at Mont Royal Park, where a teenaged boy waits for me. In his pocket, he will have a clear plastic bag. The kind you take goldfish home from the pet store in. It will contain several grams of fine Moroccan blue hash.

I will find an impenetrable blankness creeps over me as the boy, whose name I will not have remembered, pulls a tarnished butter knife and blow torch from his knapsack. No, it will not be the lovely nothing I'd once dreamed of. But yes, the experience will be everything I want it to be, which is to say, brief, intense, and forgettable.

>   >   >

The object of desire (after Calgary):

A colostomy bag.

A lovely, clear colostomy bag, as empty as the human heart, and as willing to be filled with whatever biological refuse it happens to tap into. A colostomy bag with tubes as thick as atherosclerotic veins, terminating in a various series of valves and vulvas, gaskets to fit any and every aperture that happens to occur to me.

All of them do.

>   >   >

The object of desire (before Calgary):

This lovely blank, as white as fog, not erasing us, so much as the world around us. I know this man's saliva tastes raw, sweet. I know this before our first kiss. In a crowded room, I can smell the sweat coming from this man's pores, disentangle him from not-him, as easily as a mother corrects her child's fingers, before elaborating the lesson with wool strands. Our hands, together, then, a labyrinth of threads, forming a pattern as convoluted and intricate, as innocent, as a game of cat's cradle.

>   >   >

Love (after the fire):

Of course we made love after the fire, me and H, though his hands had been re-organized like the format of a newly-sodded lawn, and were insensible to touch. We made love and we made meals, we made a lot of things, actually, the mottled-red flesh laid out in handsome strips. We made love before they healed, too, his weeping seams moving me to a rare affection. The smell was unsettling, though, so much so neither of us could cum no matter the number of plaster squares I counted over the hospital headboard, which isn't to say we didn't find comfort in going through the motions. We did. I came to love H, again, after the fire. A little unreasonably, even, this man who had absorbed my past as his skin broke into open sores with the effort. So yes, we loved, sometimes with CNN blaring in the background, our bones so desperate for connection we were wholly deaf to the number of open-mouthed dead in Rwanda, or the plague-fattened flies that collected there. We, too, were fat with a spoiling wealth, and we knew it.

But somehow, after the fire, his tongue stopped.

Oh yes, his flapping ounce of meat circled whatever dizzy bit of flesh I offered up, but his story, the story of H, had congealed and hardened like the scars on his body, this at the same time my own story had resolved into the kind of suspect liquid that refused all containment and seeped up from under the most unlikely of surfaces, the skin of H's hands. So, we pretended not to notice the changes overtaking us as we watched CNN, laughing at the value of pork bellies, a value we knew well, because that is where they take the first skin from, for burn-grafts, the bloated bellies of domesticated pigs. It was only lately they'd casually reupholstered H with portions of his own flesh, grown over a three week period in a distant petri dish, from a sample no larger than a postage stamp. In the meantime, his flesh had been covered by a modernist collage of pork-bellies. Pork rinds, at any rate.

But before the auto-grafts, before the portions of his own skin were returned to him, made large by a mystery I can only guess at, there were temporary bandages fashioned of living pigskin, and nightly, I lay in the empty bed next to H, dreaming.

Every night the same dream, and the dream always went like this:

H's hands and arms and most of his chest wrapped in a weeping quilt of pigskin. The skin does not die and slough off, as the doctors have led me to believe, but takes. There seems to be no reason to remove this animal skin, causing trauma to his body a second time, so the doctors simply send him home, to me. The porcine blanket is a cut thicker than grafts usually are and something of the deeper epidermal layer, containing the animal's sweat glands, hair follicles, and sebaceous glands, has under-written H's flesh. H's hands begin to sweat. The smell is fattish, muskish, the humid reek that clings to the under-bellies of pigs. After a week, he begins to sprout small, pig-gish hairs.

I shave his hands and forearms, careful of the gnarling seams, clipping away the telling hairs, the ones that shock bank tellers into mouthing the word: inhuman. Somehow, the gross extrusion of scars never affects strangers in the visceral, primitive way even a single thick and pinkish hair does if missed in our weekly trimming session. With each successfully clipped hair I approach redemption.

The hairs grow back at an incredible rate. They even begin to sprout, thick and blunt, from what remains of H's original skin.

We try everything. Electrolysis, hair dyes, depilatory creams.

I want to pluck them out, each by each, but am terri-fied. I don't know if I am afraid he will not wince, and I'll know he will never feel touch again, or if I am afraid to see him wince, unnaturally, from this relic of a laboratory pig. So I shave him, but no matter how he begs, I will not pluck.

I shave him each Sunday evening, to begin. And then twice weekly. Finally, it becomes a daily event. So, each evening, after dinner, I clip these bestial remnants from hands he is frantic to bury in me that night, only to gently disinter them from this wet hole in the cold light of morn-ing, searching out the least untidy bit of pinkish hair that might have been pressed flat, for instance, in the crease surrounding newly implanted fingernails that themselves, at least, will never again require a buff or polish or trim.

michelle berry

FUNERAL HOME

Hilary.

"Hilary."

All she can hear is her name being whispered in her ear. Over and over. Dick can't stop saying it. He's stuck on it. Hill — aaa — reee. Hilary.

Whisper.

They are sitting side by side on Dick's large bed in his apartment above the funeral home. Hilary walked up the stairs, walked into the apartment just above the room where her dead mother is lying, and walked straight to his bedroom. She sat on his bed. Dick followed.

Her blue dress glistens in the dim light. It is shimmery and soft and Hilary can't stop touching it. And Dick can't stop whispering. He is sitting beside her, his calves crossed at the knees, his hands in his lap, his eyes closed, and he is whispering her name into her ear and doing nothing, not touching her. He stutters often.

It is getting to be too much.

For one thing Hilary is craving that chocolate cake. After dinner at the restaurant he suggested cake and she thought he might offer her a piece in the bedroom. She thought it might be just the right place to eat chocolate cake. She didn't think they would just sit on the bed for over an hour, Dick whispering in her ear, without first eating the chocolate cake.

But she likes Dick's whisper. Soft. Gentle. Like light rain. Like a tear falling off a cheek onto a table. Wet.

Liquidy. Something lurking, a catch in the throat, a tightening of the "ahhh" in Hilary.

"Shouldn't we. . . ?" Hilary hesitates. She doesn't want to sound crude, but she wants this moment in her life to take place quickly. She's been waiting for it for so long, for thirty-nine years almost, waiting for her initiation into *Life*, into not being crazy anymore. Because crazy people don't have sex until they are almost forty. That's how she thinks of it. She knows it isn't normal to live all your life with your sick mother, to not have boyfriends, to only touch yourself lightly in the bathtub, to hide in baggy, old clothing and watch your hair, with time, become mousy and ugly. It isn't natural. She knows that. She's always known that. It's not just the things she used to hear said behind her back. Or the way her brothers, Billy and Thomas, would look at her. Or the things her mother said to her even just last week. Hilary knows. It's deep down inside of her, inside of who she is, this knowing. It's like a second skin.

And then it hits her. Dick's a bit crazy, too. Of course. Would anyone want to have sex with a man who lived above a funeral home, a man who is a mortician? She does. She wants to. Right now. She wants to pull him down on the bed and lie on top of him or have him lie on top of her. Eat chocolate cake. Something. She wants to do something and all he can do is whisper, whisper, whisper.

Hilary tries to put her hand on his thigh but Dick's slumped body jerks up, his eyes shoot open, and he looks at her. Terrified. Not terrified of her, she sees, but afraid of the whole situation. Maybe, Hilary thinks, maybe he's afraid he'll see only death, he'll see the slow numbing of her body, or greyish-whiteness, the cover falling over her eyes. Death. The soul disappearing from her body. Maybe Dick is afraid to hold onto someone, onto Hilary, because he knows how transient life is, how quickly it can be erased.

Hilary's mother's body lost its sheen, its glossiness. As if she was suddenly two-dimensional. Her soul left her

body and it was almost imperceptible, except for the flattened look to her eyes, a coat of pearl nail polish that
seemed to cross over the pupils, and the loss of shine on
her skin. It's as if in death a person stops reflecting the
light of the world.

Within minutes this look came over her mother, within
seconds. It happened so quickly that it took Hilary quite
by surprise.

Hilary stops thinking. She wills herself to. Of course
Dick isn't thinking that. He's having the typical male
thoughts about erection potential or size, things Hilary has
read about for years in magazines, things she has seen
talked about on TV.

But Dick is thinking about death. Not in the way Hilary
thinks, but in a different way. He is thinking about how a
dead body has never turned him on. Hilary's question
about naked bodies earlier in the restaurant made him
wonder. "Do you see many naked bodies?" she'd asked, as
if he wasn't the one who dresses the dead, as if they come
to him all decked out and pretty, as if all he does is put
them in a casket, bury them underground. Dick has been
to many conferences on burial, on the funeral industry,
where the back room talk has circled around the necrophil-
iacs, the lust-crazed funeral director who masturbates over
top of dead corpses or actually enters their stiff bodies. But
Dick has never himself felt any kind of need to disrespect
a body. And now that he thinks about it, he wonders if
that's a normal reaction. He is, after all, a man. He hasn't
had sex, been with someone, in years. Wouldn't he feel
something for nakedness? He has always felt himself a
type of doctor, in a respected profession. Dedicated, con-
trolled, intelligent. But now, sitting next to Hilary as she
touches him on the upper thigh, he wonders if he just isn't
normal, if the fact that dead bodies, naked bodies, don't
turn him on, then maybe that means no naked body will
turn him on.

Dick has had many beautiful women lying before him

on the embalming table stark naked. Not a hair on their head out of place. Beautiful in death. And he's appreciated their beauty, he's made them up to be even more beautiful. Coated their faces with pink, brown, life-like make-up. Even beautiful men. But there hasn't once, in all these years, been the stirring of anything in his groin. And so he wonders.

He looks at Hilary.

He has had sex before. A few times. Right now he can't remember their names or their faces or the situations. They weren't important to him. That was so long ago. Even a prostitute when he was seventeen. He knows he is fully capable of sex. With someone he cares nothing about. . . .

"Shit," Dick says.

"What?" It's the first thing he's said that wasn't a whisper, that wasn't her name. And it wasn't what Hilary thought would come out of his lips.

And then Dick turns to Hilary. He gives up all thought and just centres on Hilary there beside him. He touches her tousled hair, strokes it, he looks into those fine blue eyes, takes in the tiny body, so very small and frail, and he pulls her towards him and begins to kiss her. Ferociously. Crazily. Hungrily. Hilary kisses back in the same way. She tastes garlic and rum and seafood. His tongue and lips and chin and neck. She doesn't even think about the chocolate cake in the kitchen. She thinks about nothing.

Their teeth clank together, Dick accidentally bites Hilary's bottom lip, their tongues move in and out, squishing up, pushing each other's out. Dick drools slightly. He grunts. After this kiss they are slower. They slow right down. Little pecks on the lips, on the cheeks. Large smiles. Hilary stands. Dick stands. They take turns trying to undress the other; Dick struggles with Hilary's zipper. An awkward-shuffling dance together and then, finally, they are naked. A little shocked. Self-conscious. Hilary tries not to giggle. It's like standing before an ape, she thinks. He's covered in hair. She can't see his skin through it. Her hands are ice cold as she wraps her arms around her body, hiding it. Dick is astonished at how tiny she is, as if he peeled off layers of fat with each layer of clothing. She is childlike before him, and this frightens him. But then they slide under the covers together, looking away, one on each side of the bed, rolled away from each other. Dick turns the dim light off beside the bed, and their hands begin to roam. Hilary's hand knocks Dick's hand, and the ineptness of the situation makes it almost unbearable. Hilary wants to get up and go home. There are no smooth movements, no silky gesturings. Just bumbling, bungling clumsiness. Hilary's arm is bent back behind her neck. It hurts. And Dick is leaning far too heavily on her chest. His elbow is asleep and the shooting pains are making it hard to concentrate.

But their bodies are tight together and their hearts are beating rapidly.

Dick thinks that if Hilary says anything, if she says just one little thing, the moment will be ruined.

Hilary says nothing.

Once they start, after a few seconds of mismatched movements, they get the rhythm right and, except for the weight of Dick on her chest, the way he cuts off her breathing almost, Hilary is intrigued. She thinks about how she may be in love all of a sudden, a burst of it, like a flower, like the fizz of a pop can — it has hit her and is rocking her, affecting her, making her laugh out loud, freely. She has never been in love in her life. Not with her mother or Daddy. No one has affected her, turned her this way, touched her, kissed her, trusted her, the way this man on top of her is doing right now. And then it makes her cry suddenly to think of all the things she has missed in her life. She has missed the world. It has passed her by.

Dick watches Hilary cry. She's alive, he thinks. She's human. And in that smile on her face he sees himself reflected. He wants to laugh. He wants to burst out laughing, uncontrollably, belly-laughing, and never stop. He wants to shed his funeral director demeanour. He wants to keep doing what he is doing right now. But then it occurs to him that he may be hurting her and he mumbles, "Am I hurting you?" A look of terror passes over his face. Hilary breathes out, "No," and Dick continues on, feeling scared and wonderful at the same time. Such a tiny woman, he thinks. So fragile. Hilary rocking beneath him, trying hard to breathe, waiting for him to be finished and yet not wanting his body to leave hers but needing him to finish, for it to be over so she can lie next to him and feel his arms wrapped tight around her.

It's not that she doesn't like what they are doing, it's just not what she expected. When your life has been a series of TV talk shows, reality is hard to accept, especially when it knocks you over and pins you down, she thinks. But the moment passes and he pulls out faster than she can blink and Dick rolls over, groaning, and Hilary pushes her small head up under his hairy arm and rests it on his beating heart. She snuggles down in the fur on his chest. Now this is what she wants, she thinks. Nothing else.

Hilary lies beside the snoring Dick Mortimer and stares at the ceiling. White cardboard tiles, over 200 of them. Hilary counts them. She is trying not to think about what keeps crossing in front of her vision: her mother's dying face. Her dead face.

Her mother's eyes. The pain.

Etched into her forehead, shooting through her pupils.

Hilary watched those eyes.

For some reason she couldn't cover them up. She watched those blue eyes as her mother gasped for air, for a breath.

Oh, God.

Hilary shudders. She tries to turn on her side, away from Dick. He has her hand tightly in his grasp and her movement makes his breathing raspier and quicker. She doesn't want to wake him up. If he wakes up now and faces

her, turns to her, props himself up on an elbow and caresses her again, she will break down and cry. She will tell
him how her mother's eyes said "yes" and "no" at the same
time. How she fought and then gave in but then fought
again. How the whole thing seemed to take hours when it
was only minutes.

Minutes. Stopped minutes. Time stood still.

She's below me now, Hilary thinks. Right underneath
my naked body. Hilary moves close to Dick, trying to take
away his heat, use it for her own cold body.

Take the pain away, Hilary thinks. Take it away from
me. From the years of housekeeping and dish washing and
grocery shopping, from the years and years of sitting on
the porch late at night, knitting, and watching the rest of
the world pass her by.

Hilary squeezes Dick's hand. He groans in his sleep.
He turns over, lets go of her, and stops snoring. His breathing is deep and peaceful.

The doctor said that Hilary's mother would soon lose
consciousness. He said that she would drift into another
world. He said that she would stop crying out all the time,
begging for morphine, begging for release. But she didn't.
And Hilary couldn't stand the sounds. Hilary prayed all
Thursday morning long, prayed until her arms hurt from
holding them up and clasping her hands together, prayed
until her faith stopped. Until something in her body gave,
like a dry leaf breaking in half, a bitter, crackling sound to
Hilary's ears. And she took those two chaffed, aching
hands into her mother's spotless room and put them to
use. She stopped the pain. She extinguished the light. She
took matters into her own hands. Hilary's mother gave her
life and Hilary took her mother's life away. It was simple,
really. Except for the eyes staring back at her in wonder-
ment, questioning her choice, pleading for something.
Why didn't she just close her mother's eyes? That would
have made everything easier.

Dick begins to snore again. The trucks on the road in

front of the funeral home rush past. They rumble and their brakes scream and they chug and huff and puff. Hilary listens. She listens to the trucks and thinks about how she should have jumped on one, or in front of one, when she was younger. She should have shouldered her own self, taken care of her needs, not the needs of others, and broken out alone. She should have given herself the gift of a life lived.

Now she is thirty-nine and in a bed above her mother's dead body with a funeral director named Dick. And she likes him. She likes him a lot. And she wants to fulfill things with him, things that will change her life, give her back the gift, wrapped in gold crepe paper and a silky blue bow. Hilary just hopes that when Dick wakes up he feels the same way she does now. She hopes that he, too, wants to change his life just a little, live in the middle for a while instead of right on the edge.

III

elise levine

DRIVING MEN MAD (SCHEHERAZADE)

TELL ME SOMETHING, HE SAYS.

We have clematis. Alyssum. At one we nap. Drinks at three. Her bathing suit is pink. Pink splash borders the pool.

He doesn't laugh.

We have a white porch, a swing. A ghost called Lady Jamais, famous on the island. Nights calling in the garden, voice soft as water from the sprinklers beneath the grass.

I say, I'm making this up as I go along.

Dogwood leaps, tongue and stem. I admire his arms. His smooth skin.

Lean against me, I say.

> > >

She hooks a finger, two, a fist into me. Shouts, Bitch. You goddamned bitch.

She's got these big eyes.

We've been together for a long time. We're in love.

> > >

A woman lies on another woman. Lies and lies. A woman. A man. A woman. Nothing I say can make it any better.

Tell me about yourself, he says.

> > >

All those Pre-Raphaelites pored over, first menstruation

and its lusts. We thought we were alone. We thought there were gardens. We thought there was a ghost, unrequited lovers, we made one up and called her Lady Jamais, death-blurred, tragic as stars, tongue studded with sinking moons.

I obsess over her breasts. Hips. Till death us do part. Teenage girls are like this, better believe it. It is always a matter of life and death.

I visit her on the ninth floor, nomenclature of girl suicides: Ninth floor, please, psychiatric. At the nurses' station we ask permission to go to the cafeteria where we load up on tiny bags of bite-sized Oreos, man, we work that vending machine as if playing pinball. She tells me she hides her pills under her tongue. Swallows fast. This is the kind of girl I really go for. Of course she's upbeat, you'd be too if you scarfed down a couple hundred of your mother's best Ativan, the happy drug of choice.

Make an effort, the nurses exhorted yesterday when she refused to attend the group session. Sounds like a bowel movement, she told them.

Bam-smang, goes the cafeteria vending machines. Five bags, six bags. We've got five minutes left. Or else, the nurse had said.

We run out of quarters. We wait for the elevator with a bunch of old sick people. We take the stairs instead.

You're late, a nurse says.

I leave in the elevator. I'm carrying all these little bags. Do I toss them. Do I eat them and gain, like, a million pounds. I stand in the lobby. Life, I deduce, is complicated. Things will always, will only, get worse.

Not like this guy, I think, years later. He's simple. I lay him over and over. He's in shock, astonishment leaks from his fingertips, his toes when I rub him down.

Then I eat him alive.

> > >

It's not like he has much money. None of us do. Money

might make it easier. To go to Greece and fuck like mon-
grels. A scene of contrition in the Luxembourg Gardens.
God, what I wouldn't give for a weekend in Winnipeg.

What he and I do instead is this: meet halfway, in
Thunder Bay. The room's cold. We attract stares from lo-
cals. We're brave, we hold onto each other, drunk. I like
your arms, I tell him in the lumpy bed.

He says, I like you, too.

> > >

Tell me something, he says. We're on a bus. I hold my
breath. Exhale. Pet dogs? Birthday parties? Other men.
He's nervous asking about the women. What he really
wants to know is ordinary: does he stack up? I suspect he's
jealous. I begin to credit him with being human. I am un-
speakably cruel.

Tell me something.

In bed at his place I explete into his mouth. Nothing
random in this: I shoot, I score. He's happy as a clam. He
says he likes to finger fuck me. God, how many times do
I have to tell him. Women *don't*, I say. They just fuck. Ah,
his hand on my stomach. I can tell I'm not getting through.
Women *fuck*, I say. He taps his index finger. Guys are too
stupid sometimes. I do it — I use the *p-word*.

Phallocentric.

He rises on an elbow. He leans over me. He's hardly
got any chest hairs, Christ, I'm hairier than he is, I think.
He blows me a kiss.

I flip him the finger. Jerk.

I begin to suspect him of hidden depths.

> > >

You're losing your culture, she says. You're past the point.
You're so far beyond. There's no telling what you'll do next.

I think, My life. It's like every *Gunsmoke* rerun I've ever
seen.

We make up. She takes me dancing at Wild Bill's. A lesbian cultural evening. We two-step the night away. George Strait sings, "All my exes live in Texas." She leads, we do an inside turn, one two three, five. We do the Cowboy Hustle, we do Slap Leather. I get confused, screw up the Grapevine. I sit down, finish an Ex. I watch her. She's good, women like dancing with her. Especially the straight feminists, her friends from the Crisis Line. Especially Barbara Ann, who won't let her go for four songs. Especially Jill, who finally cuts in. Hips. Pretty face. Quite the gal, I tell her in the washroom. Through the double doors and into the cubicle where I do up my jeans I hear Patty Loveless sing, "I got a jealous bone." She sings along, waiting for me by the sink. I slap open the cubicle door. Goddamn straight women, I say.

> > >

She says she too wants to sleep with a man. She's woken me up, the streetlight bleeds through the window. Give me some covers, I say. It's been ten years, she says. She says, I can drive men mad, I used to. I say, I know, I know.

She's asleep. I get up, get a glass of water. What will she think of next?

I come back to bed. The covers are on the floor, I leave them there, all night. In the morning her back is warm against my breasts.

She meets him at a playwrights' conference. In Alberta. He's an alcoholic Newfie fag (I think), and he reads the part of a woman — brilliantly, she tells me, later. She has two vaginal orgasms with him, not clitoral, she says, knowing the distinction never fails to escape me. He beats off. He moans, I love you. That's what I think he said, she tells me. We laugh. She watches me carefully, for days.

> > >

I smell him on me sometimes. Sweat him, unavoidable. He's really there, I can't wipe him off, on my fingers, the sharp hairs of my legs.

One day we're walking to Mac's Milk.

We walk past Mr Benjamin's shrubbery. Mr Benjamin waves. What a nice day! On the other side of the street a woman in white shorts walks a Bouvier. We've seen her before, but not much, she's new to his neighbourhood. We agree we like Bouviers. We have so much in common. There's Mrs Mathilde, home from Cuba. Hot, she says. Cuba was hot. What a nice day! He says, Love me. I say, I won't. We stop in front of Mac's, neither of us reaches for the door handle. He says, So tell me something new.

He cries when he comes.

Once, when we're having sex, he mishears me say, I need you.

> > >

Of course on the way home things go from bad to worse. The stays of her bodice, her long silvery plaits of hair, undone. Oh, God, I'm going to get it now.

She is spools and hooks of her weak heart, her chest pains. She kisses my ear. I haven't got long, she says. I refuse to be threatened. I refuse to get close. She tongues fricatives into me. I'm afraid because I have no words for this.

> > >

It's bad, I think. I can't stop the lies.

I marry him; there are no children. I move back to the island with her; I never leave.

What do you want me to do? she says.

I've always liked how she smokes, even though I don't indulge. She's smoking now, white cigarette she holds lightly in her long beautiful fingers. She smokes strong, with emphasis. She's always scared me a little. She inhales. Taps the ash into the blue ashtray. The geraniums are doing fine. Exhales: I've always found it sexy, wanted to kiss it from her, like steam, I imagine. Nice lips. I like your lips, I say. It's not working, I won't get off this easy, not now.

Nope. It's Ultimatum Time. The poplar whirs. Her eyes a muddy blue. I smile inappropriately, simpleton. I squirm, she makes me feel small. I, um, like your lips, I want to say. I want to say. Smoke rises and roils. Rises and rises. Forsythia flickers in the breeze and glows. What do you want me to do.

> > >

It's bad when the story repeats too often. When they get tired of the lies. When there's nothing more to be said. Off with her head! And look: Lady Jamais, headless in the garden. A flicker. A longing of sweet basil, summer savoury powders the night air, words you can't hear but want to as she slips through the trees and into the swimming pool. She is the way roses look at night, bled of colour. She will never leave. This garden will flourish. She will slip past the cherry tree and into the sky. Fall down in a shower of stardust. Rhododendrons applaud. Impatiens, their fierce pink, spread.

I can do this, I think, I can go on and on, who's to stop me?

Oh, yeah, he says, I've heard that one before.

rachel rose

WANT

YOU LIAR, YOU TOLD ME YOU HAD IT. YOU PROMISED ME
with your hand between my legs slowly circling that you
would give it to me. Said if only I withheld nothing from
you, it would be mine.

These are the ways you made me believe you: the certain, swift knowledge that if you left me I would never get
over you. Our legs tangled, your mouth open on the side
of my face. The way your hands filled the hollows of my
body.

Nights passed like this. Days passed like this. Then one
night you untangled yourself from me. You looked at me
and said, Sweetheart, we'll always be friends, won't we? I
can't imagine not having you in my life.

And I, pushing my chilled hands between my breasts,
said, Yes. I'll always be here for you.

I should have said, That depends.

I should have said, Everything is conditional. I will be
with you as long as you love me like this. But I said yes. I
promised.

And then you turned away. And I learned that it was
not you or any other woman who could give me what I
wanted.

I quit school, got a job. This is where I am.

> > >

I got the first job I applied for. I have a good phone voice.
I have a scientific background. I got hired as a medical assistant. It is my job to prepare the patients, stripping their

clothes to make way for the doctor's hands and instruments, probing their veins with my needles and holding their wrists to catch the hummingbird pulse under the skin.

Sometimes I look at the doctor, and even though there is something in men I don't usually trust, I trust him. I want to smooth the deep creases over his face, push my palms like an iron across his forehead and relieve him of knowledge, relieve him of the accretion of pain to which his patients have exposed him.

But most of the time I resent him. Because I answer his phone and take his patients back and ready them and their faces light up when *he* enters the room. I close the door softly behind them and behind that door the doctor heals them. He heals them! I can see it on their faces when they leave, that despite their pain, he has given them what they came for.

Why can't he, then, give it to me?

> > >

I took this job just after you left. I learned how to puncture children's arms with needles and tell them that what was hurting them was for their own good. I learned that if people believed the doctor would cure them, he would. I witnessed their faith in his hands, his medical texts and charts and pills. When a cure was harder to obtain, I saw him resort to magic: the x-ray, that could show the dark spots of a lung. The electroencephalogram, that could map the dreams of an erratic brain. The ultrasound, that could show the bloom of blood around an ovary. Patients spoke of him with reverence. If they were angry at the hours they waited to see him, the doctor never heard about it, I did.

The doctor did not have the same limitations as the rest of us. He could enter the body at will with his hands and his machines. He could probe and map and name. Everyone came to the doctor wanting, needing something. I saw him perform miracles.

I was in need of a miracle.

Every day was the same. I pulled patients' charts and told them where to sit and gave them papers to fill out and did everything I could to keep from collapsing into memories of you. Your hands pressing my shoulders into the bed. Your hands covering my eyes while your mouth licked my ear and spilled promises on the sheets. *I'm here. Trust me.*

You were, after all, simply insincere. *Insanscere*, you were not without wax, not without lies. You plugged the holes of my want with stuff that would melt when I began to warm. The most ancient of stories. You said you would always be there. I believed you.

You promised what I asked you to *because* I asked you to, because this was the only way you could have me. It wasn't fair, maybe, that I wanted it from you. But neither was it fair for you to promise what you knew you couldn't give.

>   >   >

There are days when I envy the doctor his knowledge of the body. I look at every patient when they leave and imagine them helpless in the stirrups with the doctor's hands rummaging around inside them, as though searching for something mislaid. His face becomes distant, abstract. He does not watch his hands. As though what he was searching for was nothing that could bear full scrutiny.

Don't you see? Something very important to me has been lost.

>   >   >

Sometimes things slow down here; a patient cancels, the doctor leaves to check on a new mother or a life winding down in the hospital. Then I sit at the front desk and type. I type with concentration, knowing you are observing me. Presenting myself to you in this role, a woman at the front desk, typing as though nothing were missing.

The doctor has not approached me yet. I admire him for his restraint, but I don't trust it. I tell myself it must be wisdom on his part not to want my body, to see it for what it is: an uncertain structure, crumbling from within.

But what, I wonder, does the doctor want?

Sometimes I long to tell him about how many people have wanted me and had me. I want to tell him how, when I was a girl, a certain man's tongue seemed so thick I felt if he lifted his head he would hold me suspended in the air, a child on his mouth, a moth on a pin. I want to tell him too what I have learned about women, how they pretend that they are speaking love with their bodies and not just holding back the want a while. I want to ask him if this is his experience as well.

There is something in him that makes me want to confess. But I am not the doctor's patient, I am his receptionist, and I have no doctor of my own and no insurance.

>   >   >

When a patient enters the office, I ask, How are you? Their replies are shockingly honest. There is one man who replies, I'm still here, or sometimes, I'm alive. We search each other's eyes. Neither of us has it, what we need. When I wrap the blood pressure cuff around this man's thin arm I avert my eyes from the fresh and old cuts across his bicep, but he won't let my politeness pass.

Bloodletting, he tells me. Sometimes you have to. It eases things.

I don't want to know what he needs. I don't want to know any of this.

>   >   >

Sometimes I think it's as simple as malnutrition. I'm lacking a mineral. A deficit of zinc, of copper, of magnesium. I walk to the markets after work and buy myself rare fruits, raw oysters, old wines with sediments at the bottom, goat cheeses, smoked liver. I fill my belly until it is tight as a skin drum and I can trace the source of the ache in my chest. Then I sleep, I sleep all weekend, I curl my arms around my legs and dream rich dreams. I sleep until my breasts are soft against my arms and my skin has taken up the folds of the sheets. I sleep and my chest expands and deflates with unerring accuracy. I sleep from dawn to twilight and from twilight to dawn. I sleep like the princess who lost her gold heart in the dark pool and can't leave the spot where her heart went missing.

>   >   >

Today a new girl came in. Her whole family, all her cousins and sisters and uncles, waited in the waiting room. Dark eyes haunted me with the force of their collective want. I took the girl back, and because the doctor was running late, I let her keep talking. She did not push away the slippery black fingers of hair that kept falling across her face. She used her hair as a curtain, behind which, as if she were backstage rehearsing her lines, she told me the story of why she'd come to see the doctor.

The doctor came in, hurried and concerned. Here's the doctor, I said. Tell him what you told me, I said, closing the door behind me.

A few minutes later, the doctor called me to his office. He sighed and ran his hands through his hair. I could see the muscles rise under his blue shirt, the lines etched around his mouth. He explained to me how to give her the pregnancy test.

It was negative.

Thank God for that, said the doctor. We don't know if she understood. Negative, I said. Not a mother.

I saw the bruise on the side of her face as she turned away, and even through her loss I saw that she had gotten what she came for.

>   >   >

Introitus is the way a doctor says opening. *Os* is the way a doctor says mouth. I know, I type these things at the front desk. For a woman who has no uterus, swabs are taken from the *vaginal vault*. The vaginal vault: an empty chest, treasures stolen. You can't tell from looking if a woman carries the pear and figs of her inner sex organs or if she is a hollow trunk, echoes of want like water dripping onto stone. You can't tell from looking at a woman.

>   >   >

I have no pride when it comes to getting what I want. I will follow anyone home who looks at me like that, who tilts their head in such a way and says, I can give you what you want. Every time I believe it. Every time I go where they live.

It took me a long time to learn boys won't give me it. Boys won't give anything for free, they know there isn't enough of it. Boys spend their time making their bodies lean and hard. They are soldiers of denial, they never give it away. And yet, not knowing there was a choice, I went to them with my hands cupped, my mouth open. Asking for it.

>   >   >

Give it to me, I cry as you part my legs with your tongue. Yes, you say, mouthing me. Pushing me to the wall. You know how bad you want it.

Oh yes! God, I want it. I want it.

If what I wanted were as simple as fucking I would have stopped wanting years ago. Fucking only makes the times when I'm otherwise occupied more dangerous. When I'm fucking I think maybe I'm getting it, maybe this time I'm really getting it. I don't need it because I'm asking for it. But I never get it. The times right after when I'm still open I cry with how bad I want it. Still I keep on because I get to ask for it and to hear from someone else: I'll give it to you. I'll give it to you good.

These are the things I learned from you. From you not

giving it to me. That no man or god or woman or job can fill that gap beginning between my legs, the vaginal vault, rising up through my chest cavity to the hollow tube of my throat, the two sucking balloons of my lungs, my open *os*. All the empty chambers of the body. That I have to learn to live with longing, as amputees learn to live with the ache of a missing limb. I have to learn to sleep through it, the susurration of want filling me.

>   >   >

How is a doctor like God?

Today a patient brought in her kindergarten-age daughter. Her daughter with a red seam torn between her legs. A girl with hair sweet enough to attract yellowjackets, a girl with eyes black as pansies. A girl saying nothing, her mouth a chiselled line, her chin defiant. The doctor called me into the examination room. I gave the girl candy to suck and helped her mother gently hold her down while the doctor spread her legs with his latexed hands and took photographs for courtroom evidence. The girl did not scream, she did not struggle. She lay unresisting under our hands and it was only the way she retreated past us all so that even her mother couldn't bring her back that told us what we were doing to her was no different than what had already been done to her.

The doctor saw it, too. His hands were clumsy, wet with the contagious sweat of her fear. When we had finished she did not move, did not close her legs or open her eyes. We looked at each other, shocked. Accomplices.

This girl had been brought to the doctor needing a miracle. He had not healed her.

To myself I thought, this is a clue.

How is a doctor like God? Because we come wanting to believe.

>   >   >

I had taken this job in need of a cure. But there was no one who could tell me what it was. Even the doctor didn't know how sick I had become, working there day after day, seeing everyone getting better.

I thought that since a man had taken it from me only a man could give it back. I was wrong.

Then I thought that since a man had taken it from me only a woman could give it back. I was wrong.

Alone in the exam room, both hands resting on the crumpled paper still warm from the girl, layer after layer of loss wrapped around me like the onion sheets I rolled across the exam tables. Because I saw what had been taken from me was both what I wanted and the knowledge of what I had lost. All the covetous nights, all the vaulting, indiscriminate nights ahead of me would be spent on my back with my legs spread, my mouth open, and full of the dark, wanting it.

judy macdonald

THERE IS NO
YEAR ZERO

A LITTLE CUCKOO SOUND, AND IT'S TIME TO CROSS THE STREET.
They are holding hands, not watching for cars. Not making sure things are safe. Ruby looks down. She sees:

carrots	rice
beans	soap
tampons	tomatoes

That *e*. A book says that, when he was vice-president
of the United States, Dan Quayle told a kid, "You've got it
right phonetically, but you're missing a little something."
It's a pretty famous story, but some people think the former vice-president wrote it on a board or somehow spelled
it out loud. That's not right, if you believe the book.
Instead, he saw the word, and the word was "potato," written in a child's hand. And Dan Quayle hinted to the kid
that it could maybe use an "e" at the end.

Shopping lists are the same way as Mr Quayle's slip.
They can show things the writer didn't mean to show. It's
so rare to write things down, once you reach a certain age.
Lists are all a lot of people have to keep a record of themselves. Their own record, not a government one.
Something that shows what they want, who they are. Not
some kind of official thing for employment or school or
whatever. Those kinds of records just show how you fit in.

eggs

Ruby writes a lot of things down, though. She's trying to be more in touch with her creativity and also be more practical. She has read *The Artist's Way*. She has a dream journal and a daily journal and even a special little book to list the things she needs. She is looking at that now as she crosses the street with her boyfriend.

Cuckoo.

Cuckoo.

The warning is spaced out. She can't even hear this sound. She can't even hear the traffic. A police car goes by, its siren going off halfway through the intersection. Ruby doesn't slow down or look up. She is too caught up in the list. She is missing something.

whole wheat flour   soba noodles
gluten

She is barely holding hands with Andy. He doesn't go by Andy. Ever since he moved from home a couple of years ago, he's told people to call him Rep, or Repo, but nobody calls him Repo. Rep is hungry, so it's not a good time to shop, which is what they plan to do. He is spaced out, looking at the clouds and the ground. There is no view.

guava juice   sucanat
mangoes

Ruby looks at the *e*. She remembers what she had read — that former vice-president Dan Quayle also supposedly said the Holocaust was something terrible that happened this century, that we're all from this century and that he is not from this century. He was talking about the twentieth century, and he was speaking during it. But maybe he wasn't from it. Maybe he had a good point. She gets back to the list, thinking about how lucky she is to have so much to choose from.

sesame crackers   oyster sauce
tempeh

Ruby dreamt last night about one of her brothers chasing the rest of the family around with an axe. She woke up when he hunkered over her, hands clasped around the handle, arms thrown back, now coming down on her in a full-force swing. She didn't put this one in her dream journal. She got up and did the I-Ching.

The Earth below, The Mountain above. *Po*. Collapse.

The Disposable Heroes of Hiphoprisy said, "The only cola I would support is a cost of living allowance." Ruby doesn't drink cola. She doesn't know what the band was talking about, either. When she first saw them on the countdown of the best videos of the millennium, she thought theirs was okay. Rep likes it way more. Ruby has a really boring job in an office. She can't do her hair exactly how she wants. She can only put in colour that washes out by Monday. So she's pretty normal looking and she's not really part of the group they hang out with. Their friends call her a conformist. Meanwhile Rep is as cool as they come — the right shirts, shoes, hair, attitude. He won't read books because they're too bourgeois. Ruby reads —

potatoes   fucking potatoes

Rep and Ruby have been going out for a while, but they don't live together. Friends wonder about this, too. Her hair, her job, and what they're holding out for. Their friends think Ruby is both too status-quo zombie-dead grown up and not grown up enough to go ahead with an obvious thing to do. Scared like a little girl. Not that living together is really rebellious anymore. Way too many parents seem to think it's a practical first step, including her own. First step to being what they are is something Ruby's not really interested in. But anyway, it *is* something. Living together is not being alone, or just having roommates, and it's definitely not like being with parents.

What Ruby and Rep do is none of their friends' business: the couple can say this to each other as many times as they want, but how they're thought of by others actually does eat away at them. And the more time passes, the less sure Ruby and Rep are that they want to live together. Not that they really talk about it. Not in detail.

The thing is, Rep's mother just died. So the couple went back to his hometown, and he was Andy again. Andy without a mom. When she was alive, he mostly didn't talk about her. And when he did talk about her, it was all how she put him down, put his dad down, expected too much, said really hurtful things about people.

But being back in his hometown, called a name Ruby is completely unfamiliar with, this guy just kept on saying, "I won't get a chance to show her. She won't get a chance to see me make it." Like that was the whole point of his mom's life. Back at home, Rep AKA Andy wouldn't get close to Ruby. Tried not to have sex in his parents' house. Kept talking about sacrilege, even though back on Planet Anarchy he's always talking it up about being an atheist.

Ever since they finally came back to the city, they haven't had real sex. A couple of times after they went partying it got to heavy petting, but then Rep would pull away. They've slept in the same bed sometimes, but far apart. One has touched the other's cheek or thigh, but soft and quick, like children do. Since she got out of the door today, Ruby has been checking her list. She's checked it over and over. She scratched things out and added other stuff. She fixed any bad spelling. She even wrote out the list a couple of times when it looked too sloppy. Now she goes through what she needs, again and again. Looking down. Not looking around her.

Ruby and Rep have almost finished walking across the grey wet shitty street. When they get to the curb, they almost walk right into a guy waiting to cross the other way. At the last second, the couple swerves to avoid him.

Without thinking about it, Rep grabs Ruby's arm to guide
her. Ruby would complain, but at least it's something. At
least it's some kind of touch that shows he knows she's
there.

Rep says, "Careful."

Ruby says, "Yeah, right, thanks. What a help."

Rep looks hurt and Ruby's sorry. But he really is bug-
ging her ass. She's frustrated because she wants sex in gen-
eral, although not really with him if she lets herself think
about it. But she's with him, and he doesn't want it.

Since Rep heard that his mother died, they've done it
once, in his parent's house. Something took over that had
never been there before. They were sleeping in the living
room, on different couches. Other relatives were in the
spare rooms. Not that the house was so big in the first
place. Sometimes Rep . . . Andy . . . would get under Ruby's
covers for a little while and then go back to where he was
sleeping. He would talk about his mom and how much he
missed her. He talked about his dad and how everyone else
was letting the old guy down. Andy would cry, and Ruby
would hold him.

After a few nights of this, something changed. The funeral happened. The man at the front mispronounced the
mother's name. All these people came over, had coffee and
cakes, talked about what a wonderful woman she was, how
she'd be missed. So many people in wools, they gave off a
weird kind of steam. So many pinkies sticking out from
cup handles. But they all finally left, and after a few heavy
sighs and hands across his teary eyes, the father said he'd
go lie down.

"I fall into myself," he said. "I don't sleep, but I get lost
somehow. I can't really tell you what I mean. I'm always
thinking about her. How she was before she wouldn't wake
up. The last time she looked right at me." He didn't tell
them what he meant about the look. It had been so full of
hate, thinking about it made his knees weak. The father
hadn't told anyone.

About half an hour after his dad left, Andy came over to Ruby's couch. The leather squeaked a bit under the sheet. They looked at each other with try-to-be-quiet faces. When Andy got under the covers and touched her arm, electricity shot through Ruby. She had a sense that Andy felt the same thing. They held each other closer than they had the other nights. He breathed real sweetly into her ear, and his breath got deeper and deeper. Slow and loud and sweet.

She turned and licked his ear, like a cat. Not messy. She tickled his earlobe with her tongue. He jerked his head away, and pulled her more towards him at the same time. They were both lying on their backs, sandwiched together on the fancy green leather couch. Andy turned on his side, and Ruby could feel he was hard under his pajama bottoms. She didn't know what to do about it.

"I miss her, Ruby," he said.

"Yeah," she said.

"I don't know why I feel this way," he said. "You feel so good right now. I don't know why I feel like this."

"It happens, I guess. I hear sometimes it makes you really appreciate being alive or something."

"Yeah. This is different."

They were lying pretty still for a long time. Everything was tingling, wherever there was skin. The smallest move sent a shock through Ruby's body. She had never felt like this before. They were both moving their hands under each other's pajamas, slowly in circles. They turned to face each other, their noses touching. They looked at each other but they were so close everything was blurry.

At this point, Ruby felt waves. It was like her skin was melting. She was opening up and disappearing at the same time. She was so aware of everything — Ruby felt like she was more of herself than ever. They kissed lips, rubbed each others' backs.

Andy said, "I love you."

He said, "What's happening."

She said, "Don't worry," and, "It's okay."

"You're going to be okay," she said. And she really meant it. She didn't know what that meant.

She was getting into him. Everything he did and didn't do felt so right. Andy touched her crotch and she was so wet, her nightie was soaked right through in that spot. He pulled the nightie up and drew little circles right on her clit, not too hard, like hardly any guy knew how to do. She put her hand down his pajama pants and stroked his cock. Firm but not squeezing. Going down behind his balls, cupping them and rolling them.

They stayed so quiet. They listened to every creak in the house. But they were so far away. It was such a struggle to remember what the situation was. It was like they were both glowing, like they were both caught in some kind of awesome light only the two of them could see. They were so close together, and with the clothes pushed up and down it didn't take much for Andy to be inside. They weren't being safe.

Ruby got on top. They barely had to move before she came. She had to remember to be quiet, but it seemed right to be quiet anyway. The feeling of everything melting away kept growing, even after she came. Andy pushed from underneath. They were cupping each other's faces. She could feel his cock deep inside. She could feel his stomach muscles tighten and relax. She felt like she was inside him, fucking herself, felt like she was going to come again, which she did. Then Andy pulled out and came, too.

They held each other close, saying nothing to each other. Breathing sweetly into each other's ears. And she knew this would be it. The end and the beginning of something.

The next day, when she was in the bathroom for a while, she found a book about stupid things politicians say. Dan Quayle seemed to be the winner, if there was a contest. A couple of days after that, they left Andy's hometown to come back to the city. Now he's Rep again, but Rep with a new angel mother hovering just above him, watching everything he does from here on in. Rep not touching Ruby.

e

The chirp-chirp pedestrians listen for the sound and look for the light. They cross the street. Ruby adds one last item. She puts it on the list. She thinks about the century she's walking into, and about turning back.

"Want to move in together?" she asks, and Rep says *k*.

mark macdonald

PENIS

IT WASN'T TOO LONG AFTER WE MET EVEN, WHEN HE PROPOSED
that we make things official and buy ourselves a new penis. It seemed like a wise decision to firm things up like
that, more sensible than getting married, and more concrete than buying rings for each other. Something we could
share, something we could both use. I had gone out with
people before, even lived with a guy for a while, but he had
his own penis, and was more into women anyway. So this
purchase felt mature, domestic, a whole new adventure in
adulthood. We both felt terribly responsible.

We found a nice one. Not too big, but a confident size
nevertheless. I made a special box for it, lined with red
paisley fabric and with a little pocket for a twig of lavender. He constructed a shelf above the head of our bed, and
we placed the box there and felt good. We laid back that afternoon, summer heat through the blinds, and embraced
like it would last forever. Happy newlyweds.

We were so in love that we stopped noticing the dis-
tractions of life; our friends and families became near
memories. I stopped making art, and he worked away at a
job he didn't really enjoy. All the while, though, we had
our penis, in its little box, on its little shelf, like an unlit
beacon to remind us of our love.

But, after only a year or two the penis had begun to
take on a new meaning for us, enforcing the routine of our
lives. It was beginning to grow dull.

I would be away at work, and he would take it out and
stroke it into life. Masturbating our shared penis became a

kind of distraction for him, satisfying his needs alone. Eventually I caught on when he became less interested in the two of us using it together, and it sort of hurt, but also made sense to me. I had done it once or twice without him knowing, and I didn't exactly feel guilty about it. Whatever. This trivial use of the penis was hardly going to break us up. It was ours to use, after all.

Our friends all knew about our penis, and some were mildly jealous. They'd tell us how impressed they were that we were so together, so adult. One afternoon, an old chum of mine was over for tea with me and asked to see the penis. I didn't see the harm in it, so I unpacked it from the little box and handed it over. It felt strangely good in his touch, and as he admired and praised it, an erection started to grow. My pulse increased, and I felt slightly embarrassed. He just smiled and seductively ran his soft hand over the head. It felt no better in his grasp, but the difference of his touch was somehow refreshing. Again, he smiled at me like he was in total control, and I did nothing as he raised it to his mouth, licking the length, taking it in his lips.

Two things happened at once. As the pressure flushed out of the penis and into his mouth, a sound hit me like one of my bones snapping. It was the latch of the door clicking open; my lover was home. He found my friend there, with our cum on his face, and all three of us seemed to say "shit" at exactly the same moment. The shame and embarrassment of the situation hung in the air like an unclaimed fart. The penis deflated and was put down gently on the living room table. My friend left silently, and when the door closed I looked searchingly at my lover, but he turned and walked away.

I washed the penis in the kitchen sink, thinking just how quickly my bad judgment had fractured the space in our lives. How would I make this up to him? What would it mean to our future? To his credit, he remained calm about the situation. His lack of surprise, I guessed, kept

him from going ballistic. Over the days and weeks that followed it seemed more and more that my indiscretion was
more of a revelation about how things had developed without our participation. I still felt awful.

It was weeks before we took the penis out again, after
a romantic dinner, in a moment that we could both forget
the strain I had caused. Everything was going well until together we unwrapped the penis from its red shroud. We
were stunned to find it had changed during the restful
weeks. Grown less detailed somehow, its edges and folds
had sunken. It was slightly smoother, more cylindrical, the
ridge around the head rounder, and the opening at its end
less pronounced. We wondered if the problem was just
disuse, or if we had purchased a faulty one. The truth was,
it was changing.

My lover gripped the penis tightly, and I held its outer
skin in my hand, slowly pulling up and down on the shaft.
It gradually became aroused, but the lack of definition was
distracting. Prosthetic now, it had lost the character that
we were so proud of. A bit disturbed, we tucked it away,
and left it alone in the room.

The following week I found the penis lying flaccid on
the toilet tank. He said he had tried to use it while I was
at work, and it hadn't seemed enthusiastic. Neither of us
felt compelled to take as much care of it, not as religiously
anyway. The box remained on its little shelf, a reminder
of our once cherished purchase. We considered getting another one, but our attitude was different this time, like we
were shopping for a sex toy. Our lack of interest in the penis came to symbolize our gradual choice of separate
paths.

Then one morning I found him, in tears, trying to flush
it down the toilet. I didn't even try to stop him. Of course,
the penis blocked the loo, and we had to fish it out, sad
and dripping, with a bent coat hanger. We considered
burning or maybe burying it somewhere appropriate. Like
a dead pet, we felt compelled to do the right thing with the

remains, rather than just abandoning it in the landfill. Eventually we decided.

I weighted down the box with layers of molten lead, and we reverently wrapped the dead penis in its red shroud, and wired the box shut. In a decidedly funereal mood, we walked to the lighthouse north of the city. In a place we had enjoyed coming to when we first dated, we flung the sealed box into the sea and embraced. We returned home without exchanging words and began to pack our things, casually separating the records and books like proper divorcées.

We had learned more than we had lost, and the pain of our surrender to our own autonomous lives seemed worth the enduring for both of our sakes. Now alone, I know it will be an age before I consider finding another penis.

sky gilbert

SOME JAMS THAT INVOLVE BOYS

1

FIRST THERE IS THE MOST OBVIOUS MEANING OF THE WORD, like: we were supposed to meet at such and such time and you didn't show up. So now I'm in a jam. There's also meeting something that he fucked recently (or even a long time ago) when you're not prepared. That can be a jam. There's being caught in the straightest part of town with him in a dress. That can be a jam, too.

2

Then there's toe jam. This is the type of jam you're liable to come across if you like to lick his feet. I don't think I'd better talk about this particular type of jam anymore.

3

Since we're on potentially icky topics, there are other intimate jams which you may come across, if you're exploring every part of the male person. This has nothing, of course, to do with cleanliness. Well, sometimes it does. But sometimes very clean and conscientious and really intelligent people can forget about one particular area, and, if you're really doing a thorough search of the human body of a male person you may stumble over it and then you'll be in a jam. Right in the middle of it. But they say that the sense of smell is a very important erotic organ. So I say, go with it.

4

There's a jam which is really a kind of jelly. You have to imagine that a boy is a donut and you know for, like, six months or so, you may just be licking the icing. And then you may get down to the sugary part and maybe even some of the dough. Because after all, you don't want to be a pig and eat the donut all at once. And also you don't exactly know what's inside (they forgot to leave a jam trail and this was a leftover day-old and no one told you the type of jam you're in for) so you want to leave that particular revelation until the end just in case it spoils the whole donut experience. So there you go, for eight or nine months even, just licking the icing and nibbling the dough until finally you find yourself right at the heart of the donut. But the thing is, by this time, you've forgotten about the jam. You just thought — oh this is all going to be icing and dough. Pretty tough and tasty. But no, you've hit the soft, mushy centre. And it's red like his eyes and he's crying. He's crying in your kitchen and you never even imagined that. And he's wearing his glasses which makes him seem even more sweet and vulnerable and you want to hug him and you do — only what good is it because — well you've found the jam? And then you're suddenly in the position of *I didn't know boys were made of jelly, but they are, they are really, in the centre anyway, no matter how hard-hearted they act on the outside.* So, as with all jams, it's best to just lick it up because remember you're in the heart of the donut now and there's no turning back. And after all, it's the jam that you really wanted, isn't it? It's what you bought the damn donut for, is it not?

5

Finally, there is jam recovery. This is what all the psychology books call the final stage of intimacy. You have ingested the jam and now either you'll be back at some later date for more jam or you have indigestion and you won't be back at all.

6

And then of course; if you have gone past the final stage, you are in jam ecstasy. In this stage, nothing matters any- more. Even jam. And that's the way it should be. Jam jam jam. The world is a jam. Jam me. Love is a many splen- doured jam. The world is alive with the sound of jam. Stop the jam I want to get off. But if you're lucky, of course, you never do.

diana atkinson

LONGING IS MY NATIVE TONGUE

By night on my bed I sought him who my soul loves; I sought him, but found him not.
— Song of Songs 3:1

WHEN MAGGIE MET ALEC SHE WAS STRUCK BY THE WAY HE seemed so connected. So competent, with his cell phone ringing, talking into his headset, juggling his Palm Pilot, all while standing before her olive display at Zabar's.

"D'you know," he confided to her between incoming calls, "I can't make up my mind?" And he gave her a dazzling smile that made her forget she was wearing a puke-green polyester uniform, hairnet, and a nametag that chirped *My Name is Maggie. How May I Help You?*

"Try one of these," she said. And even though there were customers lined up three deep on either side of him, she handed a him a plump, dark, Alphonso olive in a little paper cup, like a nurse handing a patient a pill.

"It's purple," he exclaimed. And then, popping it into his mouth, "It even tastes purple." When he saw she was just standing there clutching the slotted olive ladle, he gave her the full force of those thoughtful brown eyes, those long lashes, that little self-deprecating half-smile. In those seconds, the room went black-and-white, so that Maggie could no longer hear the gold-toothed, heavyset woman to Alec's right badgering Rufus, her co-worker, for a pound of Bulgarian feta, nor the fair-haired, balletic-looking young man behind Alec's left shoulder, the one who kept bleating, "Don't you have cracked olives? I need them for my Chicken Phoenicia."

"Let me have half a pound," said Alec quietly, and Maggie lowered her eyes and went to work. She even made him a little olive sampler, one each of eighteen kinds, from tiny Niçoise and wrinkly Moroccan oil-cured to the great, green, garlic-stuffed.

> > >

He next came in ten days later. He was the last one in line, Rufus said, but asked for her, Maggie. So Rufus went to the back room and got her. She was wrestling hunks of blue cheese from a block with the dental floss-like contraption she and Rufus called "the cheese guillotine." (Rufus was trying to write a play about *Mme* Dufarge for his drama thesis at The New School but, he told Maggie, his characters kept ending up in cafés, eating elaborate meals.) She had just cut herself on the tiny metal teeth edging the Saran Wrap box when Alec summoned her.

"I didn't notice the sampler till I got back to my office," he said. "I really liked these." He pointed to Mediterranean Mixed. "May I have half a pound, please?" When it was dished up and sealed snugly, Rufus had cleaned up in the back and was turning out the lights in their section.

"Dance major?" Alec guessed as she rang up his purchase. She shook her head. People often asked that. ("You have a certain gawky grace," a woman had once added, enigmatically.)

"I'm a writer," she muttered, looking at her hands, which hadn't really written anything in years. They were chapped from brine, the nailbeds caked with blue cheese.

"Oh. What do you write?" Alec looked prepared to be charmed, and Maggie desperately wanted to charm him, yet the book felt sordid and pathetic to her now, as much a source of shame as pride, not for its form but for its content. Queasy with self-loathing, Maggie couldn't help but admire the smooth drape of Alec's Prada suit. She had written a novel called *More Than You Wanted to Know*, which had put her on the map in Canada, but in New York City people tended to ask, "How big was your advance?" Since this made her shrivel up like an oil-cured olive, she'd stopped talking about it. Now Alec was leaning across the counter, bending to her slightly, with the kind, interested look of a missionary street priest coming upon a homeless child.

I'm so far from home, she thought suddenly.

"I ... I. ... Oh, for heaven's sake," she blurted, "I'm pungent."

"I know," said Alec, regarding her steadily. "My office isn't too far from here. You can wash up. Shall I give you dinner?"

> > >

Before her death when Maggie was fifteen, Maggie's mother had edited a literary journal called *The Golden Calf Review*.

"It's read by sixty-five young men in corduroy jackets with elbow patches," Maggie remembers yelling. "Every issue contains at least one poem that starts with 'O Icarus.'" While this was an exaggeration, it wasn't much of one. Still, Maggie regrets her cleverness at the expense of her mother's literary aspirations. She's paying for it now. She is a writer, or a closeted writer, or a closeted, bound, and gagged writer who can't find her voice, sort of the way her father used to wander 'round the old house in Vancouver, unable to find his glasses, which were, of course, on his head.

When Maggie was twelve, her father found religion and followed it to the Holy Land, where he was killed by a PLO landmine while picnicking with his second wife. The landmine had been a leftover, an afterthought, certainly not intended for an errant humanities professor. Her mother, a social worker, took to singing under her breath. ("Work your fingers to the bone, what do you get? Bony fingers.") Now and then a man would ask her out, but she always refused.

"I'm through with men," she'd say, and pad off to the the bathtub with another library book, usually a work of fiction described on the jacket as "poignant." ("How's this?" Maggie would tease, spreading raspberry jam on toast and handing it to her. "Is this toast poignant enough for you?")

The thing about loss, she found, was that it went on and on, like a dial tone. After her mother's death, she was taken in by her father's former officemate at UBC. He was a mournful man with an only daughter, Chloe, who he loved as Maggie's father had apparently not loved her. (*So I've got a father complex*, she writes in her journal. *So what?*) It was educational, if painful, to see up close what she had missed. She got to visit at the homes of Chloe's friends, who invariably played the harp, or the lute. Chloe was in Madagascar at this very minute, studying lemurs. ("Lemur means ghost in Latin," she wrote on a postcard.)

Maggie washed dishes at Maxie's Muffins, where it didn't matter that she cried easily as long as she scrubbed the tins. She could bend her head over the suds and sob. The bakers were used to her, and it was better than sobbing in public, which had become a real problem. When people are gone you have to reconstruct them, and it's never possible to hold them in your mind the way they were, so you're left wondering who they were, and gradually the asembled clues, the Black Magic chocolate box full of photos, don't seem to add up to a person at all. I loved her, actually, and I didn't tell her often enough. Even when I did, I couldn't fill the hole in her left by a manic-depressive father and paranoid schizophrenic mother. Baby Maggie was brought in to ameliorate that longing. Here I am, pale and awkward with frizzy reddish hair. I cry in public places, fill spiral notebook after spiral notebook with my baffled observations and hopeless longing, don't know how to talk to guys, never mind get a date, never mind get married and pregnant like even the most backward of my peers. If I am the hope of my generation, my generation is in deep trouble.

>   >   >

She got a student loan and went after a BFA in Creative Writing at UBC. School, with its foreign language and math requirements, its twenty-pages-a-week minimum, was demanding. She was living on ramen noodles and working at Orange Julius. In the third year she decided a person her age shouldn't get into any more debt, so she started working at Miss Mona's Massage. Her thesis, which became *More Than You Wanted to Know*, was based on her experiences at Miss Mona's. She'd intended the setting to be incidental, almost a metaphor, through which the theme of transcendent loss would shimmer, the true jewel, just as she had been a jewel in a sordid envronment. Even though at least one-quarter of the female student body was putting itself through on stripping, on nude live internet, or escorting (pagers beeping in class from the escort agents), Maggie was the only one fool enough to write about it.

Once a young male teacher they called Snag behind his back (for Sensitive New Age Guy) called her into his office. He was holding a sheaf of papers she'd cobbled together into fiction from her diary.

"Is this you?" When she said nothing, just stared at him from behind her dark glasses, he said, softly, "What exactly are you doing to yourself, Maggie?"

"I'm paying for the enrichment of my mind with the pollution of my body." He stared, then the starch seemed to go from him, and he sank into his chair behind his desk. It was on coasters but screeched in protest, like a bad shopping cart. Yellowish stuffing spilled, entrail-like, from its cushion. He rested his head in his hands and rubbed his temples, then looked at her.

"Ah, well. Who am I to talk?" he said in a tone she'd never heard him use. "My wife's a cocktail waitress." Briefly, she considered making a too-clever-by-half suggestion that he deconstruct the word "cocktail," and then decided he seemed pained enough already. She went and lay on her stomach by the koi pond in the Japanese garden and smoked a joint.

When *More* came out, the Canadian press instantly la-
belled her, Sex Trade Worker Who Can Talk. She felt a tide
of mingled envy, curiosity, and loathing from middle-class
journalists who treated her like Doctor Johnson's dog
walking on its hind legs. Maggie didn't help herself, didn't
know that though they would listen politely to phrases like
"transcendent loss," they were really waiting for her to con-
cede, as she inevitably would, when pressed, "Occasionally, I blew one of my clients." The finer points of her
literary motivation would be left in if space permitted. But
those seven words? They'd be in bold.

School was finishing when the book was published in
New York. She had a yard sale and then went to promote
it. Though the book was stillborn, Maggie stayed in New
York, happy to be anonymous, still hoping to be somehow
washed clean. She keeps a journal, in which she also tries
to write fiction. With a mixture of despair and relief she
finds that fiction has a way of tattling on truth, and truth
always blurs into fiction.

A month before she meets Alec, she writes:

May 4th

*I've been in NYC three years now, exactly.
Still alive but haven't written a thing since
More. Just too tired all the time. I'm a worker bee,
an olive drone. Dreamed last night I was punching
the time clock at work as usual to go home and
Write Something Brilliant but then I looked down
and saw the floor beneath my feet had become a
treadmill. When I tried to leave Zabar's the treadmill
sped up and I couldn't escape. Also my knees
seem to be giving out.*

*Twenty-seven and I haven't been touched by a
man in two years. Still traumatized by the thing
with Paul. Why can't I heal?*

> > >

Alec leads her up a flight of stairs. His office turns out to be a small flat with a daybed, a lot of film reels, and lines strung back and forth, clothes-pegged with prints of sculptures. After she has washed in the clawfoot bathtub, put on the green silk paisley robe he offers, and accepted a glass of red wine, they stand together at the half-open window overlooking a dry cleaner's across the street. Beyond it, the Hudson River.

"My house is in Connecticut," he says. "My wife and daughter live there. I'm with them on weekends, but I have to be here during the week." How could I have failed to notice the wedding ring, she wonders, noticing it now. Diamond-shaped holes filigree its scalloped edges. With prescient clarity, she knows she should put on her clothes and leave now. She also knows that she will not. When she was ten, she saw a newborn fawn at the side of the road seconds befor her father hit it with the old Valiant. The thrill of tenderness followed so quickly by the thud. She vomited into the lap of her dress with the little strawberry print and all over her Mary Janes while her father wiped blood from the fender. ("I hate you! I hate you, you murderer!" she'd cried while he cleaned her up, sighing and saying, "Honey, I'm sorry. I'm sorry, kittie.")

A starling flies by with coloured wool in its beak.

"From the laundry across the street," Alec murmurs. "Maybe it's knitting a very small sweater." Maggie giggles. Alec takes her glass, sets it next to his on the sill, and, very slowly and gravely, kisses her. "You are so beautiful." He unpins her hair so it falls down her neck in thick, unmanageable waves. "Your hair is so Vermeer. I think I could love you." Behind her thoughts, an alarm light goes on. In the suicidal aftermath of the thing with Paul, she staggered to a therapist. She remembers him leaning forward in his wing chair.

"It's your father. You're looking for your father." He'd spoken slowly, enunciating into her eyes. She remembers him cupping his hands around his mouth, too, but that can't be right. In any case, the effect was of a person on shore trying to be heard by a person too far from land.

Alec's hands are large, the fingers knobby and sensitive. She is already in love with those hands. One cradles her skull, tips her head back. Through the lower half of the window comes the fresh, grey smell rain releases from asphalt.

"Look," he says, and tilts her head toward the mirror. Her head and neck are streaked. She throws him a glance — questioning, alarmed — and then her eyes close as he traces on her skin the reflected tracks of raindrops. Describes with his fingertips their shadows, then blesses her eyelids with soft, almost imperceptible kisses. Something slides inside her. Beneath his touch, she can feel her soul loosen in its shell. She holds her breath and feels the trapped bird in her heart hurl itself against her ribcage.

> > >

She lets herself into her shared flat, sees that Sasha has left her hair all over the place again, and that there isn't a shred of toilet paper. Sasha has left her a note in lip liner on the back of a pizza flyer. *Maggie Call Alec.*

"Her heart leapt," Maggie murmurs, and doodles a cartoon heart with arms and legs, leaping.

"Maggie?" says Alec. "Just a minute. I've got someone on the other line. I'll put him on hold." A pause, then, "Now. Tomorrow's your half-day, right? Would you like to come out with me and some people from my office on my colleague Everard's boat?"

And so there is Maggie, minimum wage and no insurance, smiling toothily in a red dress borrowed fron Sasha, Alec's arm around her waist as Everard clicks the shutter. There is Maggie with Alec at two in the morning at The Stage Door Deli, eating chopped liver and laughing as Alec stages small dramas with the cutlery, Mr Knife falling in love with Ms. Spoon but having trouble kissing her because he can't bend. There's Maggie smooching with Alec on the Staten Island Ferry. There they are in an all-night used

bookstore, groping each other while pretending to be en-
grossed in *The Illustrated History of Upholstered Furniture*
and *The Ottoman Empire: Footstools the World Over*.

> > >

"May I spend the night with you?"

"No. I'm married. And, Maggie, I'm in love with my
wife and daughter."

("The slimeball," said Sasha the next day. She had
hiked up her flame-coloured slip to shave her legs, paus-
ing to take drags off her Gauloise.

"He's not," Maggie wailed.

"My funny Maglentine. Always *l'innocente*.")

"Oh, all right. Just this once." And, having lit the votive
next to the daybed, he pulled down the cups of her lace
bra and sucked her nipples till she thought she'd pass out
with desire.

> > >

"My wife cheated on me with four consecutive men." He
whispers hoarsely, drinking brewed Chinese herbs from a
pottery mug. He's shivering and coughing. "The baby isn't
mine." She stares. "But I love her."

"Your wife?"

"My baby." She gets him a blanket. I'm lost, she thinks.
Self-destructive, and morally filthier than ever. What was I
thinking, responding to a man who has obligations elsewhere?
Legitimate obligations. Jealous of a baby. I should be shot.

> > >

Gradually, he stops calling. Noah, her other flatmate, becomes engaged. Of course, thinks Maggie. Pairing up.
That's what normal people do. She dreams that her
mother, now dead ten years, is digging in the back yard of
the old house with a tuning fork, unearthing dark tomes
in brown leather, their titles obscured by clods of dirt.

> > >

"I won't be able to see you any more. Work has intensified, and I must support my child." She wants to say, "Of course." She wants to be gracious. Instead she cries, "But I want to have your child."

"Be reasonable."

"Aren't I pretty enough? You told me I look like a luna moth in this dress."

"I know." He touched her lips. "You are pretty enough, and I do love you. But it isn't any of it going to happen, so please come back to earth.

"But I'm suffering."

He pursed his lips and looked at her sharply. "You haven't begun to suffer."

>   >   >

She lies in bed and listens to the phone not ringing. She curls up, rams her fists under her ribs, remembering long childhood years in beds with bars, like a monkey in a deprivation experiment. She wasn't supposed to speak of it later, because there's really no way to work bowel illness into a conversation. People look at you and think, They shoved things up your butt. It excites them to pity, as with the raped girl at school. Ultimately, it was the long hours of being alone, bolted in or tied down, that left the deepest psychic scar. Zoos still upset her.

He used to tell her stories when he visited, recite sonnets. Hold up picture books and turn the pages. She'd watch through the bars, big-eyed, marsupial. When the bell rang announcing the end of visiting hours, her father would pull off his scratchy wood sweater and stuff it through the bars. By the time he came again, days later, all his smells would've fled. Seven years later, after he'd moved to Israel, twelve-year-old Maggie found one of those pullovers and slept with it for years.

>   >   >

It's grey outside Maggie's window. Crusts of snow line the

gutters along the street; cars spray slush on the ankles of people waiting at bus stops. She stands looking down at it all through the watery glass of the laundry room. There's an ironing board behind her, an iron, a blouse on a hanger. Down the hall, on her desk, books, her journal leaning against some Katherine Mansfield short stories, Jean Rhys' *Voyage in the Dark*, and a book of Edna St. Vincent Millay sonnets, the one beginning, "What lips my lips have kissed, and where, and why," dogeared.

A cat is curled up on a cushion in the front room. Noah is out with his fiancée. Sasha is out with her boyfriend. And me, I am worse than single. I am in love with a married man. It's so trite. And I can't seem to change the channel. I'm fixated, and he's thought better of being in love with me but still visits on occasion — in order, I know, to enjoy the spectacle of me begging him for sex. For, even more than they want sex, this is what men want. To refuse you, and to watch you try to captivate them, and to experience arousal and disgust. To refuse to indulge you and their own arousal, but to use their disgust as a tool with which to push you away. And to continue to watch, fascinated, to see what happens if they step behind a plate of glass. How many times will you lunge and bruise yourself, and fall in a sore heap . . . and then gather yourself up and do it again? More than to love you, they want to master themselves. But they still want to know you're there, across the city, battering yourself against the glass.

She should be studying. She tries on clothes. This dress, just a week ago, prompted a young Italian man to tell her, "If I had a wife, I'd want her to look like you." This short jumper caused a bus driver to remark, "Looks like not much work is going to get done in your office today." But he saw her in it and gave her a pitying look. Accepted the parcel of baking ("I'll give it to my secretary, for her kids."), kissed her forehead and said, "Take care of yourself. I must run." She'd bumped along home, past the outdoor food stall, barely registering the oranges glowing like

distant suns through the thickening dark of a winter afternoon, the green hyacinth buds in their foil-wrapped
pots, mongering the rumour of spring.

Home, she ran a bath. After, she lay across her bed-
spread, worn pink chenille, and did it herself, conjuring
something she'd read about Medieval nuns not being allowed dildos and trying to feel lucky to have one herself.
Trying to stanch the thought, "Other women have babies.
I have a penis doll." His live seed. God help me.

In this self-disgusted torpor of horny loneliness, she
lay and spasmed, again and again, until the bare tree outside her window drowned in black watery dark (they say
a man lying in the bottom of a well can see the stars even
in broad daylight), and she wanted to weep but was too
numb, so she slept and dreamed that she was on a train
and that when it pulled into the station she saw him. He
was waiting for her! He was wearing a long Russian-style
wool coat, elegant on his lanky frame, and a muffler and
fur earmuffs, and he was carrying a package. But as she
descended, she saw his gaze was directed past her, at his
wife and young daughter. She woke then, and hugged her
knees to her chest in the chilly room, and wept.

> > >

In the self-help section of the Brooklyn Public Library, she
finds a book on healing the wounds of childhood, and
countless volumes berating her foolish choices. The ex-
perts' consensus is that she should complete herself.
Embrace her aloneness. She walks the streets of Prospect
Heights at night, along the wrought-iron fences of the
brownstones, and looks in lighted windows. How the hell
do people get it; wedding photos, sofa, soapdish, shared
body smell?

At work, her supervisor takes her aside and tells her
she is ". . . on probation. You've always been a good worker,
but lately you're too open, too needy. You look in the eyes
of each person who comes in the door as if you hope they

can save you." She writes a poem about a dog that falls in love with a puma at the zoo. The puma is behind glass, but the dog visits it every day, sits and gazes at it, bearing in its teeth a love offering, a hot dog found in the trash.

The poem is published in the first issue of a literary journal, *Nux Vomica*. A man at the journal's debut party tells her he is writing a book about "two famous dwarves of the Russian Rebellion." On the way home, a dwarf approaches, selling cotton candy. She thinks, Obviously I am being offered signs and am failing miserably to interpret them. She bites her cuticles raw.

One morning she recognizes in *The New York Times* the face of the author of the self-help book. He shot himself in his Upper West Side apartment, leaving behind a stack of letters, written over years, to a peep show performer named Liz who, when questioned by the earnest journalism grad from *The Times*, stubbed out her cigarette with a long-nailed hand and said, "I wish I could help you, honey. But when you've been in the business as long as I have, they all kinda look the same, you know? They spatter the glass, then they're gone." The article goes on to report that Janet Malcolm has put in a bid in for the letters. Maggie folds the paper and sighs. She is sitting on a bench in the Brooklyn Botanical Gardens, the ground around her feet littered with ginkgo nuts.

marnie woodrow

SUNDRUNK

I

WHEN THE SUNDRUNKS STUMBLE OUT TO TAN WITH THEIR browning hides and pretty hands, bending to adjust their towels and stretching, too, like cats on window-sills, tigers on sand: and their hair goes blonde in nostalgic places like the yellowing of a photograph tossed careless on a dresser covered in light, a picture taken and taken in but never noticed till it's dusting-day and the once-a-week maid lifts it up, wipes, and tosses it back to the pool of sunshine on the lemon-waxed wood next to the freshly lined-up lipsticks, and even the coins in the ashtray are forgotten, too, though they shine and penny and accumulate over a long summer of accidental savings.

The maid sometimes will pocket a quarter from that ashtray-bank, tipping herself and praying she isn't ever caught, for she is saving for her own vacation, a holiday away from the ocean and away from the smell of cocoa butter that clings to the bedding and curtains and the wadded-up washcloths she plucks from the corners of the shower-stalls.

I see your knuckles all golden-brown and your silver rings and your sundrunken stare, the salt in your curls as you laze on a mattress of faux-bamboo, your bathing suit rolled down to your hips and the white jello of your breasts leaking out sideways, discreet. Wouldn't someone just die for the chance to rub cream on your burnt parts, all the while reeling sundrunk, too, and hard in places and wet and lump-throated watching you fall asleep. Summer keeps returning, so you do, too.

2

I've been here all June and July, listening through the papery walls of this habitual villa. Dew-drops collect on my
gin-glass in the heat of the night when I squeeze the glass
hard as one holds on, tight. There is something sick and
delicious about holding a cold drink against a hot body: the
two surfaces make thunder as I sit propped and proper, my
back against a damp wall on a bed that would squeak. Cars
pull into the parking lot and their headlights pry and gawk,
the wind rattles the blinds and the bones in my spine respond to the wind-chimes that line the balustrade. Car
doors open and slam and trunks thump: people call out to
each other regarding breakfast. The sheets so cotton and
light and thin stick to my legs and I listen through the papery walls of this habitual villa and hear your pale giggle
and the rasp of your air-conditioner that confuses all other
sounds, though I manage to decide what every bed-spring
is suffering gladly under and I lay and listen with ashes
collecting in my ears, wonder at the torture but stay into
August, leaving my room only to stand on the balcony
walkway while the maid swears in Spanish at the overturned bottles and probably she notices the sour smell of
my heart dying listen-by-listen: your pale giggle, your
eleventh orgasm, your rough morning cough.

3

Once two people came all the way down here, drove all
the way down here to be alone and eat oysters and conch-
meat from each other's palms. That long drive filled with
radio music and swallows of water and squeals of laughter
and delight at the sight of a pelican. Like a bird from Mars,
and how about the pick-up trucks brimming with gun-
racks and toothy grins and violence, passing on the wrong
side, dangerously? How about the moonlit motels all the
way down, cranky breakfasts, big hair, coffee cups rolling
on the floor-boards, the maps flapping unfoldable good
fun? The stuff of honeymoons and hallucinations.

We were two people navigating the aerial highway over a seafull of shells and shark and shrimp and fake blueness. The driver drove with the passenger's hand on her thigh, as though it belonged there, always would. The sidelong smiles that were so easy that we drove 1,500 miles (more) in an effort to be alone. Together.

And if I had known that it would be our last trip together I would have driven more slowly or maybe more quickly but off the side of a bridge. We waste and fritter away the fractions of seconds, forget the names of restaurants and exactly what was eaten. Some loves travel too fast, like Floridian cars speed: we got there and the drinks were drunk, the backs oiled, the lunches devoured, magazines not really read, the fucks that happened while the maid tried the door-handle and it was all a blur, an overcrowded glass-bottomed boat tour where you can't really see much but you remember paying twenty-five dollars and it had something to do with fish swimming by and coral and Esther Williams jokes by the motel pool, later on the lawnchair with two days left.

You are right next door and I miss you more, but Florida is like that.

4

He trips down the stairs to the sandy beach, waving back at your window where you must be waving, too, with your robe open and your hair yanked back, coffee mug cupped in your two brown hands; I watch him struggle with the lawnchair, muscles rippling and shower-damp hair, his cinema-grin that I cannot bear, always looking up at you, seeing if you're seeing him: I hope that today is the day that the sun breeds a fast-eating tumour in the side of his neck — I know it isn't nice to wish such things but I imagine life would be easier if he had cancer and I burn the wish into him with my bloodshot all-night eyes, through the blinds and over the sea, up to the sun: come on, sun! Or even if he just got a very bad burn on his greasy pectorals while he slept, I would feel redeemed in my little hot room that is next door to you, Piper's Motel in this Key of Hemingway.

You know I am here, you have nodded through the wallpaper and I've heard you crying when he is out, not because you miss him. Who knows what about? But hi, neighbour, hello, old love: you consume my summers, destroy my mind with one hair toss in this Florida sea town that once belonged to two people who wanted so badly to be alone so they could take each other for granted, or a ride.

I offer you a toast through the wall: to your jello-white breasts and your. heart, half-broken, if you have one at all.

5

Adonis went fishing on a boat full of men: I saw him leave at dawn with his silly hat on, his six-pack, waving waving up at the dark window. Gone for the day. Goodbye, I whispered and raised my glass of watery gin and blew tell-tale smoke through the screen, hoped he saw it and blew a second cloud out. Late August and seventy-four sleepless nights spent watching the silvery moon and getting odd, old, even.

I hit the jackpot: you alone in your next-door room because he is a man and men must fish. I willed myself not to sleep through your unexpected solitude, my intended, unattended. But I did fall asleep after a too-hot shower that was meant to make me look irresistible. Instead I was dizzy, swooning with anxiety and old love and gin on an empty stomach. Sleep clubbed me and dragged me to the sheets where I lay in sexless sweat, in a gin-slick, all the morning eaten up and the sun high when I rolled over and realized the clock. And wept, baby-bawling and disappointed enough to wash my face and go to lunch.

I had given up on lunch, years before, the pain of sandwiches too great. But I walked past the motel restaurant with its sea-view and great conch chowder, stopped horrified by

my reflection: a skeleton with a cigarette and a plump pulp
novel about other people's sex lives. I was gaunt and devoured, stumbling on white, rubber legs, white hands flapping, flesh buried under a half-dozen shirts and eyes
shadowed. And you stood watching me from the parking
lot, watched me walk into the shrimp-shack with the cold
beer and key lime pie and Cuban love songs on the juke-
box.

6

You watched me nibble and sip and butter bread, and nothing about me moved you, did it? You thought: "She's getting old," and why did you sit on the sand where I could
not see you studying, of the way I ate my crab-claws and
lingered by the cashier. Did you watch my fingers pry the
meat away from the shell? Did it remind you of how I used
to pry pleasure from your flesh?

On the sand, I thought I saw you but shook my head,
you were gone, a mirage, a sand crab scuttling fast and impossible, pursued by nothing but sunbeams; I went down
to where the sea licks the shore and sat with my feet in
the water. The pulp novel I tossed in grew fat with saltwa-
ter and I prayed for a shark to come eat me: bone by bone.
A bird cried out and so did I; I buried my face in my fishy
hands. Under my fingernails the peppery bloodstains of
lunch. I wiped my eyes and felt the fire of Tabasco under
my eyelids. You watched me blinding myself and walked
away, down the beach with your brown certain feet and
that is when I saw you and knew why that bird had cried
out. I stayed there on the sand until I was good and sundrunk: drunk enough to knock, drunk enough to talk before the fishing boats came back carrying husbands and
dead things.

7

In one version: I open my motel room door to find you
naked except for your thumb-ring, on my freshly-made

bed. You smile looking lonely and hungry, and the more I stare the more your untanned nipples heave with breathing. Come sit. My rubber legs and your staring eyes: your come hither that always worked and always will. No healing remedy for my sickness, I pounce. Old oven-mouth: your kiss could heat bingo halls in the Arctic, the featherings of your tongue could knock down buildings. The more we kiss the harder we move the more damaging my longing becomes. I weep and collapse slippery in your arms: my lunacy completes itself in the first kiss and goes further with each blasting of the horn of the fishing boat, coming in of course, nets full and the men drunk and the seagulls overhead stalking and crying. Your heart picks up speed with each blast and you wonder if you should run to the dock waving, waving. The bullet is in the revolver (me in you) and I wonder if you will do it again, run. The horn, your hand, pressing possessive against my belly, caressing faster with the blasts, drawing me in again with a breathy explanation. You left him a note, said you were in Miami visiting cousins, just overnight, a bit of whimsy. And you say, "All yours," and so I have to lock the door and take the revolver (you) in my arms again one time more, careful not to scream, careful not to cry, careful not to die till you leave the room the next afternoon. Heart attack eyes and tired smile, a liar always, sometimes in my favour: you wave and leave.

I get good and sundrunk after you blow your kiss and go next door: no absolutely, never no more.

8

In one version: You are in your room with the blinds drawn and there is music but you fail to sing along. I listen as I have all summer, every summer, ache-eared, burnt-eyed, and ignored. I weave from too much time on the licking shore, teased green by the power of the sun on my bleached skin, drunk. No words come from you when I call your name, the music does not change or fade but you are listening, I can hear your ears wanting kisses. Knocking is easy but to stand in front of a door that will open is not easy; I reveal myself, I present myself, step out of the incognito to the *in flagrante*, empty handed, no roses, no dubloons. Oh God, you say. Oh God, like a needle sliding deftly into my swollen imagination, popping all prayers with one stab: "Please. Go away," you say, and I stare, sweating crab juice. Your face doesn't crumple with regret. It twitches and fights itself, a battle of calm, while I shake and shake in obvious pain and there is no kiss to help me go mad, no final shove over the precipice of love. No, you are silent and angry and tired of being listened to, too tired to kiss. Go away, like something said to a vagrant who hovers at your door, pretending to belong there, waiting for a half-minute of mouth by the sea.

You shut the door and the fishing boat blasts its horn, coming in, of course, full of drunk men and once-alive things, and you'd rather have that.

9

In one version: I slit both your throats with an oyster-shucker's knife and there is no more listening because I leave on a fish boat and the maid finds my coins in the ashtray, my overturned bottles, my heart floating in the kitchenette sink like a dead fish. She knows and swears in Spanish, words of pity for my soul; she has seen me for so many summers, knew what I was putting myself through. She'll swear when she sees the bloody bedsheets of you and he but she'll understand, all the while crossing herself, glad to never have been loved for that many summers in a row.

I would never, not really, with an oyster-shucker's knife, not even sundrunk, but the dream is nice.

10

One version more: I never knock, you never knock, and we never know, and summer keeps returning so we do, too. The motel the same, the game the same, the listening the longing and Adonis with his lawnchair and his waving, waving up at you, making sure you see him. And he sees me, too.

natalee caple

DREAM OF SLEEP

THE GUESTS ARE GATHERED IN THE KITCHEN AS IF IT IS THE only room in the house. The brown dog forages through the forest of legs for oysters on the floor. Eva sips her wine.

"Last night" — she turns to a woman standing nearby — "last night, Marc hit me in the back with a chair."

The woman stares back at her.

Eva swallows. "I made him dinner and I sat down. I watched him eat, and he said to me, 'Eva, don't watch me eat.' I said, 'Marc, did you ever sleep with anyone else after you married me?' He said, 'Eva, why are you always asking me questions you don't want to hear the answers to? You ruin everything. We could have had one more nice meal, with you not staring. We could have slept in our bed together one more time and I could have held you. We could have pretended that I haven't yelled and that you aren't so unattractive. We could have looked at all the pictures again, and in the morning I could have left. You could have waved goodbye.' I was upset when he said that. He surprised me. So I got up and walked away and he picked up his chair and swung it and hit me in the back."

Eva pushes her glass into the crowd of glasses on the kitchen table and reaches behind her neck to fumble with the zipper of her dress.

"Stop it, Eva," the woman whispers, touching Eva's arm with cold fingertips. "You've had too much to drink. Sit down. I'll get Marc to take you home."

"Nobody listens to me," Eva whispers. "Nobody cares."

The dog steps on her foot and lifts his soggy face to look

at her. "I was at a funeral last night," she tells him. "I was wearing this dress."

"Eva, don't talk to the dog." Marc laughs near her ear. He disentangles her fingers from the bright stem of a new wineglass and places it out of her reach. He strokes the naked round of her shoulder with the back of his fingers. His brown face hovers in her blinking gaze. His soft mouth touches her lips. He strokes her hair.

"I was at a funeral last night." She stares as his pupils dilate. "I wore this dress. All the little girls were wearing white and carrying blue orchids. The coffin was cut glass and you were fogging up the inside. I asked the man sitting beside me if you were really dead, and he turned to me and he said, 'Yes, I killed your dog, too. Don't you want to know why I killed your dog?'"

Marc turns her by her shoulders and slips her dress-zipper shut. Eva leans back as his hand skims her spine. He wraps his arms around her and presses her form into his.

> > >

The air is black with heavy rain. The windows were left open a crack and the seats have gotten wet. Marc wipes the water off the door with a cloth from the glove compartment and reaches across Eva to do the same. She shifts on the dampness. Her head lists toward her shoulder.

"Eva? Eva, don't fall asleep, baby. I want to talk to you on the ride home."

"Mmm."

"We can't go out and see people if you won't take your medication."

"I took it."

"You didn't take it, Eva."

He starts the car. The wheels grind against loose gravel.

"I took it at the funeral after they told me about my dog. You can fight back. You're a man, but a little dog like that. It was just so wrong. You drove me crazy with all your affairs, Marc."

"Stop it, Eva. Who do you think you're talking to?" He pulls the car onto the road. "I love you every minute of every day. I even love you when I'm asleep, but when we get home I'm going to push those pills down your throat and you are going to take them, forever and forever and forever, or I'm leaving. I love you, Eva; I never hurt you in any way."

"How could you leave me? You know I don't know how to drive."

"Please. Say something that makes sense to me. Say something that lets me know you know what I'm talking about."

> > >

Thunder cracks the dark in half. The road appears beneath the strained reach of the headlights. The sky has collapsed beneath the rain. Eva stares at the wipers steadily knocking back sheets of water. Marc looks over at her, muttering to herself. She cannot hold her head straight.

"If we drive like this all night we might find someplace better to go," she says.

"I don't think so. I think it will be the same wherever we go."

She wipes her cheeks and nose with her fingers and then wipes her hand on his sleeve. He stares ahead, into the dark envelope that the world has become around them. She says something else, too quietly for him to hear. She raises her blurry voice.

"We could pull the car over and make love in a ditch. I could lie on top of you so that you wouldn't get wet."

"No."

"Yes. We could wait there for something to happen; so it could all end. We could lie there in the cold dirt and talk and fuck until it all ended. Wouldn't that be better than this?"

"Let go of this idea, would you? Let go." He has a sense of the wheels slipping and then gripping again. The balls of his thumbs ache but he cannot relax his hold on the steering wheel. The windshield is fogging white from the heat of their bodies and breath. Marc rolls his window open a crack and the rain immediately beads along the frame.

"Nobody listens to me."

"I listen. I'm listening all the time, Eva."

"You could drive a half an hour further out of town and just release me and I could walk through the fields until I found someone who was brave enough to kill me, and then you wouldn't have to feel responsible."

"Eva, you're going to make me cry."

"Everything is wrong. Look, look outside. Not at the way it is right now. At least the sound of the rain lets you know where you are. But look at the night sky the way that it usually is. When we're camping the landscape goes black at night but the sky glows — studded with stars. When we come home everything seems inverted. It's as if all the stars fell onto the buildings. And nothing was left over our heads."

"Hush, Eva. Think of something that makes you happy. Don't you remember anything that makes you happy?"

"Do you remember the first night I stayed with you?"

"Yes."

"What do you remember about it?"

"You stayed with me. I was very happy that you stayed."

"Do you remember how we had sex?"

"No. I think I was on top of you. What do you mean?"

"We were sitting together on the couch. We had drunk two green bottles of red wine on purpose. There was no more food and the video was rewinding. We couldn't think of anything to say. The moment was evaporating right in front of me and I started to cry. I turned around and knelt against the back of the sofa and cried until you pulled me onto your lap and stroked my hair and I heard your breathing change. I lifted my mouth to see what would happen. My lips felt heavy and my eyes stung. It took hours to get there but then you kissed me suddenly. The weight of it, the speed of it, made it seem as if we were racing to overcome the chance that we might realize what we were doing and stop.

"Your hands dug under my shirt to cover my breasts and I was breathing in your mouth because we couldn't stop kissing to breathe. I took off my shirt and I watched your face. We made it to your bed by crawling on the floor together. I was suddenly afraid. I was suddenly afraid that I was hurting you, and I said something about that but you weren't listening. I laughed when you pulled off my pants and they hooked on my feet. I held your back, your skin was so shockingly hot, and I looked at your face when you entered me. I moved against you. I held onto you and when you came I held your chin and covered your mouth. I knew that I was going to ruin your life and that's what I was thinking when I fell asleep."

"We're home."

"Can I stay in the car?"

"No. That night, Eva, looking at you for the first time, I wanted you to ruin me; I wanted you."

"Marc, you hold my hand in your sleep."

"I know. You hook your legs over mine."

"You breathe on my eyelids."

"You ball your fists."

"I'm going to kill myself tonight."

"Let's talk some more about the first night, or the second night. Let's talk about the morning when we woke up."

"I told you everything."

"You didn't. You didn't tell me everything. You can't kill yourself, Eva, because there is always going to be something else I need to know."

"I'm so *sad*. I spend all day imagining things going

quiet. I spend *all day* dreaming of falling asleep."

"I know; I know you're so sad. And I dream *all day* of waking up beside you and knowing that you're just asleep, and in half an hour you will roll your sweaty little body over against me again and we'll have sex. We'll fall asleep together for another hour and then wake up. I'll make breakfast and you'll sit with me and be your happiest self, your best self, Eva. The jam will fall off the toast onto the floor and you won't care. The phone will ring and you won't care. The newspaper will come and you won't care, because I love you, and there are people in the world who never wonder if they're happy. There are people who never even wonder if they're starving. I love you, Eva. I love you. It's okay; it's okay for you to want to die. Just sit with me and tell me why."

alison acheson

WITH ELIZABETH

THE TRUTH THEN — ONE CAN DRAW NO OTHER CONCLUSION — is that Elizabeth has never believed him. All those words — *you are a beautiful woman* — and she's never believed. And if actions speak louder . . . well, he's been yelling for a long time. Now he's lost her to this, this room with its white walls, the paint thick and dull, and metal folding chairs. The cold passes from the metal through his jeans until he shivers. The carpet is indoor/outdoor variegated browns and greys intended to hide, but Keith's eyes find a dark stain under the first row of chairs, and he wonders what happened. Someone laughed too hard, coffee sloshed over the side of a mug, or was it wine and too much? At the edge of his thoughts there is another stain: a possibility. She's been unhappy all these years, and has spoken nothing of it. That possibility is horrific.

The smell of public bathroom air freshener invades his nostrils. The windows are too high to see from, and tinted so no one can see in. The fluorescent lights make him miserable, as they always do. In their whiteness, the faces in the room are like plaster. Not unlike the walls. The only colour in the room is the banner pinned to the front wall. WE WIN WHEN WE LOSE, it reads, in pink and orange. Pink and orange are oil and water. Keith shivers. His ass is numb. He shifts in the chair and it squeaks. And it has been not even a quarter of an hour. He turns, tries to find Elizabeth. He can't hear her voice among the muted talk. Usually his ears can find her, his eyes can see her, his . . . whatever it is, that sense that men aren't supposed to have . . . he can feel her nearby. He can't now, yet he knows that she is in the room somewhere. It is strange to him, this disconnection. He resists the urge to stand and look for her. It would be too much like a mother. He could get a coffee from the narrow table set up in the far back corner. A coffee urn and a tea carafe take up most of the table, but there is a plate of untouched sandwiches, their egg filling probably warm, the bread growing soggy. They look abandoned. There should be cookies at a meeting like this. There should be people gathered around this table, chatting. "Try this with the walnuts." "It's delicious." "The chocolate is positively sinful."

> > >

They had made cookies when they were young. It was a mating ritual, peculiar to the religious. Something to do with keeping curious hands busy. Every seven minutes a full pan sliding into the oven, and in between the process of rolling, cutting, filling another pan. Even then, Elizabeth had a way with a rolling pin; she never made drop cookies. He could see her, leaning over her work: a gentle push on the cutter, and there was a tree, branches sharply pointed. A tap, and the tree dropped neatly onto the cookie sheet. She always rolled the dough so that it was perfect. Smooth. Not a crack, no change in colour. Creamy, and one-quarter inch exactly.

> > >

Like a blow to the side of the head, it comes to Keith: how it was, out in the church parking lot, the August sun still bright, the guys gathered before the Friday night youth meeting. "Did you see that new one?" Josh had said, shaking his head, his hair feathered just so.

"Which one was that?" Brad asked, even though they all knew what Josh was getting at.

"Last week. The one who needed two seats. Who blew in like a balloon." Josh laughed.

Keith didn't. Even from the start there'd been something about Elizabeth. She'd sat just ahead of him and to his right, and as the sun set, she became a silhouette before the red, the green, the blue of stained glass windows. Finally, someone had thought to turn on the overhead lights, and Keith had spent the final half-hour of the meeting looking curiously at her skin. She was wearing a sundress of sorts. (Wasn't that what you would call it?) Yards and yards of light, gauzy cotton, loose. He could see the curve of her breast in the armhole, and most of her back was bare. Such skin. Smooth. Full, he thought. So much skin. You could begin somewhere on that skin, and end up someplace else. *Generous*. The word came to him. Then she'd turned and smiled. Her lips red; full, too.

It was the first time in his life he'd felt like that. That happy. A kid word: happy. He'd had the word included in their marriage vows.

>   >   >

He watches as the women find seats under the pink and orange banner. He wonders if the word *happy* is in any of their minds. They sit stiffly, straight-backed and scratching: perhaps their clothes are new.

"No more black for me," Keith overhears one.

"I've always been afraid to wear white," says another. "Afraid I'd be called a cow." But Keith notices that she isn't wearing white now.

There is another kid word that Keith has in his thoughts. Not that adults don't experience it. They just don't experience it as kids do. *Hate*. He thinks: *I hate this place we've come to. The west coast. Lotus Land. Vancouver. The city in which to live, with mountains and sea.* They live just outside the city, but now Keith suspects that the inside isn't any different. It is still a place where you can be built up and ripped down in the same day. A grey place whose inhabitants don't know what to do in the sun, and when it begins to rain, it is impossible to remember how it has been with the sun. A place where everyone works time over.

But Keith has always had the idea — perhaps from his religious upbringing, or at least his interpretation of it — that to a great extent, there is a path for each life. Sure, some turns of the path can be shaped, but not changed. Rather — he has believed — embrace the path, follow it, reach out and pluck the fruit that grows in the tree overhead. (There's always been a tree and fruit for Keith.) Don't push or fight in line. Accept what is offered.

He'd thought the coast was in his path. He knew Elizabeth was. He'd known that the first minute he saw her. *You are . . . you are . . . you are. . . .*

This feeling he has now — this feeling of hate, of wanting to fight — this has nothing to do with following, accepting. It is frightening and strange. Even the cold of the metal chair makes him want to leap and shout. He does stand, but he doesn't shout. Instead, he heads for the soggy sandwiches.

He catches a glimpse of Elizabeth, standing among some women. One speaks to Elizabeth and motions to him. Another turns to look at him, and her eyes travel slowly from his face, down, up again. She does this as if he cannot see her. Some part of his mind questions if he has ever been examined in quite this way before, and he thinks not.

She does not look approving. He looks down at his jeans. They're crunchy-new, too, not unlike the other clothing in this place, come to think of it. Nothing wrong with his hooded sweatshirt, is there? A bit young perhaps, but is that so bad? Shoes clean. He could use a haircut, true. And yes, his beard's a bit scruffy. He looks up to catch Elizabeth's eyes on him. She is smiling.

He can feel an unexpected chuckle within him, from some part he doesn't recognize. Some part finding a momentary salve from this unaccustomed need to fight. Why, he could probably pick Elizabeth up now. She's that light.

He could take her in his arms and he could carry her from this place. The laughter escapes him. He covers his mouth, chokes on a bit of egg filling.

He tried to carry Elizabeth over the threshold when they were married. He couldn't, and they'd laughed then, too.

"We'll have to consummate right here!" he'd said, pulling up her skirt in the doorway of their basement suite. If he'd thought for a moment that she'd be shy and pull him away around the corner, he was mistaken. She undid his belt right there in the doorway, put her hand inside his pants. Behind them, in the entry room, the clothes dryer suddenly screamed that the upstairs neighbours' clothing was dry. But Elizabeth didn't seem to hear it at all, and the neighbours ignored it.

Keith learned something about his wife that day: there was so much to Elizabeth that sometimes he could make love with her, and at other times he could fuck her, and still other times the line blurred perfectly.

Now, with a pain deep in his gut, he hears again the words she'd spoken standing in the yellow-green garden after they'd bought their home in Brandon. They'd spent months searching for just the right house. "What did I do to deserve this?" she'd said. Her tone was light; she wasn't looking for an answer. But now he wonders about the words that had passed through her mind and crossed her lips.

What did you ever not do?

> > >

They were pleased when Elizabeth found a job so quickly after his transfer. *Was there anything, anything, he could have done to stay back home where everyone knew them, liked them. The way they were. Was there some newspaper ad he'd overlooked, some WANTED posting? Why had he dismissed retraining so quickly? Why had it seemed so unnecessary? And they'd thought life on the west coast would move at a gentler pace, less complicated. . . .*

> > >

It was less complicated. At dinner, after Elizabeth's first day, she told him. "Your name has too many syllables," a woman at the office had said. "Let's shorten it. Liz or something," said another. "Eliza would be interesting," from another. "Nope. Too old-fashioned." Elizabeth couldn't remember that woman's name; there were so many of them.

"Eliza's too much, too."

"How about Beth?"

Elizabeth stopped them. That was enough. "Beth's fine. One syllable," she'd said.

"Quicker to write," began one as she tapped her computer keys.

"Easier to say," smiled another. "Beth." She tried it out.

"What are these women like?" he'd asked, trying to imagine who would want to change the name Elizabeth.

Elizabeth bit the end from an asparagus spear. "Oh, nice," she said vaguely. "One gave me the phone number for her hairstylist."

> > >

Did you see that new one? All year, since the move and Elizabeth's first day at the office, Keith has heard Josh's voice, his words from all those years ago in the church parking lot, under the August sun.

> > >

"I noticed a jewelry shop on Duffy," Elizabeth said.

Keith nodded. He knew the shop. Was she going to mention the golden hoop earrings in the front window? He'd put a deposit on them almost two weeks ago.

"I need my ring sized." She handed a box to him. He wanted to catch her bare fingers in his, but she dropped the small velvet box into his hand. She was going to be late for work.

"Three sizes smaller." She paused.

"Three sizes," he repeated. He really wanted to sound pleased.

> > >

"Three sizes?" The man behind the counter squinted at Keith. The man was the jeweller, the owner, and not the salesperson Keith had left the earring deposit with.

"That's a big change." The jeweller took the ring to the window and looked at the inscription. "*For Elizabeth, my beloved*. This'll go," he said. "Can't redo this. Too many letters. They'll never all fit. But you want it changed now anyhow, I guess." He looked sharply at Keith.

"No, I'd like it to read as is," Keith said.

The jeweller threw the ring into the air, caught it, and walked away with the slightest shake of his head.

"My wife's lost a bit of weight," he found himself explaining to the man's back. He wondered about the jeweller's day off, when he could come back and reclaim his deposit.

The man disappeared into the room behind the curtain and came back with a numbered stub of cardboard. "Think about a new inscription," he said.

>　　>　　>

Keith had always marveled at how light on her feet Elizabeth was. She'd figure-skated for years as a child, and he guessed that had something to do with it — pulling oneself into the air, turning up and away, defying gravity if only for a brief time. Sometimes she awoke in the middle of the night, and he never felt her leave-taking; only later, when she returned from her prowling, half in his sleep, he'd realize the coldness that had been the other side of the bed. She'd return, with her warmth, and her toes would find his and form a nest. He'd wrap himself around her, feel the round of her calves.

Her ass was a full moon. He could touch the moon, hold it in his hands.

When such a thought came to him, about Elizabeth, he would play with it, turn it over in his mind. He could feel such thoughts with his fingers, his senses.

The last time they'd made love before coming west:

The movers were arriving in an hour. There were stacks of boxes, waiting, black letters describing their contents. "This has been a fine old place," Keith said.

"Why are you whispering?" Elizabeth asked, her own voice low to match his, but her eyes bright.

He raised his voice. "Am I?" *Am I?* the room echoed back to him.

Elizabeth gave a startling whoop and took Keith's hand. "Remember how we said hello to this place?" She pulled him into the middle of the living room and began to undo the buttons of his shirt. She pulled gently at the hair on his chest. She liked it. He liked to keep his shirt buttoned, and avoided v-necks. "Come on," she urged, "let's say goodbye."

The chairs were stacked, the coffee tables and the chesterfield were covered with boxes. There was always the floor; Keith was quite familiar with the wool rug.

"What are you smiling about?" Elizabeth asked.

"The time we've spent on this rug." He reached for the tie that held her skirt in place. Elizabeth wore clothes made of filmy, voluminous fabric. She designed most of them. And they were easy to remove. One button, a tie, and the fabric would tumble to the floor. Then her bra, and she stood before him, completely naked, white in the flat light that reflected from the late winter snow beyond the window. Somehow, she always looked larger without clothing. Perhaps she stood straighter. With clothing there was a wholeness to her that was hidden, or broken. Keith massaged red marks that her bra had pressed into her shoulders. "Too bad we have to wear clothes at all," she said, as his broad thumbs worked her shoulder smooth again. He passed his hands over her skin, her perfect skin, her creamy, wondrous skin. As always, the sight of her skin aroused him, made him feel almost dizzy. He knew if he fell forward, she would catch him. Instead, he pressed her to him and they stood there together until another feeling overcame him: the feeling that he had when he was with Elizabeth, that they were one. Body parts were no longer parts. It was as if his soul were inside her, and he could feel himself touching her. His fingers knew better than his mind, and he could feel moans rising from her before they passed her lips. When he entered her — like so many other times — it was like pulling a door closed behind them, in some deep cupboard where there was a world for only them, a Narnia without threat. There was always a sense of being home.

The doorbell rang. It took Keith a long moment to remember the movers. Oh yes, the boxes rising on either side of them from the floor; he realized suddenly that it was his own shoulder he was kissing, not Elizabeth's. Seconds before, he couldn't distinguish between the two. He could have felt foolish, but he laughed and slowly kissed her even as the bell sounded again. And again.

"In a minute!" called out Elizabeth. She reached for a packing quilt from the couch and wrapped it around both of them, but Keith grabbed for his pants, pulled them on quickly.

"Just saying goodbye to the old place," she explained to the amazed moving men. One quickly averted his eyes, but the other — a tall fellow who appeared capable of handling the piano alone — seemed equal to Elizabeth's unabashedness. His eyes followed her up the stairs, then he turned to Keith. "You lucky bastard."

"I am."

It was that feeling — of his home being with Elizabeth — that made it possible to say a quick yes to the transfer. It didn't matter where they were. At least, he'd thought so.

> > >

Three months after the move west, they breakfasted on a Sunday. It was notable in Keith's mind because it was the first Sunday ever that they'd not had pancakes with maple syrup and three strips of bacon roasted with brown sugar.

"What's this?" he asked stupidly.

"Corn flakes. Grapefruit."

He poured milk from the jug, took a spoonful of the cereal, chewed, swallowed.

"Skim milk," she added, her tone an odd mix: embarrassment, pride, even defensiveness.

She'd always cooked, but he'd never taken that for granted. People ought to do what they enjoy and, if possible, pay someone to do what they don't. He was fond of annuals himself, and of the smell of freshly cut grass, the shape of a pruned bush, the surprise of a bulb in spring. So he did the gardening, Elizabeth did the cooking. They paid someone to come and clean once a week.

Back home, her kitchen — and it was hers — was a place he'd liked to be. He'd grown herbs for her in the garden during the brief and hot Manitoba summer. She chose the herbs; he tended them. There had always been some hanging, drying, in the kitchen, musty fragrant. She'd made braids of garlic and hung them as well. The walls were lined with her collection of ancient metal jelly moulds, tarnished cookie cutters, and rolling pins with worn painted handles. They'd begun the cutter collection when they were young and Keith had added to it for each birthday, finding them in odd corners of secondhand stores or at estate sales. In the old house a shelf as long as the table had held cookbooks. While they had a few favourite meals, it was not often that they had the same dish. A gift for her kitchen was never unwelcome, and when he'd proposed renovation — a room with a glass wall, and with space for a set of wicker and a small wood stove — she'd quickly agreed. They both had spent hours there, he in the armchair, stove fire crackling, with his eyes closed when he wasn't reading or studying, listening to her hum. She'd never allowed a radio or television in that room: it interrupted her humming, she said. He loved to stand behind her and catch the scent of rosemary or mint in her thick hair, loosely pinned up, though always with strays around her face and trailing down her back. New and surprising grey hairs emerged, that last year in

Brandon. Crinkly, uneven strands, given to heading out in directions all their own. When she hummed, he'd wrap his arms around her thick waist, feel the hum pass through her to him, and then she'd laugh and press her hands over his. She had always been happy in that bright and warm kitchen. In a most un-North American way she had another sense: the sense of food. Rich, satisfying food. Sauces to bathe in, poached fruit to sit on the tongue, syrups to drip from one's chin. They liked to eat with their hands, and on cold winter nights they had often sat on the floor by the fire and fed each other.

That Sunday: corn flakes and skim milk.

"Coffee's good," he said. She never forgot salt. She even did some strange thing with eggshells: suddenly he wondered what it was, and if it was something he should know before a time came when she would hand him a mug of boiling water, a spoon, and a jar of instant coffee. He looked at her, over his cup: Elizabeth, magnificent in her open ruffled pirate's night shirt with legs bare and the fold between her breasts deep. Somewhere to be on a cold winter's night. *You are the most. The most alive woman I've ever known.* She was reading the paper — on weekends they had two delivered because they liked to read the same sections — and he saw that her spoonful of cereal didn't make it to her mouth. Halfway, then she lowered it, returned it to the bowl as she read on. It was singularly unsatisfying, that cereal. The woman in the commercial, running along a sandy beach, then sighing contentedly as she sat at her breakfast table — that woman with the thin-lipped painted-red smile — she was only a well-paid actress wannabe who ate butter-dripping waffles to prepare for a long day's film shoot. Or maybe she did eat the cereal. She was damned skinny. The air could whistle between her legs, play a tune like a saw.

But there was something amiss with Elizabeth. She looked up from the paper and met his eyes. Self-consciously, she gathered her robe around her and tied the belt tightly.

He sat for a moment, stunned. He had an urge to leap up, fling open the windows, shout, "Where's my wife? Where have you taken my wife? Who are you?" but instead he asked: "When do you put the eggshell in the coffee?"

"Pardon?"

"The eggshell. When do you put it in?"

"You've never noticed?"

"Not really," he said miserably.

"Then it's my secret." Her eyes teased, and he felt she was with him again at that moment. The small white kitchen with the gray rain out the window didn't matter then. The cereal was all right; corn was sort of sweet, no?

> > >

Another month later, Elizabeth had painted the kitchen grey and new magazines were stacked at the end of the table. Elizabeth copied recipes from them. Recipes with four ingredients. "This one takes only ten minutes to make," she said, not lifting her eyes from the page. "Syl loaned it to me."

Syl was the woman who had given her the hairstylist's number.

Keith asked: "Shall I get some hooks from the hardware store to hang the jelly moulds and cutters? The walls look so bare."

Elizabeth looked up at him blankly. "Oh," she said, as if remembering where she was. "Too much dust." She was finished; she picked up another magazine, opened its pages at a marker and copied another recipe.

Keith began to dread meals: more corn flakes for breakfast, and pale bloated boiled things for supper. He would poke at them with a fork, wonder what they were. The salt was never on the table. He'd find it in the cupboard, sprinkle it generously over the . . . whatever it was. A box of Elizabeth's cookbooks went to the local thrift shop. There was an exercise video in the VCR. There was a quietness in their house, an unfamiliar quiet. For the first time, he began to think about the possibility of a child.

The quiet scared him. No, it was the disco beat of the video. One, two, three, STRETCH, said the skinny girl with earrings striped to match her bodysuit. That scared him.

He riffled through one of the magazines one morning. *Have an energizing breakfast, a good lunch, a light dinner, and an evening walk* read the sidebar of an article titled "Change Your Life." He thought he'd surprise Elizabeth.

"Walk?" he asked after supper. It wasn't raining. There was a light breeze — nothing like what they were used to — and he held out her cardigan.

She seemed pleased. They drove to the river, walked along the bank. He reached for her hand; the missing ring reminded him. "It needs a new inscription," he said.

Leaves blew at their feet. "Do you remember when we were young?" she asked suddenly.

"Of course."

"And you broke it off with me again and again."

He remembered, though not like that. He saw the young Elizabeth, filled with misgivings and tears. He'd tried to find words to hold her. He'd walked into Eaton's and chanced upon some sheepskin slippers their first Christmas.

"These are for your cold feet," he'd said. She cried then, too, but there were no more break-ups after that. He found the old slippers in a packing box when they'd moved. He didn't recognize them at first, the exhausted skins, dirty sheep's wool hanging from the edges, seams missing. Couldn't believe she'd kept them all those years. Could hardly call to mind the girl he'd bought them for.

"How about *Elizabeth, beloved*?" he asked. "For the inscription," he added, to remind her. The silence between them had been a lengthy one.

"What about *Beth*?" she said.

He shook his head before he could even consider it. He'd never called her by that name.

>   >   >

She hung a note on the cupboard door to celebrate the first ten pounds gone. "You are a beautiful woman," he told her. "You are beautiful as you are." But she reached up and touched his head, where his hair was beginning to follow his father's. "You're beautiful, too," she said with the gentlest laugh.

There is a sudden laugh near him now. He turns, and the metal chair creaks. The woman behind smiles apologetically as she catches his eye. He nods to reassure, turns back.

How long has it been since Elizabeth laughed while they were lovemaking? She does laugh once in a while — at some bit in the newspaper about someone getting a deserved end, or some such thing — but her laugh no longer burbles from deep within her. It has become a self-conscious sound, no deeper than her throat.

The last time they made love. . . . No. That sounds sad. The most recent time. It was a desperate ten minutes in the dark, scrabbling about, reminding each other of body parts, ending in a too-long embrace. She'd pulled away finally; he was aware that he was clinging to her. He'd just wanted to feel she was there. That's how it had been for the past six months.

If she was pleased with her new body, her pleasure was not apparent. He chanced upon her one day, before the full-length mirror that was the closet door in their room, looking over her shoulder at herself. There was, on her face, an expression utterly unforgiving.

Before she could know that he'd seen the look, he reached out for her with his arms. "Ah, my love," he cried with a tone deep and playful, but she slid from his hands and darted away like a shy young girl. She closed the sliding bathroom door behind her and left Keith standing, looking at it. He knocked gently. "Come out and play," he whispered.

"I have to go to work," was the muffled answer.

He rested his head against the door. "Why are you doing this to yourself?"

"I've needed to," she said. "For a long time."

"You don't need to."

The door slid open. "I do."

He watched as she pulled clothing from her drawers. Socks, bra, underwear. At least the socks were familiar.

"Dinner out tonight?" he asked.

"My meeting," she said.

Of course. The Meetings. At the Clinic.

Finally she had her clothes on, and stood rigidly in front of him. "Next week," she said, "we have a meeting of celebration. For all we've accomplished."

"Would you like me to come?" he asked.

"That would be nice."

He felt a moment of sad pleasure; wondered at himself.

She smiled, with lips closed, pulled tightly over her teeth.

>   >   >

She had a way of baring her teeth when she came, snarling. Almost as if she had to prevent something from coming out, something wilder. His Bear, he called her.

A bear just couldn't have a body like the reformed Duchess of York, packed into jeans that could only be called "pert." A bear couldn't have such breasts: punctured-looking. That's how Elizabeth's were now, with nipples pointing from shriveled areolae. She said her body — her skin — needed time to adjust, and she used creams and massaged her thighs and her neck. She'd hand him the jar, and he would dutifully massage it into her back, her upper arms. Though his own hands pulled away from the sad skin hanging there. Waiting, it seemed.

They'd never needed words as they made love. It had always been a language of body, a dance. Now there are words with Elizabeth's body: the words of numbers — caloric values, pounds. And the language of clothing — fashion, even — as boxes of clothes are dropped off at the local thrift shop, replaced after a parade of shopping dates. And there are unspoken words that snag like barbed wire, dull silver in the twilight that their marriage has become. Words such as *why?*

He'd always thought that it would be something like falling off the edge of the world, sex with a skinny woman. Just nothing there. With Elizabeth, there'd been curves, rounds, not angles. He could bury his head in her breasts; come gasping for air from her thighs; fall asleep, his head on her belly. *The most beautiful. You are.*

> > >

He watches as Elizabeth crosses the front of the room to accept her certificate from the woman. He watches the motion of her walk, notices the change, tries with his heart to memorize it — tries to replace the old memory with a new one.

She turns to face the Loved Ones in the room, waiting in their folding chairs. He has to memorize that face, too: her neck has fallen away; cheekbones have emerged; eyes so pronounced, darker, bigger than he is used to. There is a hunger on her face, he thinks. With shock, he recognizes. It is she, the girl he bought the slippers for. Her full bottom lip is clamped between her teeth. Her hands seem to catch in things. Here is the knotted-up teenager he'd fallen in love with. But back then, it had seemed easy to look past, to see the person hidden: a joyous person, an unfettered one. It had been easy to buy some slippers, and say "till death." Now, he can't see anything behind Elizabeth's expression. The door — Narnia, Eden, whatever the hell it was — is closed. A tree has fallen across his path.

steven heighton

WINTER EARTH

HOW DOES IT HAPPEN FOR THE LAST TIME? THE LOVEMAKING. Two bodies joining once, twice, a thousand times, then never again.

> > >

Over the city a vault of winter clouds as grey and cold as limestone. Like the walls of the old house, the walls of the garden, where the raised beds of frozen earth pushed up through snow like islands in an ice-bound lake.

Through a circle he had cleared in the frost of his study window, Alden looked out across the garden and over ranks of snowy roofs to the lake, where the ferry was cross-ing to Wolfe Island. At this distance it seemed to glide above the ice and only the mist rising around it from a slim, tenuous lead of open water proved otherwise. The newspaper open on his desk advised commuters that tonight the channel would freeze hard in the few hours the ferry docked; from tomorrow until the lake warmed in early March, the much longer, winter route would be used.

Perfect. Yes! And those scales — the ones in D minor? You won't forget? So — next week at the same time?

Holly dismissing her last student downstairs, playing her own voice with virtuoso skill — touching all the lively, pert, high trilling notes.

Alden? Alden? Her own voice again, weary and disso-nant, tuned back to the cracked muffled chords of old age by the departure of outsiders, the front door's slam.

Alden got up from his hard chair and stood facing his

great-great-grandfather Caleb MacLeod, the "rebel and ex-ile," who glowered out from his framed old charcoal sketch as if from a prison casement. Chastened, Alden pocketed his glasses, crossed the small dim study, and pulled open the door. The glassed-in parchment map on the back rattled softly as the door swung to. Alden's study was papered in maps, framed and unframed, contour, weather, and relief maps, ancient, old, or recent, the former tools and current momentoes of thirty-six years in the Geography Department at the college. Alden had been — and in retirement remained — an authority on historical cartography, especially as it applied to the mapping of southeastern Ontario and the Thousand Islands. *The Garden of the Spirits*, the Iroquois had called it, *Garden of the Gods*, before they and their names were written over or erased.

After Holly's Sunday afternoon lessons, a blessed silence settled over the house. After eighteen years with his own children at home and with students at school, then fifteen more among the swelling undergraduate hordes, Alden had been ready for retirement, for the cozy undemanding silence and setness of the old limestone house, for a study untrespassed by students who sprang lately from a world for which he had no maps, and which continued to spawn junior colleagues of an increasingly remote and radical stripe. *Post-colonial revisionings of the mapping process. Marxist demography. The cartographer as rapist.* Before his departure, Alden had made a few listless bids at befriending and understanding his new colleagues, but they had not really wanted that any more than he had. He did have a few friends — one left in the department, the others retired — and they still met sometimes for a drink or two, at the faculty club, Friday afternoons.

He had always been more comfortable with maps than people anyway.

Alden?

He started downstairs. Holly had taken on the piano

students soon after Caleb and Annie had left home, within a year, one after another, the house suddenly silent after all that time. She had said the students were to give her something to do besides the garden and her winter reading — and he had seen her point. It was good for her to get out of the house and to meet new people. But over the last few years her back problems had worsened, and her students had begun to come to her. And, inescapably, to him.

He could hardly object, out loud, to such a necessity.

She was waiting for him at the dining room table, a dull grey cardigan over the ochre paisley dress she had worn for her lessons. He sat down across from her. Her three students, who came one after another for an hour each, had made distressing inroads on the plate of biscuits she had set out earlier in the day — but a few of his favourites remained. He heard the kettle steaming in the kitchen. Snow fell behind her, beyond the picture window giving onto the garden, and it seemed to fall around and onto her head, whitening her hair, which had been white now for a decade and grew whiter each year so her shrinking face seemed each year redder against the white, her blue eyes refined to an eerie radiance.

"Alden, really, there's no need for you to hide away in your study whenever they come."

He selected a small piece of her shortbread.

"Or to look at me like that."

"I was watching the snow. Behind you."

She half turned in her chair and winced, her rouged mouth pinched and puckering. Alden started to his feet, and then, seeing she was all right, settled back down.

She said, "I would have thought it was too cold to snow."

"Well, the paper predicts the ferry channel will freeze tonight and they'll have to change to the winter route tomorrow. So tonight would be better for the island."

"Yes."

"Is your back too painful? We don't have to go."

"Alden, *please*." That faint, exasperated quaver that betrays deep weariness. A yellowing key, accidentally touched, on a worn old piano.

"I only meant—"

"No, I want to go, we go every New Year and we'll go tonight. I want to."

"I realize the food isn't as good as it used to be."

She smiled. "That's us. We don't taste things the same way." She started to get up for the kettle but he waved her off with a brisk, teacherly sweep of the hand. He rose and strode smartly past her as if entering a crowded classroom.

"To hear you talk," he chided from the kitchen, quickly finishing his shortbread, "you'd think we were in our nineties."

He poured a stream of boiling water into the white stoneware pot she had already sprinkled with leaves. He checked his watch. Beyond the kitchen window, snow was sifting down into the garden, filling the furrows between the raised beds; tucked invisibly under the sill, the stiff frozen stalks and clenched faded flowers of the snapdragons would soon be buried.

Alden brought in the teapot and cups and saucers on an heirloom tray. As he served her, Holly frowned and fidgeted with the brooch pinned over her thin breast, the grey cardigan that grew looser by the week. How much longer, he wondered, would she be able to go on teaching? He did wish she could still go out to do it.

They drank tea in silence. The room went darker, the clean corners growing dusty with shadow and the dust seeming to creep outward and suffuse the whole room. Above the piano there was a small Krieghoff that had been in Alden's family for years and by the time he had finished his third cup of tea the voyageurs heaving their sledge through snowdrifts, pipes pluckily chomped in their mouths, were almost imperceptible.

He squinted again at his watch.

"Shall we get ready?"

She swallowed the last of her tea, as if bracing for an ordeal.

"You really don't want to go," he told her, sensing her fatigue and how it mirrored his own and accusing her of both. But her back, he thought, her spine — the bones there dissolving. A woman who loved more than anything else *to go out*, for dinner, for walks, for drinks and dancing when a sitter was found and it was a Friday night or even on weeknights when the children were older and Alden willing to go along. To the theatre, then, or a pub by the harbour — or, more recently, on her own to the warm rooms of students where she would be offered such delicacies, Alden, such delicacies, you can't imagine! Things we never had when we were young. *Sushi*, *samosas*, blue corn chips with homemade *salsa*, pickled ginger. How our old city has changed!

Each New Year as they got ready for the drive to the ferry and the island for their annual celebration she would grow spry, sprightly as Caleb and Annie years before at Christmas: the drive down Princess Street crowded with students under the green and spruce-blue lights and then aboard the ferry, pulling out, the half-hour passage with the boat grinding through the ice-clogged channel or taking the longer route past Fort Henry and the lights of Marysville to the winter dock, then a short drive to the old limestone inn, the Sir John A., and the table they reserved each year by the window with the city lights mirrored in long, tapering rays over the ice.

He helped her upstairs and in their bedroom turned on the dim lamp on the oak table between the beds. Her idea, those matching single beds; not long after his retirement she had pointed them out in a catalogue and said that with her pain and her waking at night for pills it might be better for him, he might rest a bit better. "Well," he'd said after a time — a short time during which his mind flashed over a broad, sombre spectrum of feelings — "I suppose it's a good idea. It would be better for you, I suppose, your back."

STEVEN HEIGHTON 295

And he'd added, "Besides, we never really make love anymore."

"We never much did," she'd snapped. And after all there had been a time when only he was indifferent — once the children were born, and his academic standing and responsibilities increased, when sex had seemed, as often as not, just too much fuss. He wondered sometimes if he had left his most passionate efforts in the lecture hall — or perhaps at his desk? He could not be sure. He couldn't say. He could only wonder how a man put in thirty-five years at "an esteemed institution of higher learning," reading and thinking and teaching, and forty-one years in the institution of marriage, perfectly faithful (in marked contrast to his colleagues, or most of them); how it happened that he raised two good children and cared for his wife in health and now in sickness and did everything one is supposed to do only to end up so baffled, bled dry, alone in a study scanning the legends of priceless old parchment maps for a clue to where he was and what had happened. *One of the country's leading authorities on. The author of respected volumes concerning.* Lies, on one level. *A stranger to his most basic desires.*

He eased shut the bathroom door and shaved for the second time that day. The light above the mirror granted, as usual, no quarter at all: his dull eyes trapped in a cobweb of wrinkles: deep shadow in the wattled folds of his neck. But a full head of silver hair, swept off the forehead and back from the sides, still handsome.

When he stepped back into the bedroom the lamp was off, the room almost dark. Holly sat on the side of her quilt, her knees in the furrow between the beds — her knees bare. She was naked. They always undressed separately these days, not exactly hiding from each other but with a kind of coy, Victorian stealth, discreet contortions and turnings-away, Holly stiffer, more clumsy all the time, Alden more precise and methodical.

It had been a while since he'd seen her naked. Thinner

now. Sitting on her bedside in the near dark.

"Alden?"

Faint stirrings, a quickening in the belly, not the rush-ing spring-melt of early youth but an echo of that, muted as so many things now seemed, as if age were gradually cooling, burying him in drifts of softly falling — what? Not only snow. Cheques and bills? A storm, maybe, of calen-dar leaves blown from the old black-and-white films of his youth. Blurring his eyes, frosting his brows and hair. His eyes filling up. His senses shrouded, deadened — but alive.

He undressed. Snow slipped past the darkening win-dow and for a moment a gust rattled the pane and snow whirled and flocked against it.

"Of course I want to go," she said softly as he eased down beside her. "I still look forward to it. Every year. Here, kiss me."

Her face looked different, smoothed out by the near-dark; in bright light, her papery skin seemed almost translucent, as if she were melting from outside as well as from within, but this dimness filled out and deepened her face so she seemed now more solid, more substantial, less likely to fold up and crumple if he held her.

As they lay back together on her bed and began again, with great patience, for the first time in a year and the sec-ond time in three years and for the last time, a thought drifted through Alden's mind and he wondered if it mat-tered and thought it must but then he lost it, he let it go and only recalled later, when they arrived an hour late at the Sir John A., that he'd been worried about missing the next ferry. Their pale bodies stirring like snow outside the window, blending, settling through grey air then churned to life by occasional gusts and floating down again to sift white over the frozen earth like seed. But cold. And as Alden made slow and difficult, blissful love to Holly, he wondered why they had never much done it and why they did not do it more often now in spite of everything, to let it heal and bind them, and he vowed he would not let the intensity and purity of this moment melt away, he would keep it alive inside him, he would make this happen more often, again. But afterwards, as they lay on her bed, he felt the warmth and the rapture begin to fade and bleed away: stored heat drawn from the body of the earth as summer ends, and autumn, and ice embalms the dead stalks of flowers and glazes over the lake — an old woman's eyes dulled, glassed over with time.

So they came home later that night from the island to their separate beds, and went on as before, and Alden failed to keep his vow. And kept on asking himself how, and why. How it was that love and gravity stored in the lodestones of the body — the organs and the brain — were strong enough one day to draw two people together and the next day not quite strong enough? Or the next, or the next. A threshold crossed. The body's brief half-life ending.

He holds her arm tightly as they come downstairs, he in a wool suit, dark grey, she in a pleated maroon skirt and jacket. Telling her he wants to clear snow from the steps he carefully bundles up and hurries out around the house for a shovel. The air is clear and cold. Orion's belt hangs over the chimney like three sparks and, in the back garden, light from the picture window maps a gold square on the beds of soil. Huddled by the limestone in deep shadow under the kitchen sill are the stalks and wizened heads of the snapdragons; each year he records the date they last until and this year has been the latest ever. A few hardy survivors, closest to the wall, were still waving gamely from the snows a month before.

A faint high trilling of music. Through the dining room window Alden sees Holly at the piano, hunched painfully over the keyboard, her face flushed and her lips, half-open, budding into a smile. He can't quite make out the piece she is playing but he stands a long time, leaning on his shovel in that parcel of light, and watches.

contributors

ALISON ACHESON has written a collection of short stories, *Learning to Live Indoors* (Porcupine's Quill), as well as two novels for children: *Thunder Ice* and *The Half-pipe Kidd* (Coteau). She lives in Ladner, BC, with her husband and three sons. She thanks you for reading this anthology. She'll give you a hug if you actually bought it. She'll consider more if you buy it for two friends.

SONJA AHLERS currently lives & works in Victoria. Staying true to the inside flap of her last book *Temper, Temper* (Insomniac), her band Kiki just opened for Modest Mouse. Her favourite joke is why did the girl mushroom go out with the boy mushroom? B/c he was a fungi. From now on all her work will be dedicated to the Canadian who apologizes too much: *I want to be / in the opening band / singing about / the artist / working in the art supply store*

DIANA ATKINSON (née Wigod) was born and raised in Vancouver. Author of *Highways and Dancehalls* (Knopf Canada), which was nominated for the Governor-General's Award, the Chapters/Books in Canada First Novel Award, and the Commonwealth Prize, she has a BA in English from Concordia University in Montréal.

MICHELLE BERRY has published two collections of short fiction, *How to Get There from Here* (Turnstone Press) and *Margaret Lives in the Basement* (Somerville House). She has also published her stories in numerous literary magazines across Canada. "Funeral Home," was originally from her first novel *What We All Want*, forthcoming from Random House, but, as the editing progressed, was finally taken out. She lives in Toronto.

CARELLIN BROOKS is small and niggardly. She likes to ride. Brooks lives in Vancouver, where she writes and edits. Her most recent Arsenal publication was *Bad Jobs: My Last Shift at Albert Wong's Pagoda and Other Ugly Tales of the Workplace*.

CLINT BURNHAM lives in the Mount Pleasant district of Vancouver. He also teaches, and does puppet shows with Mark Laba. Recent work includes *Airborne Photo* (Anvil Press) and *Buddyland* (Coach House Books). "Free Country" is reprinted with the permission of Anvil Press.

NATALEE CAPLE is the author of two books of fiction: *The Heart is its Own Reason* (Insomniac Press) and *The Plight of Happy People in an Ordinary World* (House of Anansi), and one book of poetry: *A More Tender Ocean* (Coach House Books). She is the Literary Editor of *The Queen Street Quarterly*. Her poetry and fiction have been published across Canada in *The Malahat Review*, *The Capilano Review*, *Descant*, *Canadian Literature*, *Grain*, *The New Quarterly*, and many other magazines. She lives in Toronto.

MARTINE DELVAUX was born in 1968 in Québéc City and grew up in and around Ottawa. She is now an associate professor in the Literary Studies Department of the University of Québéc in Montréal. She has published a book, *Femmes psychiatrisées, femmes rebelles* (Paris: Les empêcheurs de penser en rond), as well as narrative essays in *Sites*, *The Canadian Review of Comparative Literature*, *Post*, and *The Midwest Quarterly*. New work is forthcoming in *Open Letter* and the *South Central Review*. She is currently working on a book-length project tentatively entitled *Fragments For A Broken Subject*.

TAMAS DOBOZY is a recent graduate of the Ph.D. program in English at the University of British Columbia. He has published one novel, *Doggone* (Gutter Press), and numerous short stories and poems in journals such as *Grain*, *Chicago Review*, *Prism international*, and *Short Story*. Currently, he resides in Toronto and teaches English at Seneca College, which leaves him less time than he'd like to engage in acts of inhuman carnality.

TESS FRAGOULIS' collection, *Stories to Hide from Your Mother*, was published by Arsenal Pulp Press, and was a QSPELL First Book Award finalist. She's been a writer-in-residence at the Berton House in Dawson City and at Hawthornden Castle in Scotland, where she completed her first novel, *The Sun Has Teeth*. She has also been a guest of the Helene Wurlitzer Foundation in New Mexico, and is currently conducting research for her next novel.

CAMILLA GIBB is a writer living in Toronto. Her first novel, *Mouthing the Words* (Pedlar Press), was selected by *The Globe and Mail* as one of the best books of 1999. "On All Fours in Brooklyn" is an adapted excerpt from her forthcoming novel, *The Petty Details of So-and-so's Life*.

SKY GILBERT has published two novels: *Guilty* and *St. Stephen's* (Insomniac Press). Presently, he is working on his Ph.D. in Drama at the University of Toronto. He also writes a column ("The Pink Panther") for Toronto's *eye* magazine and is working on his third novel, about an AIDS-infected serial killer, tentatively titled *I Am Kasper Klotz*. Sky's memoirs of his eighteen years as artistic director of Buddies in Bad Times Theatre — *Ejaculations From the Charm Factory* — is forthcoming from ECW.

R.W. GRAY is a Vancouver writer. His prose and poetry have appeared in journals and magazines such as *ARC, Absinthe, Event, The James White Review, Grain, Dandelion, Other Voices, Textshop, Blithe House Quarterly,* and the anthology *Quickies 2* (Arsenal Pulp). "Back" is an excerpt from his forthcoming novel, *Things to Put in an Open Mouth*.

BRETT JOSEF GRUBISIC was a late bloomer. Lately, he lives in Vancouver, where he writes book reviews while completing his Ph.D. dissertation. *Contra/diction*, his first editing project, was published to acclaim in 1998.

STEVEN HEIGHTON lives in Kingston, Ontario. He is the author of a novel, *The Shadow Boxer*; volumes of poetry, *The Ecstacy of Skeptics* and *Stalin's Carnival*; story collections, *Flight Paths of the Emperor* and *On earth as it is*; and a book of essays, *The Admen Move on Lhasa*. "Winter Earth" is excerpted from *On earth as it is* with the permission of The Porcupine's Quill.

MICHAEL HOLMES writes fiction, poetry, cultural criticism, and literary journalism. He has published three books of poetry: *James I Wanted To Ask You, Satellite Dishes From the Future Bakery, Got No Flag At All* (all with ECW), and one novel, *Watermelon Row* (Arsenal Pulp). He lives in Toronto. "Last Call" is reprinted with the permission of Arsenal Pulp Press.

LARISSA LAI was born in La Jolla, California but grew up in St. John's, Newfoundland. She is currently based in Vancouver, where she works as a community organizer, writer, and critic. She received an Astrea Foundation Emerging Writers Award on the basis of a draft of her first novel, *When Fox Is a Thousand* (Press Gang), which was nominated for the Chapters/Books in Canada First Novel Award. She recently spent a year as the Canadian Writer-in-Residence with the Markin-Flanagan Distinguished Writers Programme at the University of Calgary. She is currently at work on a second novel entitled *Salt Fish*.

ELISE LEVINE'S short story collection *Driving Men Mad* was published by the Porcupine's Quill. Her fiction has appeared in the *Journey Prize Anthology*, *Concrete Forest: The New Fiction of Urban Canada*, *Coming Attractions*, as well as in numerous other publications including *THIS Magazine*, *Gargoyle*, *Malahat Review*, *Quarry*, *Canadian Fiction*, *Grain*, and *PRISM international*. Originally from Toronto, Elise now lives in Chicago, where she recently completed a novel. "Driving Men Mad (Scheherazade)" is reprinted with the permission of The Porcupine's Quill.

"Stars" is from ANNABEL LYON'S first short story collection, *Oxygen* (Porcupine's Quill), and first appeared in *The New Quarterly*. A graduate of the MFA program in Creative Writing at the University of British Columbia, she lives in Vancouver. "Stars" is reprinted with the permission of The Porcupine's Quill.

SUZETTE MAYR was born and raised in Calgary, where she graduated from the University of Calgary with an honours degree in English. After completing a MA in Creative Writing at the University of Alberta, she returned to Calgary where she now teaches at the Alberta College of Art. Suzette has published two books novels: *Moon Honey* and *The Widows* (both NeWest Press). "The Education of Carmen" is excerpted from *Moon Honey* with the permission of NeWest Press.

DEREK MCCORMACK is the the author of two short story collections, *Dark Rides* and *Wish Book: A Catalogue of Stories*. *Wild Mouse*, a book he co-authored with poet Chris Chambers, was nominated for the City of Toronto Book Award. He lives in Toronto.

JUDY MACDONALD is a writer, journalist, editor, and producer. Her first novel, *Jane*, published by Arsenal Pulp and The Mercury Press, was shortlisted for the Rogers Writers' Trust Fiction Prize. Judy was born in Guyana to missionary parents. She grew up in Saskatoon, Saskatchewan, Edmonton, Alberta, then in both Windsor and Aurora, Ontario. Judy has lived in Toronto since 1983.

MARK MACDONALD'S stories have appeared in *Quickies 2* (Arsenal Pulp), and *Bar Stories* (Alyson). His first novel, *Flat*, was published by Arsenal Pulp Press. Mark is a keen horticulturalist, a verbose drinker, and an unrepentent high school dropout who lives in Vancouver with Puss and Pet.

HAL NIEDZVIECKI is editor of *Broken Pencil* magazine, the guide to alternative culture and zines in Canada (www.broken-pencil.com). He is the author of a novel, *Lurvy*, and a book of short stories, *Smell It* (both Coach House Books: www.chbooks.com). He is also the author of a work of cultural criticism, *We Want Some Too: Underground Desire and the Reinvention of Mass Culture* (Penguin Canada) and the editor of *Concrete Forest: The New Fiction of Urban Canada* (McClelland & Stewart).

Born in Vancouver, ANDY QUAN is a third-generation Chinese-Canadian and fifth-generation Chinese-American writer and singer-songwriter. His short fiction and poetry have appeared in anthologies and literary journals in Canada, the USA and the UK including: *Take Out: Queer Writing from Asian Pacific America* and the gay men's anthologies *Quickies 1 & 2*, *Gay Fiction at the Millennium*, and *Best Gay Erotica 1999, 2000*, and *Best of Best*. He is the co-editor of *Swallowing Clouds: An Anthology of Chinese Canadian Poetry* (Arsenal Pulp). He has lived in Toronto, Brussels, and London, and is currently in Sydney, Australia working as the International Policy Officer for the Australian Federation of AIDS Organisations. He's at andyq@unforget-table.com.

TRUMAN LEE RICH is the author of such KDM titles as *Sex Picnic Freakout* and *Terraplane Pussy*. Rich also writes under the name Michael Turner. Turner's titles include *Hard Core Logo*, *American Whiskey Bar*, and *The Pornographer's Poem*.

RACHEL ROSE is a somewhat hysterical new mother who has finally gotten all she wanted, and then some. Her first book, *Giving My Body to Science*, was published by McGill-Queen's University Press. "Want" won the Bronwen Wallace Prize for fiction and was first published in *THIS Magazine*.

MICHAEL V. SMITH is a falsifying autobiographer. His work also appears in Arsenal's anthologies *Contra/diction*, *Quickies*, and *Quickies 2*. He lives alone in Vancouver.

ERIN SOROS has published fiction, poetry, and articles in Canadian and American anthologies and journals, most recently *West Coast Line*, *Open Letter*, and *Queen Street Quarterly*. A double columned piece incorporating narrative and philosophy was the lead article in a special issue of *differences: A Journal of Feminist Cultural Studies*. New work is included this fall in the Australian publication *Journal of Intercultural Studies*. She lives in New York.

NATHALIE STEPHENS writes in both English and French. She is the author of *Somewhere Running* (Arsenal Pulp), *UNDERGROUND* (Éditions TROIS), *Colette m'entends-tu?* (Éditions TROIS), *This Imagined Permanence* (Gutter) and *hivernale* (Éditions du GREF).

ANNE STONE is author of the novel *jacks: a gothic gospel*, and the chapbook *Sweet Dick All*. Her most recent novel is *Hush* (Insomniac).

R.M. VAUGHAN is a Toronto-based writer and video artist originally from New Brunswick. His books include the poetry collections *A Selection of Dazzling Scarves* and *Invisible to Predators* and the novel *A Quilted Heart*. His videos and Super 8 films appear everywhere.

MARNIE WOODROW is the author of the short story collection *In the Spice House*. Her short stories and poetry have appeared in *THIS Magazine*, *Canadian Forum*, *CV2*, and *The Algonquin Round Table Review*, among others. She has just completed her first novel in which almost every character has sex, even (or most especially) the Canadians.

Carellin Brooks and Brett Josef Grubisic are Vancouver writers and editors who never came to blows while editing this book. It was a surprise to them, too.

photo: Laura Jane Petelko